The Thrillbilly Magnet

Annie Love

iUniverse, Inc.
Bloomington

The Thrillbilly Magnet

iUniverse books may be ordered through booksellers or by contacting:

iUniverse
1663 Liberty Drive
Bloomington, IN 47403
www.iuniverse.com
1-800-Authors (1-800-288-4677)

ISBN: 978-1-4697-7645-3 (sc)
ISBN: 978-1-4697-7647-7 (e)
ISBN: 978-1-4697-7648-4 (dj)

Printed in the United States of America

iUniverse rev. date: 3/30/2012

SPECIAL THANKS

Simon

Earl

Jerry

Ursula and Ramiro

Harley and Marianne

Acacia

Cheryl and Steve

Ethan and T

Jeremy

Bryan (my editor)

Chapter 1

I walked into the cigar shop on August 1, 2005. It was tucked away in the deep crevice of the seedy part of town. Since I had just arrived there, I didn't know exactly what kind of people called this place home. My cousin warned me not to move there. She had contacted me in Spain and told me the population in this particular beach town consisted of only junkies, hookers, and trailer trash. She tried to talk me into moving to Cocoa Beach, near her own home. Jo, my cousin, is a nerd and an X-File fan.

I thought to myself, "I have lived everywhere. Nowhere can possibly be as bad as she is describing this place."

I am not shocked easily. I have lived in the bowels of Mexico and Amsterdam, and nothing bad has ever touched me. Yet despite my confidence, I was about to experience how right my cousin was.

The reason I went to this particular place was because it was a cigar shop, and I was out of smokes. I smoke all-natural cigarettes that are rare, exotic, and expensive. I had to seek places like this, which usually carried expensive cigars and my personal brand.

There was a miniature Ducati motorcycle on the sidewalk outside the door. At the time, I owned a miniature Harley Davidson that was always in the way. My guitar player had given it to me for Christmas when I lived in Spain. I had so many keepsakes from my life of adventure that I was on a mission to get them out of my house and distributed to their new rightful places. I was honestly running out of room and so I thought that this cigar shop would benefit from using my bike as a physical advertisement, serving the sucker yuppie cigar smoking crowd. Little did I know, I had just entered the "insane cracker zone".

I walked in at noon on that hot, sticky day. The place was so tiny and utterly filthy. Inside reeked of sweat and stale cigar smoke. I looked around and noticed a stripper pole in the back left corner, with a warm, sweating keg of beer by its side. It had beat-up, ugly rust-brown vinyl couches while old porn and astrology books were littered everywhere. The floor was sticky and slippery all at once. It felt as though it had never been mopped. I wandered around slowly towards the counter and humidor. I noticed a pile of photographs depicting nude women in lewd positions lying on the counter like souvenirs for everyone to gape at. There were a lot of dusty antique bar knick-knacks everywhere. In fact, everything there was dusty and grimy.

There was a large screen T.V. displaying graphic porno. The sound was turned down but the images were unavoidably in-your-face. What kind of cigar shop had this on display? I had never been in a place like this anywhere. I felt very uncomfortable to say the least. However, the shop owner did carry one pack of my exotic cigarettes. He also had quite a full-stocked bar, though it was not a legally-operating bar. I saw an older, stinky, grungy-surfer-man sitting in an old beat up chair smoking a big stogie in one hand and holding a martini in the other. I asked if he was the owner and he said, "Yes", obnoxiously. He was incredibly rude and nasty, resembling his shop very well. He acted like, and must have believed he was, the king of the universe. Even the least decent of women would have considered this guy a pig.

I was dressed in crisp, summery white linen that day. He took an attitude towards me before I could open my mouth to ask my next question. He was tying to intimidate me right off the bat. Little did he know, he was dealing with me, 'Ruthless'. It's my nickname.

I asked him if the little bike outside was -- he interrupted me and barked, "It is not for sale!"

I coldly said, "No, I don't want to buy it." I was very stern with him in order to not be bullied and added, " I have a miniature Harley".

He said, "Really?"

I replied, "Yes. Do you want to buy it for your shop to help generate customers for bike week?"

He was stunned for a moment and replied, "Yes!"

I showed him a photo of it and he lit up.

"Definitely a great idea!" he exclaimed like a child.

'Bikertoberfest' was eight weeks away and he really needed to generate some real profits to make up for a dead summer with hardly any customers. I told him it would be coming off the ship in a week or so, and that I would bring it by in my truck.

Well, as we were shaking on the deal (350 dollars to

be paid at twenty dollars a week), the owner of the little bike that stood outside came swaggering in. He was dressed like a beer distributer, wearing a Miller Beer shirt. I noticed a keg in the back of his pickup outside. He seemed buzzed, with an ultra bright smile and glazed, sky blue eyes. He held a stack of tattoo magazines in his arms. He acted like he had partial ownership of the shop. He had an arrogant attitude too and, at first sight, seemed like a typical asshole .

The owner told him my name and informed him of the deal we just made for my little bike. He didn't seem interested, rather he appeared jealous. Then he threw down the stack of tattoo magazines and cranked the sound on the TV playing porno to a deafening level. I was on my way out the door, thank God.

As I was getting in my rental car he went outside to fetch the keg from his pickup. I forgot all about him instantly.

(Sorry, but when there is porno and alcohol playing during lunch hour, I am repulsed instantly). This place was a regular 'Pandora's Box' tucked away in the crevice of town.

I continued exploring the town for the future. I kept telling myself I could have a great life there - if only I found the nice, worthwhile people. I knew that good folks exist in every town. It would take time and effort, but I always have great luck wherever I go.

Chapter 2

My belongings were delayed a whole month because they were mistakenly shipped to Russia. Thankfully, my things were still to arrive before 'Biketoberfest'. So one afternoon I went to tell the cigar shop owner of the delay on my way to the health food store nearby. He was fine with it.

The man with the little bike appeared out of nowhere, genie-like. I had a glass of water and asked where the hot spots were.

They barked, "Here!"

I only asked for their reaction. I kept a straight face. I noticed on the postcard wall that there was one from where I just moved, in Spain. The owner told me it was from a Norwegian man named Nils. I asked if he had a photo of Nils since he had photos of everyone else all over the place.

He said, "Yes."

Well, turns out he was my Spanish neighbor. We had hung out with the same crowd for five years. The storeowner was astounded.

I thought to myself, "Nils spent the winters hanging out here?"

Yep, same Nils. Then, the owner decided he liked me as he saw me to be a friendly person. Now I was accepted into the dark world of the cigar shop, and not just for our business transaction. Well, I felt differently.

I never went there except to drop off the bike and get paid my twenty dollars once a week. I never stayed longer than five minutes, ever. Each time I dropped by, the shop owner offered me a drink and a smoke – and each time I declined.

I always acted as though I was late for an appointment or pretended someone was waiting in the car so as not to lose the deal or offend him. Clearly he was a control freak of sorts. I got a bad vibe from this place. It was a sick place.

Because he thought he had won me over, he gave me gummy Christmas candy and Evian water as gifts. But every time I went in there, there was some nude girl bearing it all while being photographed in the humidor. It was that or a bunch of drunk, wretched-smelling, bragger men watching porno in the middle of the day. And the same guy with the beer shirt would always show up to cheer on the revolting behavior.

I ride a Harley. I have seen it all in my life; I've even witnessed death right before my eyes. I know boys will be boys, too.

I had long, wavy, platinum blond hair to my waist. It had many color streaks flowing throughout. My clothes were rock 'n roll, but tasteful. When I looked in the mirror, I liked the image I projected. I didn't resemble any other women in town, in any way. In fact, I think they thought I was not only from another country, but another planet. I stuck out like a sore thumb in this place and I liked it.

I think because I was so mysterious, they wanted to know why I was always busy and not partying. However, I saw their partying as drowning. They had to know I was never going to be one of the lewd, nude recruits, no matter what.

One day I saw my female doctor at the cigar shop. She was visibly uncomfortable and freaked out because I had spotted her there. She just so happens to be married to a Sherriff. I didn't linger; I just ran in and out as usual.

Well I started noticing after a few shocking months that no matter what time I visited the shop, the beer shirt guy would always appear, but he would rarely make eye contact with me.

Chapter 3

The boat shipping my belongings was very late but it did finally arrive in time for 'Biketoberfest'. My friend was bringing my truck on a trailer from Hurricane Katrina. We took the miniature Harley to the cigar shop together.

Coincidently, the guy with the beer shirt materialized as soon as we arrived. He didn't speak to us as we unloaded the bike off my truck. However, he was drooling all over it - everyone was amazed that the bike was made in Spain and not in the U.S.A. It immediately drew a crowd as we placed it in front of the cigar shop.

The rough owner was gleaming with happiness. He handed me a twenty dollar bill to initiate our deal. My friend loves cigars so he bought a few and enjoyed a free cocktail. I went next door to the health food store until he was ready to go.

I returned to a crowd gathered around my truck and the little Harley. The crowd was seedy. I wanted to get out of there. Nobody could believe this was a "girl's truck". It is a 1950's Chevy, hand-painted with gold leaf motif. It looked very rough but it still ran great. No one could believe it survived Katrina. Since it has a Corvette engine, it is both loud and fast.

My friend was telling the folks gathered the history of my truck and recounted what I had lived through during my cross-country travel in it. He loves to talk. He continues to tell them he is going to marry me by New Years Eve.

I hear this while approaching and say, "You wish!" and I started laughing. "We have to go," I said.

We actually did. We had to get new tires. The old tires were rotten from the sewer water after being submerged for eighteen days during Katrina. The tire place was across the street from the cigar shop and police station, as well as all the stores I frequented.

We headed back to my house to start working on cleaning out all the debris and wasps nests from the car. We had to gut it and take the engine apart and clean it. It was pretty bad. The first round of work lasted ten days. Ten more days for the second round to strip, scrub, and restore for safe driving.

My friend is a very well known mechanic from California who I have been a good friend with since I was in college. He really did want to marry me, it turns out.

I thought to myself, "We'll see. Time will tell."

My friend left after the first ten days to go back to California. He said he would be back for ten days of Christmas and for New Year's Eve to give me an engagement ring. He said we would have an engagement party and complete the work on my truck.

In the meantime I unpacked and decorated my new beach house. Once a week I would stop by the cigar shop to pick up my twenty dollars for the Harley. I would drop by any time of the day. The shop is open from ten A.M. to midnight. I never knew what time I was going to be there. I'd just show up, and the rough owner would hand me a twenty and cheerfully tell me how much business had picked up. In return, I'd smile and say I had to run a million errands.

There were always seedy people in the place drinking, smoking, and watching porno. That beer shirt guy would continue to magically appear every time. He still didn't speak to me. I thought it was especially odd because I once heard him say he worked at the local paper as a printer. If someone has a job, shouldn't they be there? I thought he was quite peculiar. He always appeared and pulled a draft beer and lit a cigar seconds after I appeared. Well this went on every single time of the day or evening.

My friend who wanted to marry me loved that little creepy shop of horrors. When he came to town I took him with me to get my money. He and the rough owner had hit it off. This was my red flag to not marry him.

He left the day after New Year's day. He asked to take me to Mexico for our birthdays in March to see if we were compatible. I was uncomfortable. In my heart of hearts I knew it wouldn't work out. During Christmas, he was over drinking and wanted things I couldn't give. I loved him, but was not in love with him. It was time for me to have a boyfriend. I had been single way too long.

Chapter 4

I had already made friends with my neighbors. My new neighbor was a party girl who loved to dance and see live music. I didn't drink; but I am a singer and love to dance. I agreed to go out with her and a group of women every Friday night in order to meet musicians and be a guest singer.

Well, it worked. I met great local musicians and arranged my own band after some time. I was blessed with some of the best musicians in the area. They liked my voice and I started to enjoy a very fulfilling musical life there. I was really happy.

My band grew bigger and better with every Thursday night practice at my home. I found an electric violin player who is a woman my age. Her name was Rika. In fact, we looked like sisters. She rode on the back of her husband's Harley. He wouldn't let her learn to ride. My own Harley was still in the shop being repaired from the Katrina damage. It took six long months to get it just right again.

I missed riding to 'Biketoberfest' that year. I just kept preparing for March with my music. The holidays came and went really fast. All I wanted was 'Bike Week' to arrive so I could sing and ride.

The opening day of 'Bike Week' this year was unusually cold and windy, but I was determined to go on my bike. I put all my leather on, happily got on my bike, and blasted off into the unknown. First stop was the cigar shop for my twenty dollars and to see the expression on those freaks' faces when they witnessed me riding a bike of that size.

There is no helmet law in Florida but I wear one no matter what. I wear a police helmet so that the folks in cars respect me. I had my hair tucked into my jacket so no one could tell I was a woman when I rode. I pulled up and they all had to look at my bike. Gawking was a normal reaction for these bored folks. After the gawking, they all had to analyze and compare it to their own - bla, bla, bla.

I took off my helmet and jacket. That is when the jaws dropped as the crowd saw that it was me, Ruthie. I just walked, glib as usual, past everyone and into the shop.

The cigar shop was packed with the usual yuppie bikers smoking cigars and drinking. The rough owner announced that I had sold the little bike to him. He was in disbelief of my Harley I rode in on. I never told them I had one. The beer shirt guy appeared like a genie again. He stared at my bike, and rightfully so. My Harley is an antique. It is beautiful and simple. No chrome.

I got my twenty and did a monster burn out as I left, headed for the big event. I had a huge smile on my face this time. I was going to meet my female friends at a certain place. The gigantic biker bar was only one mile away up the road and was packed to capacity. It is set outdoors with booths, bike exhibitions, and a huge stage where bands played all day and night. It was louder than you can believe. Folks come from all over the country for this crazy biker frenzy. You could see each and every kind of motorcycle in the universe there. The "beer girls" were really young and practically naked. The biker men were always drunk, fat, foul-mouthed, and sweaty. They bore me to death. I only cared about the music and singing with the bands. That's my rush.

My female friends are in their late forties and single. They were looking to meet biker men for relationships. I invited them to come hear me sing and prowl for guys. I never saw a man I liked there, yet.

I parked my Harley in front and was heading over to sit with one of my friends, when BINGO here came the beer shirt guy on a huge, police-style Harley. He parked next to me. He was talking to the parking guy like they were old buddies. They both looked at my bike for a few minutes. My friends were already having drinks there. He didn't bother to acknowledge me: nothing. He did however sit at the next table over, alone, and watched us. He had a huge mug of draft beer. I had water as usual.

Our other friends met us and we all danced in the back with the band and ate Gyros. The beer shirt guy mulled around us the whole time we were there. There were about five hundred people there all dressed like wannabe bikers. The women traditionally dress like a hybrid of bike-hookers and strippers in attempt to allure men. The event was like a biker Halloween party for ten days. It was really kind of funny to me. Everyone tried to look like a Hell's Angels gang member when most of them were actually dentists and doctors or just plain, old working stiffs. They all thought they had license to get bombed and act trashy. It cracked me up.

The band asked me to sing "Roadhouse Blues". I did and it was great. Everyone went nuts. I was so happy. My friends loved it too. I was becoming known as an entertainer. The only unsettling part was that the beer shirt guy was watching and creeping me out. I went to leave on my bike and I checked to see if the beer shirt guy was going to follow me. He was invisible for once. This party was huge. I was not used to this volume of people, noise, bikes, music, and singing all jam-packed into one day. I was exhausted after everything and it was getting dark, so I left and rode home happy as a clam.

Chapter 5

My friend was at home working on my truck. We were leaving for Mexico the next evening. I had to finish packing anyway. I had been going to this particular place in Mexico many years and my best friend and I were going to celebrate my birthday as we had done for years. Her boyfriend would love my fiancé. They were the same kind of men. They loved to drink and tinker with things.

When I arrived home from singing and riding, my fiancé had four men, who happened to be my new neighbors, in the garage helping with my truck, hanging around, and drinking. I had met a few of them already. They were very helpful when I was moving in but, there was one man who I didn't know yet. He was just standing around with a beer and a cigarette, talking as if he knew everything. He was tall and lanky with an enormous, beet-red nose and Brillo Pad, textured, short hair. His teeth were florescent yellow like a swamp rat. I wouldn't have been surprised if they even glowed in the dark. He wore thick, ugly wire-rimmed glasses.

The ugly stranger looked at me as I rode up on my bike like I was straight from of a dream.

My fiancé blurted out, "Here comes my baby!"

The guy with the beer was visibly bummed when he heard that. I burst into the garage as loud as a rocket and hit the kill switch. The bike sounded like a sonic boom going off.

I yelled, "Hold your ears!" I started laughing hysterically as I turned off my bike. I took my helmet off and said, "Hi," in my innocent girl voice.

Everybody was cracking up laughing. The creepy guy was smiling like a psycho at me and said, "My name is Gus and I live behind you."

I replied, "I'm cold. Burrrr!" and ran into the house. I got a bad vibe immediately. He was creepily checking me and all of my stuff out. I went in the house to peel all my bike leather off because it was windy and the temperature was only in the sixties that day. I changed into my velour tracksuit and put on some Brazilian music to finish packing for Mexico.

Somehow my fiancé let the guy weasel himself in for a beer. I was very uncomfortable. It took forever to get rid of this guy. He told me he lived directly behind me. I was wondering where all that loud Pink Floyd music was coming from all the time. He also said he was unemployable and mentioned his wife would love me. He then told us that his wife is bi-sexual and that together they are swingers.

I pulled my fiancé aside and whispered, "Get him out of here right now!"

So he gently said we had to get cracking to go on our trip so he had to leave. I was freaking out truly.

I thought, "Oh great! I have just bought a house with freaks for neighbors. OH NO! Help me GOD!"

I had a pool and Jacuzzi in my back yard. He would be able to see through the fence and watch me all the time. Now I was upset. I felt stuck; trapped. I packed and went to bed with a bad feeling about all of this. It was now March and I imagined this guy had been watching me in my pool since July. He could hear and see me twenty-four hours a day. He said he just hung out at home, drank beer, and smoked while his wife cleaned houses and pulled weeds with a lesbian friend. How did these folks pay their bills? And on top of that, they partied like rock stars everyday.

I said to my fiancé, "I have to move."

He said "Don't worry, I told him we are engaged and getting married."

I said, "He and they don't care! They are swingers!" I said, "You come back and forth from California. I am here living alone with my music and Harleys. I love to work out in my pool every day and go in my Jacuzzi. They don't have a pool and I know they are going to be trouble for me when you're not here."

He said not to worry. Well that's impossible for me since I was alone. They were compromising the perfect lifestyle I had so carefully planned out. I was really bummed out now.

Chapter 6

My fiancé had become an alcoholic. I had known him for twenty-two years but had not seen him since nineteen ninety-nine. It turned out that he had gone down hill during this time.

In Mexico he had gone overboard and partied until he was so sick that he couldn't get out of bed for ten full days. So, we broke off our relationship amicably. When we got home from Mexico, we left each other as friends and I never saw him again. I got to keep the ring as a gift for having to put up with all of his addictions. He was a great mechanic but a lousy fiancé.

I had grown up clean and, sadly, he went down hill. He was exactly ten years and one week older than me. He never cleaned up from the eighties and was on a path of total self-destruction. As if this wasn't enough, his ex-girlfriend started calling him every time she was drunk – which was just about everyday. All of these elements made it clear to me that it was time to say, "See ya." I was on a different path, one aiming to become a famous singer and writer. I was all-too-ready to devote all my time to my band, singing, riding my Harley, going to the Hot Rod events, and meeting all the really good folks.

I had a band with excellent musicians from the Music Society. I sang on Wednesday nights at the open jam and we had rehearsals at my home on Thursday nights from five 'til ten P.M. My neighbors loved the live music. They loved me for bringing life into a retired neighborhood of old folks. We played a lot of classic songs so the neighbors would come to our rehearsals, drink wine, and revel in the nostalgia and happy memories that the music invoked. I was so happy. Life was becoming all I ever wished for.

Chapter 7

I had a darling old Jack Russell Terrier that I walked around the block every evening before sunset. We would walk one way around the south block one evening and then around the other north block the next so she wouldn't get bored. I had been walking her with this same regime every day since I moved in. Well the neighbor, Gus, behind me has a front porch that was hidden by many large bushes and trees. We had been walking by his house every other night since we arrived and moved in and I didn't even know it. Gus sits (lives) on the porch. I never saw him, but I did actually smell him many times. After I returned from Mexico he started saying "Hi" to me when I walked by. He asked if I wanted a beer or a smoke but I always declined. I tried to pull the same trick I always use to handle the cigar shop folks. I was always in a hurry or had someone waiting for me in order to avoid him... anything.

This man was obsessed. I could feel it. He would ask questions like, "Where is your fiancé?"

One night he came over, plastered drunk, with his wife and asked if they could swim in my pool. She fell flat on her face in my next-door neighbor's yard.

Thank God my neighbor came out and yelled at them for cutting through their yard. They didn't like Gus and his wife either.

My next-door neighbors ended up being my adopted parents. They hang out in their yard or garage sixteen hours a day. They noticed Gus was always walking and driving by my home slowly and were very worried that he was infatuated with me. I had no idea. I was too busy; in and out all day trying to live my life long dreams.

My saxophone player introduced me to friends of his who were forensic psychiatrists. Their hobby was playing music and I sang jazz with them the last Thursday of every month at a local Italian restaurant. The same regular crowd of locals gathered every time. I guess the band was bored because they asked me to sing with them regularly. It was a nice alternative for me, as I could dress up really pretty and sing softly for a change. I enjoyed the gig the first few times until I saw the beer shirt guy hiding in the corner of the bar.

"What was he doing here?" I thought to myself.

Then I saw him all buddy-buddy with the owners and bartenders. I decided not to sing there for awhile after that. Just when I thought I love my life outside of my home.

I sang blues and rock with the other bands regularly. I was invited to be a guest singer at many events in town. It only took six months start making my dream come true. On Saturday and Sunday afternoons we would all sing karaoke at a famous beach bar to practice and keep up our game. Life was becoming fun. I was popular and had a nice group of friends who all played music and loved it. In between I would ride my Harley and go to all the hot rod shows. I had a few nice friends and was having a blast. I tried to forget about my creepy neighbors and the beer shirt guy, but they refused to forget about me.

Chapter 8

It started one hot night when I was watching a movie around ten p.m. my doorbell rang. I looked through my peephole and there was Gus.

I said, "What do you want?"

He said he wanted a beer and to take a swim. He was plastered already.

I said, "I do not have any beer and I do not think it's a good idea for you to come here. You are married."

He told me he was "in love" with me and wanted to leave his psycho, bi-polar drunk wife.

I said, "Sorry! I am not the answer to your problems." I refused to open my door.

Well the next day his wife Dodie called and left a very nasty message on my cell phone saying, "Are you fuckin' my husband?!"

She has a very slurred, Southern red-neck accent too. I was so flabbergasted! I thought I was being "punked". I wouldn't have been shocked if Jerry Springer appeared at that moment, out of nowhere. I have never been accused of anything like that in my life. I took my phone to my next-door neighbors' and had them listen to the message.

After all the trouble I was going through to avoid her husband, how could I be the victim of such an accusation? My next-door neighbors were astounded. They knew I was nice and would never do a thing like that. After their own encounter with the drunk couple, my neighbors placed a NO TRESPASSING sign outside their house to help keep Gus away from me.

I thought, "Great! Now I have a drunken, swinger "peeping Tom" obsessed with me who lives ten feet away with only a one-inch thick fence separating us. And now his whacko wife thinks I am committing adultery. Sheesh! What did I do to deserve this, God?"

First impressions are significant. I was right at first sight. This guy had totally creeped me out. Now what? She was drunk as usual. The whole neighborhood was in an uproar. A week later, Dodie finally sobered up and apologized to me, but living there was still a nightmare. I was stuck with crazies.

Two weeks later I was walking my dog around the block when I came around the corner to see two sheriff cars parked in front of their home. Gus was in handcuffs and being forced into the back of one of the cars. I found out that he had pulled a handgun on Dodie. In turn she brought out her shotgun and promptly dialed 911. Gus was hauled off to jail and subsequently admitted to the mental ward for overnight observation. He is a serial con artist, so he managed to be released.

I went down to the courthouse and checked public records. I discovered that he had three pages worth of women abuse accounts, as well as other various arrests. Married five times... etcetera, etcetera. Crazy as bat shit. Now I was really nervous. I had a few psychopaths living behind me so far.

I own my home, paid for it in cash, but the market was in the gutter. I paid high for my home as it was now worth half its original purchase price. If I tried to sell and move to a safer place I would lose half of my life savings. I was upset, worried, and felt like I was being stalked.

Whenever I was out by my pool I could hear him coming toward the fence to look at me through one of the openings. I found all the peep- holes and I promptly plugged them all up. One day he was trying to sneak over to the fence to look through a new hole he had made when he slipped on dog poop. He had to grab for the hanging rubber tree branch to keep from sliding into more poop. He was cursing up a storm. He must have been covered in it. They never let their three dogs out, ever. There were landmines of dog shit everywhere and the grass was wet because it rained all the time in Florida. Shit gets slippery when on wet, unmowed grass. This made me laugh a little. The downside is that now he would have an excuse to spend more time in his backyard, cleaning up the innumerable mounds of old, stinky doggy doo. Any excuse would do for him.

I did everything to avoid this guy, everything possible. He could hear me warm up my bike, truck and car. I had high performance vehicles. They require T.L.C. to function properly. Gus had nothing better to do so he always knew when I was coming and going. It was stressful to say the least. I even started walking my dog in a different direction to evade Gus and his antics. I would even vary my schedule and go at different times of the day. However, Gus eventually figured that out and started driving around. He would drive up and down all the streets with a beer in his hand and a smoke dangling on his fried, cracked lips. He was looking for me to say anything to him. I tried my hardest to be polite and ignore him but the situation was escalating.

All of the sudden, dead squirrels and rats from his yard started appearing on the other side of my fence. Gus and Dodie were hurling dead animals at me to get my attention. I'm talking about five different kinds of rodents, poisoned and bloated, landing in my yard all throughout the day and evening. My dog would bring them to my attention. It was bad. I called the police and tried to make a report only to be blown off by them. I ignored it and let it go the best that I could. I photographed the evidence in case it would get any uglier. Now, I didn't want to go in my own backyard anymore. He would do anything and everything to get my attention.

Chapter 9

I had better things to do than deal with this elementary school prank. I still had to do my errands and stop by the cigar shop once a week for my twenty dollars. As usual I went by the cigar shop randomly. And, as usual the beer shirt guy was always there.

My friend told me that her husband had put a GPS tracker under her car so he could know her whereabouts at all times. She warned me that it could be done to my car, Harley and my truck very easily. She said if the beer guy was inexplicably appearing everywhere I was, that it was possible he had been tracking me with a similar GPS device. Well he really did show up every time I went to get my twenty dollars, no matter what time of the day or night. Now I had two stalkers.

I have never had this kind of thing happen to me. I was so confused and stunned. Everyone else noticed that I was being followed too. It was not subtle. I was astounded. I didn't know how to handle this kind of bullshit. No one had ever bothered with me anywhere else I had lived in the world. Never. What was this all about? How could I politely keep them away from me? They drank and did drugs. I didn't. How and why would they be obsessed with me? I am so boring and I walk such a straight line. Why was I alluring to these drunken, adulterous, drug-addicted swingers? None of this made any sense to me.

As the days went by, Gus and Dodie's music and parties got louder and louder. Dodie had a very loud laugh like a cackling witch on Halloween. It echoed across all of the neighboring swimming pools. Everyone in the community had pools, except for Gus and Dodie. In fact, they had a party everyday after work for all the local stoners and alcoholics. They continued to drunkenly and nakedly stumble over to my house and ask to use my pool. They must have forgotten about the dead animals they were throwing into my yard.

I said, "Why are there a bunch of dead rats and squirrels in my yard?"

They said they had a rat infestation in their garage and had put poison out to get rid of them. The animals probably just ran up the rubber tree and keeled over, falling into my yard by chance. A likely story. They persistently tried to invite me to their parties and I always declined politely. I was still trying to avoid them at all costs.

Finally, a neighbor across the street from them threw a fourth of July party and she invited me. I accepted. She was older and her husband had died at Christmas. Her son was a landscaper and had become my friend as I walked my dog. He was very nice. They were originally from a place not far from my own hometown.

I went to the party and Dodie & Gus were amongst the attendees. Dodie had butch-short, frazzled bleached blonde hair and oval wire rim glasses that complimented her deep fried tan. She had gone to Wal-Mart and purchased some matching shorts and a tank top for the occasion. She found Gus a Tommy Bahamas shirt and khaki shorts at a thrift store nearby in attempt to blend in with the regular neighbors. I was trapped and had to be friendly to them because the party and neighborhood was small. Dodie politely told me what plants I should put in my yard. Gus loved to hear himself talk and brag about his whole life. He would tell everyone. He was always holding a beer and was stoned out of his mind, continuing to chain smoke. I was very quiet, listening and piecing together exactly who these people were. It turns out Dodie had been married three times and her children and family didn't speak to her. She said she was bipolar and an alcoholic. Gus rattled on that he had been married five times and hated Dodie, but was broke and needed a woman to take care of him since he was fired from every job he ever had. He was committed to the notion that he was unemployable, and would brag about this. He hated Dodie, but his own family was sick of him because he was a crack addict and alcoholic. He was stuck now. Dodie had owned the home they lived in since the nineteen eighties. She was Gus' "sugar mama", allowing herself to be taken advantage of because he was reportedly good in bed. Dodie was bi-sexual and was even having relations with a woman from our neighborhood.

Gus was able to fool around too. I always wondered who he was fooling around with, because Dodie was always so psychotically jealous. The couple also bragged about how much fun it was to be swingers. If it was so great, why were they so desperate and miserable?

And why were they bothering me? Gus and Dodie kept telling me how gorgeous I was. It creeped me out, giving me chills.

After hearing about Gus and Dodie's swinger exploits, I had to go home and throw up. At least I heard it from the horses' mouths. Now I knew I had to batten down the hatches and tighten security. I knew Gus had been watching and following me. He was running into me too often for it to be a coincidence, I felt like they were preying upon me. He had nothing else to do and I was becoming increasingly paranoid.

Chapter 10

I tried to engulf myself in my slide guitar lessons and band practices. We had seventeen songs we had to learn and perfect for our first debut at the Music Society. I was so excited to have a saxophone player, electric violin player, a famous bass player and guitarist and an amazing drummer. I lived for Thursday night rehearsals at my home. We were taping every practice and we sounded good. It was my goal to be the best at what I was passionate about. We had so much fun and got along so well. Our bass player used to be a music teacher so he helped all of us grow as musicians. On top of that, he was a car mechanic was helping to perfect my truck since my fiancé and I had parted ways. Things were coming together in every other aspect of my life.

Time was flying by in a happy blur. I still had to go by the cigar shop to pick up my twenty dollars once a week. I had built up more self-confidence since I had my own band and friends. I was not shy anymore. I was still glib to be honest. I have lived all over the world and have learned that the best way to be was quiet for the first year, watching and listening the local people and learning their ways. The goal was to try to be polite and to keep a low profile, which would make me mysterious. It was also important to smile often. It was a sure-fire way for the folks to eventually show their true colors. There were opportunities to hear things in the ladies' room and discover what is really going on.

If anyone asked me anything, it was wise to always respond, "I just moved here from Spain and do not know anyone or anything." They couldn't compete with a foreign country transfer. It worked, every time. It had kept me safe many times. Plus, I do speak Spanish fluently. I was mysterious and confusing to the locals for quite some time. It was great for my self-protection and security. Most of the folks had never left their hometown. They were clueless in regard to trying to strike up conversation with me. That helped me. Since they could blatantly see why I moved (to pursue my hobbies), I appeared to be an open book.

I hadn't been by the cigar shop for a few weeks so when I dropped by unannounced and, as usual, the beer shirt guy showed up within three minutes of my arrival. His appearances were like clockwork. He ignored me as usual. I received sixty dollars and gracious thanks for all the business my little Harley was bringing in. I exited quickly as usual. I knew that little bike would bring the tiny place customers.

I had started making friends with the health food storeowner. I was going through menopause and suffering severely. This was another reason why I wasn't going out too much at the time. The owner of the store was wonderful. His name was Ike. He and his employee smoked and I would see them randomly at the cigar shop. He cross-referenced my rare blood type with my symptoms and administered four things for me to take. Within six weeks I was done with the regiment and had lost sixteen pounds. I was overjoyed. This man was amazing. He knew everything and really cared.

The girl who worked there was a lesbian and a smoker. I noticed she was friendly with the beer shirt guy. She probably overheard my problems when she rang me up at the cash register each time I went to purchase my remedies. She seemed alright enough so I tried to be friendly with her. Her name was Pistol. She seemed very shy and put her hand over her mouth when she smiled or laughed. She was a chubby, mousy-looking girl with a few tattoos, brown hair, and glasses. Quiet, but with a good sense of humor. I thought she seemed okay. She was there many of the times I went to collect my twenties... and so was the beer shirt guy. I tried to ask her about the beer shirt guy and she would roll her eyes and not say a word. Very suspicious. Now I was extremely intrigued. And why was he following me? People he knew were trying to be friends with me suddenly.

Summer was very hot. I couldn't go outside in this heat except to swim in my pool to cool off. My pool guy who came with the house was not doing a good job cleaning my pool. I have been a swimmer since I was a child. I checked the filter. It had not been cleaned in a year. I was angry. I started taking note of all the other pool cleaner trucks in the neighborhood so that I could have a new one. Oh, well the next week I went to get my twenty at the cigar shop as usual and the beer shirt guy showed up and ignored me. He stared at the woman who was sitting in the big leather chair, smoking a stogie and drinking a Martini. She was talking as if she knew everything and was named Red. She was a natural, copper redhead. The Beer shirt guy tried not to stare at her like she was a dream goddess. She announced that she was getting breast implants soon. Then she flashed her new enormous lizard tattoo, located just above her shaved beaver. The beer shirt guy told her not to get bigger breasts. He said hers were already perfect. She flashed him her breasts anyway, right there and then. She didn't have to; she was an exhibitionist. There were hundreds of nude photos of her all over the place already. She was very hairy and must have had to shave a lot.

I had seen her in the humidor photos nude since the first time I entered the cigar shop last summer. Now she was blonde. By the looks of them in the photos, she had the same size breasts that I did. However, she was heavy-hipped and had very thick thighs. She had freckles all over her body. She wore thick glasses and had green eyes. She was bragging about all the fabulous things she had done in her life. She always added sexual connotations to everything in attempt to be funny. She would brag on and on. Red had a very loud, lingering laugh. She loved to hear herself talk, much like Gus and Dodie did. I just sat, smiled, and listened. She was waiting for her husband. I had finished many errands and actually needed a smoke and Evian water, so I sat down. The place seemed cleaner and more upbeat than before. I thought maybe I should relax and listen to the local chatter here. Maybe I could learn something I didn't know already.

Deuce, the owner, told Red about my little bike

outside and how its presence had quadrupled his business during the last two biker events. He felt the urge to tell everyone. She was amazed it was mine. She was all about sex. She asked me what I did, and I said I had a band and was a blues, rock, & jazz singer and that I had just moved here from Spain. She went on to tell me that she was also a jazz singer and segued into telling her whole life story. She was initially married to a man who ignored her. Then she met Rave, her current husband. And she told how he divorced his wife for her and that she also divorced her husband for him. They just moved here from Michigan and own a pool cleaning business. She seemed fun and kooky. She asked if I had a husband. I blew off the question and was saved by her husband's entry on his Harley.

When anybody showed up, the townspeople made a big deal about it. He came in and introduced himself to me. He had terrible halitosis and brown stained teeth. I had to back up in this tiny, crowded place in order to not pass out from the stench. You think I'd be used to stench by now.

He looked at me like I was a dream goddess. There were no nude photos of me in the humidor but as we were all chatting, Rave flipped through the stacks to make sure. Apparently I was the only woman in town who was not in or on the pile. How could he let his wife do this? She was portrayed in some pretty sick, crazy poses too. Seeing them accidentally hurt my eyes... call me old fashioned.

I told them I inherited my pool guy from the previous owners and that he was not doing his job. They offered to come by and see if it was in bad shape and whether I should fire him and hire them. I gave them my address to come by the next day. They did. It was terrible. The filter had not been cleaned in at least a year. As a result, the pump would break and cost me five hundred dollars.

I knew the drill. I have had many pools in my life. I have had large and small pools. This one was very shallow and small. They did all the work in front of me. They seemed legit. They had many clients and were doing well. I called my pool guy and they told him off. I fired him. I hired them. Cool Pools was the name of their operation. They gave me a discounted price for both the pool and Jacuzzi. I was satisfied.

Red was fun and similar to a little sister at first. She made me laugh my head off. If a telemarketer called, she would pretend to be an angry Asian housekeeper and yell with a crazy accent, telling them to never call again. It was hilarious, but she drank practically a whole six-pack of beer before lunch while cleaning my pool and never seemed drunk. She also swam and went into my Jacuzzi as though she owned the place. I encouraged her so that Gus would have a new woman to spy on. She loved an audience and now had one, and also now had a pool to use because she and Rave were without one at their home that was half an hour south.

Chapter 11

They started going to karaoke with me some Saturday afternoons and singing all kinds of great music and having a blast. She really did have a nice voice. Unfortunately she flashed her boobs and got asked to leave once. I didn't drink, but Red and her hubby sure could pour them down. They never seemed to be worried about the strict cops and D.U.I.'s in this part of town at all. It was strange. The cops were everywhere. These folks were always way over the limit. They drove drunk without any semblance of worry. I always wondered how they got away with such activity.

It turned out they were friends with all the cops that hung out at the cigar shop. I guess they liked the nude photos of Red in lewd poses. The word must have spread about Red and she was immune to trouble, if you know what I mean. I never connected it until later. I had my own agenda. I never drank around these people. I tried to remain very mysterious. These people were full of surprises and somebody had to be sober.

I kept to myself and had to do a million errands to get my house just right. I was always running around town grabbing things and plants for my beach house. I noticed that the beer shirt guy was appearing at some of the other places I went. He just glimpsed at me then disappeared. I lived twenty- three minutes from the mainland shopping area. The speed limit was only 25 and 35 mph. There were only two roads to my house. One was the beach road and the other, the river road. It was like an island. How could he know where I was going to be all the time?

One beautiful Saturday afternoon I met a really funny guy named Harry while I was out with friends at the karaoke place I went to regularly. We really hit it off and ended up talking for five hours and laughing our heads off. He was a Harley mechanic. As it turns out, my neighbor across the street was his instructor from the motorcycle mechanic school. Small world. My neighbor was the one who was redoing my Harley for free. Harry was his student ten years before. He said he was a very nice guy and an amazing mechanic. He liked him as a student and as a person. I asked if I could know his last name so I could call and ask him to go riding together sometime. My other friends didn't have bikes. I called him and he said he would like to show me all the beautiful riding areas in the nature reserves around the area. He also wanted to take me to lunch. I was thrilled.

One Saturday we made plans to go out together. He made me ride to his house downtown where all the dead main street biker bars are located. We got ready to go and rode all over the place. We must have gone fifty miles that day. We stopped for sodas and joke telling at a number of the biker hangouts along the way. We had a blast. I thought to myself that I'd like to date Harry.

Well, I was not very thin at the time. He told me the truth and said he preferred slim girls. I was a little hurt at first, but I had tried every diet and nothing worked except for the one I was currently on. I thought we could just be great friends until I overcame my current health situations. I was suffering.

Harry was six foot seven. He was very handsome and kind. His brother played in a rock band and we went to all of his shows and had a great time. We rode to Bike Week' together and as soon as we arrived, the beer shirt guy did too. In fact, we were taking a group photo and he slipped in the back of the photo. I couldn't believe it. Later I found out his girlfriend and brother worked at the place we were at. As a matter of fact, the beer shirt guy's girlfriend served us. She made a big, loud scene about my coke order and tried to bully me into having some alcohol. It was eleven in the morning. Her bloodshot eyes bulged out of their sockets when she barked out loudly, calling me a "pussy". She was a mammoth woman, standing tall at six feet and one inch. She had deeply pockmarked skin and weighed about two hundred and eighty-five pounds with dark, bobbed reddish brown hair and a bellowing, gravel man-voice. She was very abrasive. I even thought she was a man at first glance. I will never forget her as long as I live.

The guy that directs the parking for hundreds of bikes was apparently the beer shirt guy's half brother. He is the garbage man usually. I found all of this out later. The beer shirt guy was everywhere Harry and I went. Harry noticed without me even saying anything.

Harry is really funny. He thought she, the bartender, was a man in ugly biker woman drag. We never did see them together. I asked Harry if he knew him or ever saw him before and he said he had seen him a couple of times in bike bars here and there over the years. Harry was very perceptive. Being very tall didn't hurt, either. Harry and I had a summer of barbeques and laughter at his house, hanging out at my pool and riding to listen to his brother's band. Meanwhile, I was slowly but finally shrinking.

One evening in the late summer, Harry and I were walking my dog around the block. I told him about my peculiar neighbors behind my house. Well whenever Harry was over at my house swimming, their stereo was always cranked to ten on the volume. They were real "thrillbillies". They wanted everyone to know what was going on in their life everyday - as if it was exciting. They wanted everyone to know no matter what.

Harry had the most amazing stereo system I have ever heard, except for the one in Studio 54 in N.Y.C. from the 1980's. He said theirs sounded horrible. We laughed. The barbeque was getting started at my house, so we took a quick walk before dinner around the block that I usually avoided.

As we walked by Gus's house, Gus came shooting off the porch with a beer in his hand, as usual, and said "Hey! I know you" to Harry.

Harry said, "Oh ya. You worked at the bus station. What happened to you?"

Gus said he was fired. We tried to keep walking and Gus followed us, trying to get "in" with us, friendly style. He offered us a beer. Harry thought Gus was a creep since the moment they had met at the bus station. Harry was a mechanic. Gus was a driver. Gus met Dodie while she rode the bus to work every day for five years.

Tonight, for our viewing delight, Dodie was wearing a lacy polyester lime-green teddy top with matching hot pants on her front porch. She was gripping a huge freezer mug filled with boxed wine in her hand. The cooler with the box was at arm's reach. Dodie was smiling like she was on glue while flirting and laughing extra loudly. She really did laugh like a witch, her cackle was unreal. It was scary to Harry and me. I nudged Harry and he said we had to go. Dinner was on the grill. Gus tried to invite himself over and Harry said were romantic together to get him off of me. Whew! I was so relieved.

But later, Gus thought this was a new connection and tried to friend me again. Thank goodness Harry and I were always on the move with our bikes. Harry knew what Gus was like. He suspected that Gus was spying on us through the fence too. He remembered why Gus was fired - he had sexually harassed many women on the bus. He was never wrong. Harry told me to call him anytime if I was nervous and he would come by. Harry was a great friend to me.

Gus was miserable in his marriage. I had another antique Harley in my garage that I had promised to bestow upon my friend, who is a Special Operations agent for the United States. I used to keep it in my living room when I lived in New Orleans. I had promised that if I ever sold it, it would be to him so that it could be mounted on his living room wall. In fact, my ex –fiancé had already delivered it to him in March after we returned from Mexico. Gus had seen it in my garage when my ex-fiancé let him in. He wanted it badly and wouldn't stop talking about it. I had moved it into the living room so Gus couldn't have another excuse to drive by and look at it. As if he would ever be sober enough to ride a bike. Plus, this one was for decoration. It was a collector's item with no wiring harness or battery. Gus is two feet too tall for this model, anyway. No matter what, he could never ride any bike because he wouldn't be able to hold a beer and drive at the same time.

Well, Gus whined and whined. He would go on and on arguing until he passed out from drinking. He tried to put me on the spot in front of folks about how he should have my little bike. As if that would get him any closer to having it closer to riding it. It was already long gone.

Chapter 12

I was very blessed as a child. My father restored classic cars in our garage. He loved motorcycles too. He taught me how to drive anything and everything. Dad was very popular and we had many friends over everyday, they would hang out at our house and in the garage. Our doors were never locked. Between my dad and the regulars, I learned everything about cars, cycles, and bodywork.

My Dad was a photographer for all the Indie, Daytona, Bahamas, and Grand Prix races. He was friends with all the famous drivers and everyone loved him. He was really fun and told thousands of jokes and was always nice to everyone. We were always going to races and parties all over the place.

Dad had Narcolepsy. It is a disease where you fall asleep randomly and wake up, not knowing you lost time. He could be in the middle of a joke and dose off without warning. It actually made the joke even funnier. I had to learn to drive about the age of eight because he would doze off and I'd have to grab the wheel as we started to drift off the road. He just put big telephone books and a pillow in the car which allowed me sit up there and drive. No problem. He said I was a natural. Roger Penske and Evil Knievel were my heroes. I was a full-blown tomboy. I loved hanging out with my dad in his dark room while he developed photos of the races. He taught me how to do that too.

My Dad was associated with a group of car dealers who he played poker with and had a big band that played at all the local weddings. He sang beautifully. He taught me all the songs and we sang all day in the car, garage, and everywhere. When I was about thirteen, the band was playing at a wedding and I got to sing. I wore one of my grand mother's antique dresses and looked the whole part and sang. It was great. They were amazed that I could sing like that. After all, this was during the 60's and I was singing music from the 40's. From then on I was always invited to sing at every party. Then, when I got older we sang at piano bars all over the place. I sang jazz too. We loved to sing no matter where we were. We sang all the new songs on the radio. Everything.

I had an entourage of boyfriends who worshipped my dad and had crushes on me. I never let a boy touch me unless I was arm wrestling them for money. We had a pool table in our basement and my dad taught us how to be pool sharks. I never lost at pool. My dad loved to gamble. He had an interesting assortment of eccentric friends who he gambled with. They would bet their cars, furniture, and even dogs sometimes. You never knew what car would be in the driveway when you woke up in the morning. It was literally a crap-shoot at our house everyday. There was never a dull moment. Dad taught us how to make stencils and paint hippie vans. He was good at everything fun. Our house seemed like the center of the universe. He was the King of practical jokes. We had every, 'booby-trap' and 'whoopee-cushion,' kind of prank gag in our house. My dad lived for pranks and laughter. As a matter of fact, I do not remember ever going through periods of not smiling or laughing while he was alive.

His motto was, "We are here for a good time. Not a long time." He was the best dad in the world.

So being brought up the way I was had made me street smart. I ended up traveling all over the world alone, but I was able to do so because of my life's worth of invaluable lessons. Sometimes I shipped my bike. I have friends in practically every country. I have met some very remarkable folks in my travels. I thought I could handle practically any situation because my dad groomed me for adventure without fear.

Chapter 13

It was a gruelingly long and hot, sweltering summer of paranoia. I was already playing daily cat & mouse with the pervert in my backyard. Now I had to listen for him to go on his beer runs so I could work out in my pool in for the only twenty minutes of peace I could get at home. Thank God that the cheap beer and gas station was further than the first one, so he had to drive about four miles to chat and brag at the "hot dog stand". Like I said, Gus loved to talk and hear himself talk. He had an unprecedented self-importance complex that constantly needed nurture. Plus, he was the local smoke connection and had to meet up with folks to drop off the "stink" in order to make money to fund his daily drinking. He basically lived on a "weed to be" basis.

Dodie was a shop-a-holic at Wal-Mart, so money was like water through her hands. She had to keep up with the latest trashy lingerie and gardening equipment. Gus had refinanced their home for the seventh time so he could buy the smallest BMW he could find. The car was a lemon; it broke down daily. Dodie was furious. This anger was festering like an underground swamp fire and was sure to escalate into a traditional Florida style "sink hole" soon. It was just a matter of time. Like I said, everyday, after other folks work, they would basically hold court on their porch and discuss the latest neighborhood events and try to intellectualize and analyze the surrounding happenings. This went on from 4 PM until Dodie hit level three and was plastered. She would try to bounce off the kitchen walls and attempt to cook dinner.

Some days Dodie would intercept Gus. This was when the deafening Pink Floyd music came on. It turned out that the music's purpose was to mask her screaming, cackling orgasms. I was always wondering why the screaming part of Dark Side of the Moon was off key. I didn't do drugs in High School. I am not tone deaf either. I knew something was "hinky" about their copy of this epic hit, but I couldn't put my finger on it right away until I heard Dodie say it was their mating music. It began to all make sense to me after talking to them at the fourth of July party. This also provided me a short window to work out in my pool for an extra five minutes, I had to take whatever I could get. Now I was getting, the skinny on their schedule of insanity to make my life barely sane. My dad used to say that "information is power".

There was another factor that plays into all this. 'Charlie.' Dodie had a beautiful and tragically neglected McCaw parrot named Charlie. She refused to talk to it, so it impersonated her when she was not at home. I am sure owning the bird was her way of irritating Gus, who hated it. I think it kept him on his toes. He would yell "shut the f@#$k up!" at poor old Charlie all day. When I heard him leave to go get beer I would talk to her. They kept her out in the backyard by my back fence all day, along with the three dogs they never walked or cleaned up after. Their dogs loved my dog and the bird loved talking to me, it even started talking back to me.

My brother used to have birds like that and would train them. I loved them, and they loved my voice for some reason. Well, I got Charlie to start talking to me everyday during my swim of freedom. So, when Gus & Dodie would land in their drunken, drug induced fog in the late afternoon, they would be shocked that the bird was smarter than they had given credit. It just needed someone to talk to. I loved it. The bird, however, did have Dodie's voice, unfortunately, and its cackling laugh was a given.

I taught the bird to say "gimme a drink." I thought it should impersonate Dodie's orgasms with Pink Floyd. Gradually, Dodie thought her meds were wearing off and thought she was hearing her own voice in her head. She decided to go off of the meds completely. Oh no! Well, when she did, all hell started breaking loose over at their little love shack. She started getting drunk and passing out over at the lesbian house two blocks away and threatening to leave Gus and take his car and truck away, which she owned. She started accusing him of everything he is, daily, and the fighting was escalating to where the sheriff's department was dropping by on a daily basis. It was a regular fiasco just to walk the dog around the block, but it was worth the hilarity. They were drunk out of their minds and as high as Pluto. They never got busted for drugs or anything. Like I said, Gus had a police record three pages long. Dodie put restraining orders on Gus, then dropped them weekly.

It was a war zone in our peaceful little retirement community. Unfortunately, for me, Gus got more focused and infatuated with me. Now that Dodie was all over the place physically and mentally, he decided to try ten times harder to confess his undying love for me, daily, anywhere and anytime. It was a nightmare.

I, at this point, couldn't even hide inside my home. He was on "crack", and had delusions of grandeur that he could just drop by and ring my doorbell to cry about his lousy life. I would never open the door. My neighbors would shoo him away, daily. It was getting ridiculous. It was getting more and more difficult for me to concentrate on my work. Now, I wanted a restraining order, too. He was a whack-job.

At one point, I had to blatantly say to Gus, "You are not my type." He asked why. I said I only liked mechanics and bikers. He was neither, and never going to be either, ever. That's how thick he was on the juice. Gus was as thick as a brick.

Chapter 14

It was still sweltering hot by the time September was floating by. Summer just wouldn't free us from heat bondage. Everyone seemed on edge, especially myself since I was not allowed to move about freely in my "paid in full" cash life. I never thought I would have to have an escape plan running through my brain at all times. Why did this insanity trap me? I was, constantly being interrupted by the doorbell and Gus.

I was trying to have band practice and get ready for 'Biketoberfest' joy. My band was irritated that I was being harassed in my own home and during rehearsals. Gus wanted to join the party every week. He actually thought it was a party. My home was soundproof but since Gus had no life and just drove around he dropped in whenever he saw the cars and vans in my driveway. We just ignored the door and kept on rehearsing. It was getting to be ridiculous. My bass player is six foot five and explained to Gus that his presence was inappropriate and told him to please buzz off. Gus needed a hobby. Dodie had given Gus a Fedora hat for his birthday and he started to wear it and walk one of his dogs obsessively around the hood to spy on folks.

Now he was dry, bored, grounded, and desperate. He gained the nickname of "Creep" by the neighbors. Now, all the riff-raff had to come to him. He even had to get folks to bring him his beer. He drank at least a twelve pack a day. The booze was like speed when combined with his crack intake. He would fiddle with his crack pipe when he was craving his next hit. He was like a freight train out of control.

So, the daily party grew larger and louder. Gus had guilted every person who he had ever known into "mercy deliveries" of all kinds. There were so many new hillbillies in pick-up trucks arriving at their abode that the neighbors couldn't park or get into their driveways. The noise was unbearable. Then, the sheriff would have to come for that fiasco next. This guy would do anything to escape boredom at any cost. These folks lived for drama at any cost. They sure kept the Sheriff busy.

I guess Gus wanted to have his own form of redneck jam session to try to get my attention, now. It was so noisy that I couldn't read or hear my television or stereo over it. It wasn't fair. All my other neighbors had hearing aids and could turn them off, technically.

I figured, well, this might be a new window of four plus hours of distraction when I would be free of Gus being in my rearview mirror. I took advantage of all of it. I needed a place to hide out and think and chill. It was too hot to walk my dog until dusk.

Chapter 15

I should have filed Chapter 11, at this point for bankruptcy of both privacy and sanity. I decided that this would also be my new shopping time on the mainland.

My pool cleaners were always calling me and asking me to meet them for a smoke or a drink at the cigar shop after they finished work at four o'clock. They were funny and quirky, so I started hanging out with them a little. There was a nice bar and café next door to the cigar shop that was outside and had a bizarre clientele as well. You couldn't spit without hitting "bizarre clientele" in this town, as it turns out. This place was upscale for the area, surprisingly. You could actually wear real clothes there, as opposed to cut offs and flip-flops. Red and I loved our clothes. That's probably the only thing we had in common that I knew of, other than the northern sense of humor and singing. I agreed only because it was not the cigar shop.

We started to go out regularly to have a few laughs and wear higher fashion clothes. They invited some other kooky folks to join up with us who were funny, too. Red had to be the center of attention wherever she went, so it was good because I was thinking about other things or practically nothing at this point in time. They let me be. They could see that I was in my own world. I just sat quietly and laughed at the buffoon court she was holding and was happy to be released temporarily from hillbilly hell. It became a regular thing until one Friday, when everything changed.

We were really getting into the fashion thing at this point. I was getting ready for 'Biketoberfest' and new outfits to sing in and all. I had on a new outfit that I was planning on wearing on stage in a few days and Red had one of her trashy biker wannabe outfits on and we went to the little bar next to the cigar shop to have appetizers and she had tons of drinks. And I mean a lot. Then all of the sudden the Beer shirt guy came over and plunked himself down at our table. I was bummed. He was buddies with Red. Rave had the "oh shit" look on his face. Nobody said anything to me as usual. I just could watch people and read them. Their body language was blabbering to me. The beer shirt guy acted like they were continuing an earlier conversation. Turns out they were. I always played dumb and still held onto the old 'I just moved here and don't know anyone or anything' clause that had been working like a charm so far. And the "look at the time, I have to go home and let my dog out" routine. The beer shirt guy hardly looked at me and never acknowledged I was there as usual. I said "adios" and split. That genie gave me the willies. Since they were all hardcore drunks, I left them with no further adieu. Just when you thought it's safe to try to upgrade. This town was shrinking around me.

The mainland is twenty-three minutes away from

my house, without traffic. After you get there you have another distance of the exact same length to get to the south end of town. It's on a grid and very simple. I had to take two roads and a bridge to get to my house. The mainland only has four roads that run north and south, as well as two more bridges. That's the lay out. It's either crack motels and strip clubs or seedy bars in the center. Then, there's the airport, track homes, and trailer parks and the main highway. I lived up north out of town where the beach homes and old retired folks were. It's pretty basic. There are only a few large money making events per year. The rest of the time it's dead as a desert and as hot as one too. I chose it because it was cheap and allegedly easy.

Now that I had been out there for a year and two months I thought I had it all figured out. Yes. I had it all figured out for me in my world. I thought what I wanted to do was what the brochures advertised, but it turned out I actually wanted less than they offered. It turned out that the town wanted more from me, though.

I learned that these redknecks loved drama and hated mystery. Also as it turns out, I was too mysterious and they were demanding drama of some sort. I had no idea. I just went on singing and writing and riding. Why did they want to keep messing up my secret plan? They must have really been eavesdropping through my fence while I was on my phone. I never told anyone locally about my dreams and aspirations. I am a very secretive and quiet person. I always acted like I didn't care about anything. The British folks teach you in Europe to ignore everyone, because folks just gossip, so this prevented anybody from getting under your skin. I liked what I had learned from them: just smile and act interested; picture something really pleasant in your mind instead. It is hilarious and effective.

Chapter 16

All I could smell was BBQ. Now, I couldn't get Sam Rockwell's face and visualizing *The Green Mile* scene out of my head. I could hear him singing the BBQ song while the guy was getting fried without the wet sponge. Oh boy. Then I started singing it out loud. Then I had to re-watch it for the forty-fifth time just to clear my head. What was going on in this seedy little town? What were these folks living for? Was every day just another cocktail hour in their lives? Or was there some kind of magic I couldn't see or feel? Was I not in the loop? They were happy as pigs in the sludge as their misery escalated. They laughed as though things were all hunky dory while swilling back their body weight in booze. They would fight and make up like it was a routine thing. I had never seen this anywhere. I just wanted normal, please Lord. I was thinking that there must be some creed that they lived by that was to have knock-down, drag-out fights and then celebrate the outcome with a drunken, slap-happy BBQ to laugh it all off. This country was more foreign to me than Morocco. I just wanted what I came there for.

I knew I wouldn't stay longer than five years. I never

do. I was already planning where to move next. The real estate market had already slid down the slope to where my home was worth thirty percent less than it was previously, so I was in a real financial bind. I was looking at other homes to see if I could move to a quieter, more remote place for less until my other house would sell. But, because I was so serious about my band and music goal, I didn't want to cut loose completely, yet. After all, I had just gotten the best musicians in the state to form a wonderful band. I was not willing to give up my dream because of an inconvenience. I was stuck. And it stunk to high heaven.

I thought to myself, maybe I should give in a little and see if I can fit in with these jack-asses as a performance art project and not let them know they were being punked. I decided that I would give it a whirl. I would accept the first offer that came along. It could end up being a laugh. After all, all you had to do was have a few drinks to fit in. It couldn't be that hard. I am like my dad. I don't need drinks. I act so nutty that folks think I'm drunk half the time if I am in a good mood. I faked being buzzed many a time in college and was surprisingly, the designated driver at the end of the night. I get high on ginger ale. I am very blessed. It was settled. I had no choice. This would be good. No one had seen me drink at all yet. I am a George Thorogood fan if you know what I mean. As my dad would say, "If you can't beat 'em, punk 'em." I can usually pull anything off.

Chapter 17

My hiding place on the weekend was a beach bar downtown that had a huge Karaoke scene. It was perfect because it was during the redneck cocktail hour in my backyard. The funniest locals and tourists would go there and sing. Most were very good. I loved this place on the sand. You could eat on the beach and swim in between songs. It was paradise. The regulars were cougars and guidos. They had all been around a long time. And I mean around and around and around. They were all party animals. It was really fun. You could get away with a lot of crazy at this place. If they had a "crazy thermometer" on the wall, it would've blown the mercury sky high. The master of ceremonies was the cutest man I have ever met. I had the biggest crush on this man. I was like a teenager when I walked through the door and laid eyes on him. And he sang my three favorite songs to open the show one Saturday. He was not aware of it. I got chills up and down my spine. His voice could sing any song perfectly. I was in the ecstatic zone when I went there. I forgot about all the nut jobs for four hours, two magical days of the week and I got to practice for my band while having a great time. It was perfect. My sanctuary.

There were these women who came to meet men. They were local cougars who dressed theme and had blingy glasses and clothes. They were friendly to everyone because they were hammered and horny. They were so flamboyant and danced, doing insane shit in public. They rode bikes, too. Hammered. Always. There were three blondes. Two were tall and one was short and fat. They all had a hundred miles of bad road written all over them. But they made me laugh until my face hurt, God bless 'em.

Well, the fat one thought I was the BEST singer she had ever heard in her life. She was always really drunk and buried me in compliments. She'd give me flashing ice cubes to put in my drink and hair bands with bunny ears that flashed, or whatever the "theme" that day was in her kooky world. She was trash, but sad. She reminded me of the Smokey Robinson song "Tears of a Clown". You could tell she was manic, too. I was beginning to think that something was in the water in that made all these people crazy as bat shit. It turns out they never drink water because fish fuck in it. That's their excuse for being bombed all the time. Moanie was the fat girl's name. She had her own house cleaning business for thirty years. She told me she'd come clean my house. I had to see this in action so I took her up on her offer.

I could get the skinny on that other group of cougars and other folks from the other end of town where Moanie lived. She grew up there and knew absolutely everyone who was anyone, as she stated. In Europe, the older women got all the guys. In the U.S., the old gals were sadly made to suffer humiliation. She had self-importance issues like the rest. She had to be the center of attention, too. But, since I was this singer who just moved there, she had to hook me into her friend group if she could.

I am a lone wolf. I don't do high school cliques. Never did. Never will. I like to stay in my own galaxy. She was hell bent on making me her new best friend. I was new and mysterious. There it is again: mysterious. I always thought it was a good thing to be.

I had stayed home the first year and worked in my home. I guess it was time to venture out to try and experience what was really going on beyond our two local bars.

Moanie loved to bar hop. She showed me every hole in the wall bar in the town. They were beyond sewers. She had no sense of smell since she was a house cleaner and had burned her nose from inhaling blow for thirty-five years. Therefore, she couldn't smell the urine and vomit-embedded bars. It turns out that the rage was the "cheapest beer in town" nights. And this was every night. They had the place set up for dollar beers in a close radius so you could crawl around from breakfast up until last call and only have to park once if you were downtown. Different bars in different sections around the areas did the same thing, so the partying was more convenient. It seemed like they were aiming for a few "mini Bourbon Street style" areas.

There was the humongous mall dedicated just to bikers that had yuppy biker bars and stripper-attired bartenders. Their uniform was an assortment of styles that were very revealing. This place made Hooters look like Sonic burger on glue. Clearly, it was a freak show out there. No one looked like regular people. They all had an issue they were dealing with and they told the world their sob stories and hustled dollar beers for sympathy. And they lived happier ever after and never walked on the beach and enjoyed the beautiful weather and sunshine.

I, on the other hand, would only go to an outdoors place on the water, where you can smoke and eat with live music. I loved the little places I found. They were perfect for me. Outside, on the river or inlet or ocean. Why bother going out unless you could have a perfect, uninterrupted relaxing place with a view. Now I had to get outside my box to get inside their heads. All of the other places were dirty and dangerous.

Well, the seedy biker bars had salmonella and "Ptomaine poisoning" on the menu. There was also 1970's décor and live music. Unfortunately, every band played the same music. It was like Ground Hog Day no matter where you went. You would see the same trashy women and horny men just cruising the same scene every day and night. I was hoping there was more. They were the locals. And that's all there was to it. What you saw was what you got.

I had to wait for an event like Bike Week to see a new crowd. And that crowd was just as seedy, if not worse. I really had to try to fit in now. I was a little too straight from my past. I had to dial myself down a few notches and relax to try to get in. Thank God my band was more upscale, and they were my only friends so far. They also were all happily married. All of the songs in our venue were different than the other bands, but they were still popular, fun ones. We were trying to break the boredom barrier.

Moanie was single her whole life. She was the "village party girl-idiot-drunk". She loved to drink and drive, so she was my driver. I would buy her a few cocktails and she would take us all over the place. She loved to brag about what a great singer I was. Every time we were at a bar with a band, she would request the band to call me up to sing a song. It was fun at first. I had a great time blasting out an oldie or two. I could do it in my sleep, after all. Now that she was my driver, I could start to drink a little. I was a little looser than usual. This was beginning to be fun. I started to become a small town celebrity. My poison of choice has always been Crown Royal and soda water with a Marachino cherry, so the drink it looks like a Shirley Temple. As a matter of fact, I called it my "Big Girl Shirley Temple" as a joke. The bartenders thought it was cute. I had Evian in my purse to water it down. After all, I was the new girl in town: the "mystery girl". I had now created my new, out-of-the-box image. I was a whiskey drinkin' and rockin' blues singing biker chick, as they referred to me. Publicly known now. I liked it. I was faking it while making it. It was important for the locals to actually see you party here. It was important to have some kind of reputation in this cracker box beach resort if you did anything of significance. They had to label folks for fun.

October was crawling by, it was just the second week. I still had twelve days left until I was going to try to be a star while singing and riding, finally. I was counting the minutes for the new fun and crazy activities ahead. I was excited. It was my first official 'Biketoberfest' singing that I had rehearsed and waited a year for. I was totally prepared now. I had the hair, clothes, song list, everything. I knew what the crowd liked and how they liked it. I thought my dream was coming true. I am a perfectionist at heart.

Chapter 18

It was a cool Friday evening, when Moanie picked me up to go out. She was dressed in a long top with leggings and a jacket. I was dressed like a biker chick in black leather pants and my leather biker jacket.

We cruised down to the cigar shop at about nine o'clock, with our flasks to get my twenty bucks from Deuce. We parked at the nice café next door and walked five hundred feet to the smoke shop speak-easy.

There was a huge full moon above us. It was beautiful. You could see the whole town when you crossed the bridge glowing like it was powered by another energy that night. Everything twinkled. The river and the ocean were lit up by the moonlight. It was breathtakingly beautiful. I loved this place just for the beauty it possessed, it allowed me to forget the seediness of the lifestyle. I can see why my Dad loved it here in the nineteen fifties and sixties. It had a magical ambiance when you were outdoors. It glowed and smelled of night blooming Jasmine. I guess that's why all the bikers came here year after year. It had a sentimental smell and warmth for a tortured, overworked soul who worked in a factory or an office job all year. This was paradise for folks who only had two short holidays a year and needed to breathe fresh air and relax in a fantasy world for a week, on a motorcycle.

Tonight was unusually different. Moanie and I were a little buzzed while laughing and joking around with Deuce as I got my twenty bucks. Nobody was there but Deuce when we walked in. Usually he was holding court with all the locals and a full strip bar atmosphere was happening with porn and loud music. Like I said, tonight was different. It was dead as a door- nail. Judging by the rare ambience, I thought he had been raided by the ATF as we walked in. This was unusual. In fact, he was closing early.

We actually sat down and poured ourselves a drink while he was counting his money. He was astounded that I had a small Crown bottle in the purple bag and a Crown plastic cup, soda, and cherries to make a drink. I had half water and half Crown in the flask. I always watered down my booze. He made quite a big deal about it. He said he had offered me drinks before that I never accepted. I said I didn't drink before dark. He was fine with that, and not offended. Now I made sense to him for once.

Moanie had never been there, so she was mesmerized by all the naked women in the humidor photos. She knew most of the women, naturally, since she had grown up there her whole life. She had a great sense of humor, so she was cracking up, laughing and gossiping about who they really were. I just sat in the big leather chair and lit a smoke and sipped my Big Girl Shirley Temple and laughed hard. Full moon. Moanie, Deuce, twenty bucks and a cocktail were proving to be a fun combination for me. We had plans to see one of my favorite bands at our local watering hole afterward.

How much better could it get being a local? I had a big smile on my face. Life was getting more interesting at last. I was feeling more relaxed. I was cracking some of my dad's old jokes that they had never heard before and we were all on a laughing roll. We were all lit up in smiles, like the moon. All of the sudden, as Deuce was turning off the smoke shop's neon light, the beer-shirt guy appeared like a genie as usual. He just slid through the door as Deuce was approaching to bolt it shut. He sat down next to me. I was suspicious.

We were all in the middle of a joke so the beer shirt guy had to wait to say anything. He laughed at the joke really loudly as if he had heard it told from the start.

Moanie screamed, "Hi Beau!" and proceeded to jump up and run over and hug and kiss him. She asked where he'd been and how long since they had seen each other last. She told him how gorgeous he was and asked how his job was , etcetera. She went on and on. Apparently, she knew him well.

I just sat there in total shock as Deuce poured cocktails with the outside lights off . He put the CLOSED sign on the door and locked it. I tried to compose myself and listen to every detail.

I finally learned that the beer shirt guy had a name, Beau. His beer shirt today had a name patch on it that read "MOE". Apparently it was a joke from *The Simpsons* TV show. He was wearing a Harley Davidson brown leather hat, black jacket, blue jeans, and ugly boots. He also sported yellow-and-black-framed night driving glasses. His goatee was a lot longer now, and grey. He said he just bought a new Harley Davidson and it was just delivered from up north. It was outside. He actually looked sort of different tonight. He didn't look as buzzed as usual. I stayed quiet while he bragged and told Moanie about all of his new news. He said he was retired from his job after twenty-three years at the local paper and his friend had just brought this new bike, which he got a good deal on, from up north. He unzipped his jacket. He looked a little different, not as bloated.

Now he was purposely looking directly at me. I froze and then I jumped up and swerved through the clutter to the tiny dirty bathroom. I had dressed extra special this particular night because I was going to sing with the band in half an hour. I checked my make-up and did inventory of my outfit and lipstick. In fact, I looked and felt great. Full moon too, it was great. Now, who was this guy who had been appearing like a genie for a year and three months? I finally had him cornered.

Moanie is a nosey gossiper, along with being a clingy and loud drunk. This was my chance to get the story. I was in a position of power at last. I could try to figure out this genie now. I thought of what I was going to ask him while I was in the tiny toilet. I started to wonder if he had GPS'd Moanie's car at this point. How in the wide world of sports was this man finding me? I asked the moon and just got a crazy smile in my mind's eye. I freshened up and came sauntering out with a carefree attitude.

Meanwhile, while I was five feet away, in the tiny toilet I could hear Moanie bragging about being my new best friend. She went on to talk about what an amazing rock and blues singer I was and told him that I had an antique Harley and hot rod. He already knew a lot of what she was blabbering about since he had been following me for so long. Bla, bla, bla.

I came out and sat down and opened my "port-a-bar" and made a fresh cocktail. Moanie asked him if he knew me. He said he didn't. "But, if she drinks Crown, she's my kind of woman," he said.

He now couldn't take his eyes off of me. He was smiling and flirting with me. He purred and growled at me like a loud panther in front of all of us. I almost fell right off of my chair. Moanie couldn't stop laughing. He asked my name. I looked at him and rolled my eyes. As if he didn't remember. He has known my name for over a year, since the day I made the deal on the little bike for Deuce. He said he had a terrible memory. The worst. Really. For a man who coincidentally saw me everywhere for over a year, he had to be brain dead if he really couldn't recall my name.

I asked what model Harley he bought. He told me and I responded by calling him a pussy. I laughed like the cartoon character, Woody the Woodpecker. Then, he told me what he paid for it to try and impress me with the deal that he was afforded. I laughed even louder and longer which made Moanie and Deuce laugh even harder and louder.

Deuce was ready to go home, or to retreat to his Mistress'. He knew I'd eat this boy alive. I was ready to go and sing. We all left the smoke shop together. It was about ten by this time -a perfect time to show up at the bar to sing and be fashionably late.

We were walking towards the bike, which was between the shop and the car, when Moanie's phone rings. She continued walking toward her car and around the corner. I stopped briefly to look at Beau's new bike. It's one of those new plastic Highway Patrol style Harleys. I make some sarcastic jokes and comment. I told him that I ride a "real Harley".

Then I changed the subject and exclaimed, "Wow! Look at this moon. It's going to be a lucky night." I start to say, "See ya. Wouldn't want to be ya..." when he suddenly grabbed me and planted a ten-second-long, earth shaking, fireworks-inducing, dream-style romantic French kiss on me. Wow.

There was nobody in sight. It was as if I had dreamt it. Moanie was around the corner and Deuce went out the back and had already left. The street was empty, except for us. It was amazing. I was paralyzed. My legs went out from under me. I almost passed out but I looked up at the moon for guidance. It just smiled back.

I couldn't breathe or speak for what seemed like forever. I almost fainted. Then Beau gave me his name and phone number on a small piece of paper with a heart drawn on it. He told me to call him if I wanted to go out during bike week with him. I told him I am in a band and am singing. He said he'd like to take me out on a night when I wasn't singing. I was so stunned that I actually answered the question.

My legs wouldn't move. I couldn't move. I was frozen. No one had kissed me like that since my fiancé died ten years before. He told me I was gorgeous and smiled at me like he had diamonds for teeth, the light reflected off of them beautifully. Then, he hopped on and fired up the bike, hanging a U-turn and burning out, loudly, in the opposite direction. He was so slick that I didn't even have time to react in any way whatsoever. It was like life was moving in both slow and fast motion at-once.

He was like John Wayne, as a hero on a horse, in a movie. I still can't properly arrange what happened to me that night to this day.

Moanie pulled out of the parking lot and I was standing there alone with a blank look on my face. I got in the car and we went up the road to our local bar so I could sing and she could dance and drink. I took a swig of my watered down Crown in my purse and popped a cherry in my mouth. I was in shock. I kept going over it in my head. W.T.F? What just happened? Did I imagine that? Now I actually needed a drink. Possibly a real double cocktail.

Chapter 19

It was only a one minute drive over the bridge to the bar. Moanie was blabbering all about Beau. She couldn't believe I had not met him. She had known him since they were kids. She said she almost had sex with him a couple of times. She said he is pretty much married to an enormous nightmare named Gin. And Gin was apparently referred to by others in town as a coke addict, dealer, and a huge pain in the ass. What a reputation, why would Beau be with this woman? I just listened in total shock. I was freaked out. She didn't see him kiss me or speak to me other than the Crown banter and panther growl, which is normal banter in the smoke shop, and apparently his regular demeanor in public. "Was this all a joke on me?" I wondered, sadly and surprisingly at the time.

Now I was messed up. What's going on here? I am going to find out. This is strange and possibly dangerous. Incredibly dangerous. Time to do detective work. Everywhere I go, he appears. Why now after over a year, does he kiss me? Not just any kiss... a huge, very dramatic romantic French kiss. And he finally gives me his phone number after a year and three months? He knows people I know. Was I being punked? Probably, I thought.

Moanie told me that Beau's girlfriend was referred to as his hell mate. She also said that she was that same big nasty woman bartender who called me a pussy at the biker bar.

I thought, "No way!" I was freaking out in my head. No wonder he never spoke to me before tonight. I didn't want her or anyone else to know he had kissed me. I just acted like I had seen him many times and he had never spoken to me until tonight, which was the truth. She said she was surprised that Beau was still with Gin. And, that they fought like crazy, in public and made huge violent scenes everywhere in town. They were into drama. Drinking and drug drama is so boring. I had seen my fair share of it during my California college years in the eighties.

Chapter 20

I waited four days and then I called Beau to say I could go out, but only on the opening night of Biketoberfest. I was busy singing the rest of the two weeks. Also, my favorite band was playing with some of my own band members at a huge biker bar that was outside of town. I had to find out what was going on with this man away from the maddening crowds.

That particular day had a strange storm blow through in the late afternoon. It got really cold and rained. I didn't know what to wear on his bike. At first I overdressed to keep safe and warm. When he came to pick me up, I was in a sweater and all black leather. I always wore my police helmet too.

Beau showed up at seven o'clock sharp. He was dressed very nicely. He was overly polite and acting as a complete gentleman. He told me I looked amazing and asked me where I wanted to go. He told me it was no longer as cold outside. Since I live right on the ocean, it felt colder than on the mainland. I didn't go out at night very often and was not used to the necessary layering of clothes. I didn't realize that mainland was ten degrees warmer. I had been a homebody and stayed the beach at night for over a year. Plus I had not ridden a bike at night in years.

Many factors played into my insecurity, including my first date with an admirer of sorts. I had my hair in a long braid. Very little make-up, since I had never owned much anyway. I was very nervous. And I mean petrified. I was scared about my house as always. I am an artist and I owned crazy art from all of my friends all over the walls. I also had blown glass on display everywhere. I had Hunter S. Thompson books and others from various artists scattered all throughout my home. I listened to music from Italy, Brazil, France, and Argentina. I would often play Ian Drury to Dave Brubeck on my stereo.

I had my home decorated with Indian saris as curtains, Mexican blankets, and incredible amounts of art, both secular and religious. My home was furnished eccentrically with my family's nineteenth century antiques and an antique seventies disco bar with the small little disco lights to compliment it. I decorated it with loads of all the crazy and fun things I had collected from my travels and inheritance. My house was in no way "Rooms to Go" material.

I had a coffee table that was deep, filled with all of the cigarette lighters my dad brought back for me from all over the world since I was four years old... Yes. I have been smoking since I was four. My brother and I got busted by my mom while jumping on their bed while The Beatles were on Ed Sullivan's Show back before my parents' divorce in 1963. That's when I became "Emma Peel" forever in my mind to escape their fighting. Yes, she is my heroine.

I became a fashion designer. I had a studio with a

sewing machine and I made bikini tops out of Crown royal bags for the Bike Week lady bartenders. They all had 'boob-jobs - 38 C's or D's. I made the one of a kind bag-tops so that they could rake in bigger tips during the events. It worked for them. In turn, they were nice to me and protected me from drunks after I sang.

Now Beau would know who made the tops for his bartender gal pals. I was a painter and I made crazy theatres out of cigar boxes. I live and breathe art. I also sang and played guitar, sax, and harmonica.

I just played along with this so-called "married man" to feel him out. Maybe he was trying to break-up with Gin. He wa s acting as Prince Charming toward me. He was honestly really impressive. He told me he was retired and rich and he offered me everything in the world to make me happy – this was all in the first five minutes of our date. I felt like Michelle Pfieffer in Scarface. He acted like he was a big wig and very well connected. Who was this guy?

Beau was trying to act like my house was normal and nice. He acted like I was normal.

"Nice house," is all he said.

I said, "I don't own a penny of it. It belongs to the Bank."

Then he said, "I mean your stuff."

I told him it was all just junk. Later I would find out that "junk" was his magic word.

He said he loved my home. He said it was very comfortable. A place that you never wanted to leave. I took this as a happy compliment since the neighbors who helped me move in and decorate frowned as if it was incredibly bizarre. He had already earned a silver star in my eyes.

I had to figure out his "wife" story on our first night out. He announced that it was not a date, yet, technically. Not yet. He didn't know that I knew about Gin. He thought he was so slick and that I was the green new girl in town. He was sadly mistaken.

I am a natural born Nancy Drew. I watched him prowl around and offered him a drink while I put the finishing touches on my fashionably late image. Mascara.

He made a drink and browsed around my place while he waited for me. When I surfaced, changed into a new outfit, I noticed he was taking pictures of some framed photos of me that hung on my walls, with his phone camera. That was weird.

I asked him why he was doing this. He said he wanted to take the tattoo magazine to get a better look at me. I tried to take it as a compliment. I came out in black leather. I had opted to change into a leather vest, instead of the sweater.

I eventually joined him for a quick, small cocktail in my kitchen and to have a casual chat. He could tell that I was nervous. He was nervous too. He was acting too perfect. He didn't act anything like he did at the cigar shop. He was kind, sincere and gentlemanly. He was on his best behavior. I was intrigued.

We left on his bike to go to the huge, outdoor biker bar. He was taking me on a tour of the nature reserve that was on the back way to the bar. It was cool, damp, and smelled wonderful. I had ridden this way in the daytime with Harry already. It was different at night. There was no moon this stormy evening, so it was very dark. The old oak trees were enormous. The swamp was so enchanting.

He drove me through the whole scenic drive very slowly. He grew up here and loved this place with all of his heart and soul. It was a great place to escape the freaks. I truly was enjoying this ride more than any of the others that I had been on. I said he should have taken me on this ride during the full moon. Remember, he had kissed me already. I think he forgot about it already.

He knew every nook and cranny of this road and area. He also knew the entire history of it. He loved to tell me everything about it. The whole long ride was about forty minutes. I learned so much about what was my new back yard. It really did start behind my home. We arrived at the bar just in time for the first set.

We were the only ones there except for the bartenders and the band. There were crazy show bikes parked everywhere to look at, and souvenir booths with t-shirts and jewelry were scattered about. It was like the evening was custom ordered just for us. Now, the weather was changing again to a sweltering humid nightmare for me. Beau bought me a Crown and soda with a cherry and we sat down on a picnic bench in front of the stage.

I waved at my band friends and they waved and smiled back at me. The singer was amazing. I actually had a big crush on him the whole first year. He never noticed me ever. His partner from work was in love with him and she was thin and gorgeous and determined. She was hovering around as usual. He was a hair stylist for his day job. He had so much charisma that it would knock you over. I had tried to flirt with him many times and he never noticed. I was out of practice anyway. I still kept trying, just in case. I couldn't stop smiling. I actually had a "sort-of date". Plus my favorite band was playing for us. I was really happy for about an hour.

Then, I got so over heated, by the humidity, that I had to do something to get comfortable. While the band took a break I tried to buy a t-shirt but they didn't have my size displayed yet. The event technically started tomorrow so all the stock was not available yet. I was burning up and starting to feel extremely uneasy. I was so bummed because I finally had a date and was feeling awful.

Beau got me water and another B.G.S.T. drink to try to alleviate my suffering. He was such a gentleman and so sensitive and caring tonight. I was experiencing a doozy of a hot flash. I needed the fire department to put this one out. His brother was the fire chief so I asked Beau to call him, jokingly. I thought I had a temperature of 110 degrees. It was the worst fear a woman could imagine on a first date... trying to hide the suffering but being unable to do so.

I suffered and hung in there until about ten o'clock. Then I asked if we could go for a ride to cool off.

Beau said, "No problem. Your wish is my command."

He felt perfectly comfortable with the climate because he was used to it all of his life. We drove slowly back to my house the way we came. It was cool in the swamp on the bike. I hugged him like the hero he was being. He was so sweet to me. Old school sweet.

I apologized and he told me not to bother and said he

had a great time. He walked me to my door and thanked me, then left. No kiss, no hug, no nothing. He said he'd call me soon for a date. I thought I had blown it. I had no idea.

Chapter 21

Biketoberfest was great fun. I sang and went out with my friends and had a terrific time. I didn't see Beau at any of the places I visited or sang at. Where would he be when everyone else was everywhere? I thought that was strange.

A week and a half goes by and then he calls and asks me out to a fancy lunch. He showed up at eleven to take me. He said we were going somewhere special. I was still new to the area so everything was an adventure and new to me at his point. He showed up on time. He was dressed very nicely. He was very polite and proper. He opened my car door and doused me with all of that old school charm. Impressive for a Floridian biker.

He drove me through the same nature reserve and then up a crazy back road for what seemed like forever. He showed me where the Bush family has a Camp David-like retreat.

I was lost. I had no idea where I was. I think he liked to be a know-it-all with strangers. And to this day, I still don't know where we were. He took me to a European village in the middle of nowhere. It was an expensive and very 'yuppy' place. He was telling me about himself on the way to and at lunch. He was extremely polite and acted as though he had attended Yale or Harvard University. Seriously, he was like an Ivy League graduate. He was really trying to impress me. His manners were impeccable for no apparent reason. Remember, I had seen him for over a year indulging in activities like watching porn and acting strange.

Only my ex-fiancé from ten years ago, who had died, treated me like this. I thought to myself that most men are not this romantic. We ended up driving back the long confusing way, so our date was five hours long by the time we were finished. He still didn't mention that he was living with Gin, or anything to acknowledge her existence for that matter.

He still wouldn't touch me or kiss me, but he held my hand all day. Then, he asked if he could see me again. I said yes.

Well, I got an emergency call to go to Europe ASAP, and I had to bolt. I had no idea how long I would be gone. I called Beau and said I had to go. He asked if he could come over while I was packing to see me. I said it would be okay.

Well, he came over at twelve-thirty in the afternoon with a small cooler in his hand. Next, he went into my kitchen and sat down at my small table in the breakfast nook area. He asks for a glass and I gave him one. I had an icemaker in my fridge door. He went over and filled the glass with ice and returned to sit down. He opened the cooler, which had a bottle of Crown in it, along with a few Miller Lights, and he poured a full glass of straight Crown.

He took a huge swig and the glass was suddenly half-full. He was talking a thousand miles an hour, nervously. He was buzzed already. He must have had a few before he even got to my house. That's probably why he never kissed me. Breath.

He was talking about his printing business and taking care of his old blind diabetic mother who lives across the street. He still coincidentally neglected to mention Gin. Then he pulled out an ankle gun to show me.

I said, "That's nothing. You should see the guns my Uncle makes."

I dismissed him completely. After all, I was too preoccupied with my packing to listen in detail. I told him I was very busy and had to concentrate in order to get out of there on time. I really wanted him to leave.

Guns had always been a part of my life. My mom and dad shot our dinner everyday my whole life. He couldn't impress me of all girls. Plus, he was too buzzed at 2 p.m. He didn't even offer me a ride to the airport. This was my first round, and he had lost.

He tried to justify his heavy drinking by saying he was only doing so because he was nervous that I was leaving and didn't know when I was coming back. I would only be gone a month, maximum. He acted very nervous and giddy. He had to be getting bombed by the time my friend came to take me to the airport at two-thirty. He acted excited and sad at the same time because I was leaving. He had no grasp of what my life was like, at all. He was clueless and buzzed.

Beau didn't kiss me good-bye. Just a tight squeeze that lingered for what seemed like forever. I told him I would call him from Europe when I was there and checked in. He blankly acknowledged the information. He was in a daze. I was clearly a woman he couldn't figure out.

My friends and bands all teased me, calling me an "international playgirl". It was a joke derived from The Beverly Hillbillies' show. I was the Jethro Bodine of women. I told Beau that that was my nickname and he didn't quite get it, yet. He soon would.

Why was he acting so extremely in response to my leaving? Why was he so nervous? I still had not mentioned that I already knew about Gin, the secret he was not willing to tell me. Maybe he thought I had been tipped off and he was worried I'd found out about it already. I didn't know. Now he had a window of time to straighten everything out during my absence. I had one too. I kept running through what I knew already in my head. I also kept thinking about how he acted overly polite for a man from "redneck central". Why was he trying so hard to act differently from all the other folks I had met?

Chapter 22

I was gaining the title of Woman of International Mystery and Intrigue. Between the pool cleaners and Beau and Moanie, I was the talk of the town and the 'hood.

In Spain, for eight Euros you could call all over the world for 800 minutes. This was a secret card that only Europeans knew about. I had a Spanish phone. I had it for six years. I speak Spanish fluently, so I was able to cash in on the secret call card. After I arrived, I was able to call my friend who was taking care of my dog and also to Beau and everyone else I wanted to speak with all over the world. It was great.

They were all flabbergasted that I could call and talk as long as I wanted for practically a song. I called my band, in fact. They loved it. I was singing with my band in Spain and we called and they were able to hear me sing with an English band over the phone. It was so much fun. I had a blast. I got to see all my friends and go out with Nils and our group and take group photos to bring back that depicted me singing with my band. It was wonderful. My business deal fell through. But, I got to spend time with all of my beloved Euro-family and eat good food and swim in my pool and love my home for the last time there.

I called Beau and if he didn't answer, I left really funny Spanish/English messages for him. Apparently he saved them forever. He loved them. They made him laugh even though he only spoke English.

I was gone until December 2nd, 2006. It turned out I arrived home right on Beau's birthday. I didn't know it was his birthday until I told him I was home and to come over. I told him I had brought him some cigars that you cannot get here for him. He came over in the early evening. He said he couldn't stay long.

I didn't know it was his birthday until he said he could only stay for a few minutes. I had brought him the cigars for Christmas. I just wanted to see how he would react because I was ready to tell him that I knew about Gin. He acted extremely nervous and anxious.

I said, "Why do you have to go?"

He said, "It is my birthday and I never tell anyone or celebrate."

I said, "Me too. My Birthday is St. Patrick's Day."

It stinks having a birthday on St. Patrick's Day! Everyone is plastered and never remembers. It sucks!

He said he wished that day was his birthday instead. Another sign. He was not being straight with me. I gave him one of the best cigars I had bought. A Cohiba. A real one. He had never smoked a real one. He was ecstatic.

He said he had to go and wouldn't be able to see me for at least a week. He said he was very busy.

I said, "Fine. Whatever."

Well, for some reason, that word gets his attention.

I said, "Go ahead, go. See you whenever."

He left without kissing me but he gave me a tight squeeze. He seemed like he wished he had not lied to me. He looked sheepish. My brother is a pathological liar. Their Birthdays were just days apart. Sagittarius. Born to lie.

I messed up. Big time. Now I was in for it. Everything he had told me on our two nice polite meetings was a load of BS. He was trapped, like a rat in hell. He was an insincere liar and a conman who was bored and looking for mystery and drama that I could provide. He had been playing me from the day I met him. He was trapped in hell and he thought I could release him. I don't know.

But I realized since I was unknown, Gin would never catch on to the fact that it was me who he desired. It was my fault. I had written a list of the qualities I wanted in the man of my dreams. There is no way he found my list. Yet, he fit my exact description of the man of my dreams to the T, except for the "no alcoholics or drug addicts or lying" part.

I couldn't get over it. I thought God had answered my every prayer when I came to this place. It was all lies. But why? Why was I the target? The alibi. Why me?

Chapter 23

I was sad. I knew something was up. I just went on with my normal routine and tried to forget about this joker Beau. No calls for over a week. I thought it was over.

As it turned out, he and Gin were having a "melt down" over at their own "Crazy Town" version of domesticity. She apparently was the mayor of this Crazy Town. It had nothing to do with me.

They had planned a Birthday/Christmas Party at his home and he was trying to prevent it. I was told that they had officially broken up a year ago after eleven years of misery and fighting. It was announced to the whole family. She was trying to carry on as usual. She had already planned and invited around fifty of the usual coke-heads and drunks – the date was set for the 12th of December.

Beau was anxious and wanted her out. I didn't know anything. I didn't call or anything. On the 12th, I was invited to a four star bar to hear a New Orleans style musician with my friend, Brenda. We went.

We got a call, and it was Beau, inviting us to his home for a party at nine o'clock that night. Directions to his house and time were provided. We were bored and disappointed in the musician at the place so we were happy to go. We were in Brenda's white Corvette convertible when we arrived. We parked across the street and walked down the dark driveway.

I saw who I thought was Beau, and said, "Hi!"

His brother rudely said he was not Beau and that Beau went up the street to Mom's with Red to get more wine and that he would be back soon. Brenda & I went and sat on the front porch. Rave was there. We sat down and I didn't need a drink yet. Brenda got one in the garage. The bartender had poured me a double at the bar since the musician was rude to me earlier. I know my limit. I had to wait an hour to see how buzzed I was. I wanted to be alert at this party in order to see what was really up with this Casanova cling-on.

We were all dressed up and looking great when a huge woman dressed in a black midriff top and bellbottoms appeared and barked, "Who are you?"

I said, "We are just folks from the cigar shop."

She just grunted like a big old hog and turned around and stomped off back into the house. I asked Rave and Red who she was and they said, "That is Gin. Beau's girlfriend."

I was blown away! He endangered my life and invited me into his fire ant pit. I didn't deserve this. You could tell she was high as a kite and in another solar system. She was huge in heels. She was harsh and she was yelling at Beau and swearing like a drunken sailor. Just the thought of him touching her and liking me was scary.

Gin was suspicious of anyone other than Beau's

family and their inner circle of old pals. They were all there. I got up my gumption to go in to the 'loo, and Brenda came with me. We passed Gin in the kitchen as she was bent over digging something out of the bottom of the fridge. She was very tall and maybe 220lbs. She was yelling and swearing at Beau and making a scene about something. She was not happy and it was her party. Nobody had eaten her "chef style food" that she had learned to make from magazines. I looked at her and realized she owned him 'TIL DEATH. At death would they part. Ring or no ring. He was the one for her. All these years invested in Beau. And, it was true and real and WRONG AND TORTURE AND MISERY and loud screaming, insulting, degrading pain. It was the absolute worst.

Why was I his type all of the sudden? He obviously liked huge women. Moanie was huge too, but short. I was petite compared to these folks. I was completely wrong for this boy. Red was chunky too and it seemed he had something going on with her. Why was he hitting on me, then all of a sudden not? He was playing too many games. I had to get out of here. I was really sad and desperate. I had made an enormous mistake. I was not used to this level of misery.

Gin was vile and he ignored her pleas as a drunken man usually does habitually. He would smile and ignore her, etcetera This wasn't his first Rodeo with this woman and this sort of family get together. Beau and his whole family were there except his sister and brother, Terry, who looks like Uncle Fester from the Adams Family. Beau's sister looked like him in drag.

Also, she despised him because she could see what a piece of shit he really was.

I told his brother and his girlfriend that he had been asking me out. They didn't believe me. They looked at me as though I was from another planet and was not speaking English.

I felt really uncomfortable and asked Brenda if we could split.

She said, "Absolutely."

We just went out to the car and drove away. We were both in shock at the whole scene we just witnessed. We discussed, in disbelief, what just occurred on the way home. It seemed like a bad nightmare for both of us. What was this guy thinking? Was he insane?

Chapter 24

The next morning he called me around ten o'clock. I said I didn't want to speak to him. He was so apologetic. I balled him out. He said he was coming over to explain.

I exclaimed, "NO!"

He begged and pleaded to, though.

I told him he was a liar and had put me in danger. He said to please let him come over. I held my ground. I hung up really angry.

He showed up anyway with a bouquet of flowers and rang my doorbell. I looked out the window and saw him.

I said, through the door, "I told you not to come over!"

He begged and pleaded. This man had no boundaries. I opened the door so he wouldn't disturb my neighbors who were often working in their yards and hanging out in their garages, tinkering away. He had tears in his eyes. I wouldn't touch the flowers. He asked if he could 'come clean' about the whole thing.

I said, "Okay, tell me, then leave."

You don't want to piss me off, ever. Trust is my most important issue.

He asked if he could sit down. I told him he could for only a minute. He kept trying to get me to accept the flowers. I sternly told him to just put them in the sink. My dad had firmly told me never to let a man mess with me, ever.

I said, "From the beginning, the whole real truth". Everything you have told me so far has been a lie".

He said he had wanted to date me since the day he saw me at the cigar shop. The tears in his eyes were very convincing as he explained that he had never been "in love" before he saw me. He said it was love at first sight. He explained that he was having a tough time trying to deal with it, considering the trap he was in.

I asked him if he was following me and he said he was and that he couldn't help himself. He said that he was afraid I would meet someone else before he could get a chance to meet me like he did. He stated that it was his way of protecting me. I was in disbelief. He promised me he had never done a drug in his life and never would. He also promised he would never do anything to hurt me, ever.

He also told me that he had been with this woman and it was never right from the beginning but that he made his bed and now had to lie in it. He said he had broken up with her and she wouldn't move out. He firmly stated that he had not touched her in years. He said he owned the house himself but made the mistake of putting the bills in her name ten years ago and couldn't get her out, legally, until she decided to leave willingly.

She was not willing to move on with her life. They officially broke up last Christmas and she was sleeping in the guest room. Beau said he would officially ask her to leave on New Year's Eve.

In Florida, the law is if you have bills in your name at a particular address then you also have rights to stay there legally. He said she had bought a house for her son, across the street, and he hated it, didn't want it and was moving out. He said she would move over there soon.

Across the street? That's even worse in my opinion.

I said I could in no way date him until it was over and Gin was gone. But she'd never technically be gone as far as I was concerned. He wouldn't take no for an answer no matter what. He said he just had to see me and insisted that we were soul mates. He stated that he was seriously in love with me and he had never been in love before.

I said, "Talk is cheap," and, "Too bad you lied to me and put me in danger."

He said Gin would never suspect me because nobody in his friend circle had ever seen me.

I disagreed. I was everywhere singing and now pretty much everyone in town knew who I was. I held my ground. He said he would prove to me he loved me.

I again said, "Whatever. I am very busy and do not have time for your bullshit." Then I told him he had better leave now.

He still wanted to stay at my house and talk more.

I said, "No. Go, now."

He started crying.

I said, "Go now, please."

He said he would call me later.

I said, "I mean later, after she's out of your house."

I said I was afraid of Gin because of her substance abuse problem coupled with her size. She could get violent.

Beau said she wouldn't.

I didn't buy that story one bit after all I had heard of her temper and all. She was rough and psycho. I also asked how he could date someone as vulgar and down right huge and nasty.

He said she wasn't like that when he met her.

So I said, "And you haven't noticed what she has evolved into?"

He said he had tried to avoid her at all costs.

I said, "Well, throwing a party with family and friends didn't appear that way. Inviting me was a nasty and dangerous thing to do to someone you are allegedly in love with. Plus you couldn't talk to me at the party other than to say hello because Gin was on a drunken coke roll."

He said he wasn't thinking about that.

I said, "Well you better start paying attention because I am not attaining any happiness in this relationship that you say you so badly want with me." I was very angry and stern.

I said, "Please go now."

He cried and left.

The next ten days he tried everything he could to come by and hang out with me at my home. He brought me presents and cards and flowers. He called three or four times a day to see how I was. This man was obsessed with proving himself to me and trying to win me over.

Chapter 25

Christmas Eve came along and I was alone as usual. They had the karaoke party at my favorite sanctuary. I took a cab so I could have a few drinks that night.

The host, Stormin, was as darling as ever. He had a way of making folks really happy. All of us local orphans went for dinner and the after-party. It was a blast. I was singing my head off and dancing and laughing. A wonderful group of folks were there. I knew most of them. We were having a happy Christmas party.

All of the sudden, two gorgeous guys appeared. They came right up to me to compliment my singing, my outfit, and my long hair. They were funny and friendly. The one fellow had a girlfriend who bartended next door at the beach hotel. But the other was single and looked like Mickey Rourke and Bono put together.

His name was Glenn. He was sweet and soft-spoken. He offered to buy me a drink. I allowed him. I was single, after all. He was more my type than Beau. We ended talking for hours. We had a lot in common and a similar sense of humor. I was about to find out just how much.

Well, we were outside enjoying the ocean on the deck. I was having a smoke. He was becoming increasingly attractive to me. I actually wanted to kiss him right there and then. I had to contain myself. So just for fun I asked him his nationality. He told me he was adopted and didn't know. I asked his last name and he said it.

I said, "Your last name is my nationality".

We laughed. He asked me my last name and I told him. He lit up like a Christmas tree. He looked at me for a few seconds.

I said, "What? Is it bad?"

He asked me, "Do you have a brother named Swinger?"

I almost fainted right then and there. My heart almost exploded. I turned around to look at the ocean and catch my breath. I couldn't breathe or speak for a few seconds. I took a huge breath and turned and looked at him with a serious face.

All the color had drained from my face. I thought of Humphrey Bogart and Ingrid Bergman in *Casablanca*. Then, I decided to quote the saying to him.

"Of all the gin joints in the world you had to walk into mine."

He said, "So, that's a yes?"

I nodded sadly.

He said, "Sorry."

I told him we do not speak and I had not seen him in thirty years. He said he had sold him fifteen Harleys over the twenty years he had worked at Harley Davidson on the west coast. He said he did not like him much either.

I collapsed with relief. Thank You God. The karaoke party was ending. I said I had to call a cab. He said he would take me home.

We went up to his beautiful Harley custom truck and got in. It was sweet. He invited me to his home for a drink on the way home.

I said, "Sure."

It was Christmas Eve after all and we were both alone and lonely and he knew my brother. He took me to his beautiful home. It was located on a street two blocks from Beau's house and hidden in the woods right in the middle of Beau's little neighborhood. It was really private and nicely decorated. This guy had good taste. He made me my drink and we hung out and were really attracted to each other. He was a true gentleman.

We were there for an hour or so. We kissed and it was quite nice. Then we started telling stories to each other about my crazy brother. He couldn't believe the coincidence. I was floored. We were in hysterical laughter. He told me things to fill in all the years I have missed seeing and speaking to him.

My brother has been a mess for a long time. He buys insanely expensive bikes and cars. He parties like a rock star.

Glenn and I had a good buzz coming on at this point. We decided to go to my house since we had no family and it was Christmas Eve. We got in his beautiful truck and headed over to my house.

While we were driving and cracking up laughing, we decided we would call my brother and punk him when we got there. It was only ten o'clock when we got there. I had an unlisted number and a speakerphone at my house. We were brainstorming on what to say to him and laughing the whole time.

We got up to my place and I had just redecorated

my kitchen the past week. I had antique cigar label wallpaper from Cuba on the walls. I made it look like a cigar lounge from Cuba. I had all the decorations from Mexico and Spain all over and parrot lights around the small cute bar in the corner in the nook. I made a Palm tree Christmas tree with pink flamingo lights and small disco ball ornaments on it for the ambience. It looked amazing.

The rest of the house was all lit up with fun Christmas decorations of the Grinch that I had collected over the years. I had crazy lights all over the place. It was magical. Glenn came in and had a huge smile on his face. I put James Brown's *Funky Christmas* CD on the stereo and we danced like James Brown and it was great. We made another cocktail and started planning our "punk my brother" Christmas call.

We knew my brother would be bombed out of his mind at some party or bar. So Glenn dialed his number and my brother picked up his cell phone in some loud place.

Glenn says, "Merry Christmas Swinger! Do you know who this is?"

Swinger slurred, "No, but Merry Chriiiisssmmmaaass, to you! Who is this?" He was tanked and in a happy mood.

Glenn said, "It's me, your Harley buddy, Glenn."

Swinger went nuts! He was so happy that it was Glenn. Swinger asked him where he was, because he moved to an East Coast beach city and my brother was too huge to ride now and was trying to sell a Texas Chopper.

Glenn told him he works in coastal town now and

bought a home here. Swinger could hear me cracking up in the background, along with the James Brown playing.

He asked Glenn, "You have a hot babe there with you? It sounds like you're having a good Christmas, man!"

Glenn said, "I have the hottest, smartest woman I have ever met here. I just met her tonight. She's my Christmas Present. She's a living doll."

Swinger said, "Lemmmme talk to her."

Swinger absolutely thought that Glenn was a total playboy who always got the best women.

Glenn told Swinger that we were on speakerphone.

So, Swinger said "Hi! Whazzzzz yer name?"

I start laughing so hard that I couldn't remember which nickname to choose. He never called me Ruthie, ever. He had called me "Fantasia, the first wonder of the world" or "Faye".

So I said, "My name is 'Faye."

Then he said, "That's my sister's name. Wow that's crazy!" He was so roasted that he didn't recognize my voice and nothing was registering yet.

Glenn and I were losing it, laughing. Glenn described that he met me singing in a bar in the coastal town and that I was gorgeous and rode a Harley. My brother still didn't get it. They started bantering away about old times riding on the west coast for a few minutes and yucking it up.

I told Glenn to ask him if his nickname was "Swinger with the big humdinger." So he did.

There was a silence on the line for about 3 seconds

then my brother went nuts. He said, "Oh Shit! Are you with my sister?"

We busted out laughing! My brother was so surprised and pissed off at the same time that it killed his buzz instantly.

He said, "Get the F***K outa here! You're with Ruthie?"

Glenn said, "Yup. And she is amazing. You'd never believe she is your sister. What happened to you, Swinger?"

I almost had heart failure from laughing at this point. That was the same answer we have gotten since Swinger had changed drastically in his early twenties. I was crying because I was laughing so hard.

Swinger got really mad as usual after the same comment he had heard for years and years and then angrily blurted out that he had to go and said, "Bye Glenn old buddy. Merry Christmas!" soberly. I guess it was a buzz kill for him. Or perhaps maybe a moment of clarity.

We continued laughing hard for what seemed like an hour. I mean, what were the chances of one degree of separation. On Christmas of all days, too. I was so happy. The best Christmas Eve "punking" on Swinger since my friend pretended to be Jack McGee,in Seattle back in nineteen-ninety three. And that was hilarious, too.

You'd think, Swinger would be used to being punked while growing up with Dad and my grandfather. He was out of practice.

I thanked Glenn and hugged and gave him a huge kiss. We just kept hugging and laughing and imitating my brother and kissing. I thought this man should be my boyfriend, definitely. He understood me already. No creepy mystery or girlfriend.

We had not thought to lock my door when we came in. It was about eleven-thirty at this point when all of the sudden, as we were hugging and kissing, the door flew open and Beau came charging in. It scared the crap out of us.

Beau saw us and ran towards us. He grabbed Glenn and pulled him off of me. Glenn was in shock. So was I.

He yelled, "What are you doing? "Ruthie's my girlfriend!"

I said, "I am not! You have one you live with. I am single. You have no claims on me. I can do anything I want with whom I want. Whenever I want. And I always have and will. Get out of here! What are you doing coming into my home anyway? Go!"

Glenn was so polite. He said, "You heard the lady. You need to leave."

Beau was really drunk. He wanted to fight Glenn for me. I said that Glenn knew my brother and that we were seeing each other now. Glenn smiled. Beau still wanted a fight over me. I said I'd call the cops if he didn't leave. He was really jealous. He said he was throwing her out.

I said, "I don't care. I want to date Glenn, not you. You have too many lies and bad baggage. Everything you say is a lie!"

Glenn listened carefully and was ready to help him out to his truck.

I said, "What are you doing all the way up here at midnight on Christmas Eve?"

He said, "I missed you. I had to see you."

I said, "This is not acceptable behavior and to barge into my home and assault my brothers friend. Go home and sleep it off."

He loved to argue and he did so for as long as he could. He was determined to ruin my happy, lonely Christmas. And he did. Beau had just ruined my happiest evening in years. I was pissed off, to say the least. He finally left. It took an hour. Glenn lived two blocks behind him of all places. Of course now I had to tell Glenn the weird story about him appearing all over the place, etc. He felt sorry for him because he blew it with me, "the coolest woman in this town," as he described me as.

This year Beau was the Grinch that stole my Christmas. Glenn and I were both unbelievably angry that he interrupted our romantic moment. We tried to get it back but the magic was stolen that night by Beau. We kissed and hugged for a few more minutes and then he left. I went to bed with a big smile on my face nevertheless.

Later, I was to find out that Gin had stolen Beau's Christmas.

Chapter 26

On Christmas morning, I woke up at ten o'clock AM. I was happy and freaked out at the same time. I had a date with Glenn. He had no family and mine was dysfunctional and absent for thirty years. Perfect. We had the same nothingness. I was excited to have a date on Christmas day.

My friend from New Orleans was flying in around noon. Moanie's sister was having a Christmas dinner party at her house and we were all invited. Beau was invited too, unfortunately. Well of all the crazy things to happen at noon on Christmas day, a tornado went through the center of downtown and took out the police station on the main street, missing Moanie's sister's house by just ten blocks. I was driving to the Airport only twenty minutes before the Tornado. I was only blocks from the disaster. It was really close. It was a true miracle that none of us were hit by it.

So I picked up Hal at the airport and we went over to Moanie's party at her sister's house. Her boyfriend had just wallpapered my kitchen a few days before. He was really nice.   They were all plastered and stoned already. The food was amazing. She was the Queen of

BBQ. I have never had better food in my life. We were not drinking that day. The cops were all over the place with the tornado and all going on. It was a huge disaster. Many homes were hit and destroyed.

Just as we were leaving and getting into my car, Beau appeared. He was visibly pretty drunk. I introduced Hal to him and told him that Hal was a detective and my best friend from New Orleans. Beau was trying to be really nice to the two of us. He was trying to apologize for showing up last night without being invited.

I could tell that he was still drunk from last night. He was all showered and shaved and dressed nicely, but the booze was oozing out of all of his pores. His eyes were really blood shot as well. He looked miserable.

Hal and I were trying to get in the car with tons of leftovers. Beau asked if he could come out with us.

We said that he couldn't and that we were just going home to watch *Uncle Buck* and to catch up on old times. Beau looked bummed and went back into the party where everyone was bombed out of their minds and celebrating. Moanie was thrilled that Beau was there. He was in the right place now. They were all on the same level of drunkenness, drowning in booze. After all, they all grew up together in this small party town.

Hal already knew about Beau's and my situation. Hal was six foot four and two hundred and eighty pounds of solid muscle. He worked out and swam everyday at the gym. He was my bodyguard. Beau was not going to be able to mess with me until after New Year's Day. I was relieved to say the least. Last night was horrible.

In the car on the way to my home, I told Hal what Beau had done and about Glenn. He couldn't believe how stupid it all was. After that, I told him what we did to Swinger, and we both lost it laughing. Hal was my closest friend since my dad had died. We had been though hell and high water together for twelve years. He was my closest friend. His parents were like parents to me too.

Hal used to be partners with my Special Operations friend who now has my antique Harley. We had done some amazing things together for many years. You could depend on these friends forever. Plus they were really fun even when we were doing business. I could tell them anything and they knew I was telling the truth every time. No matter how crazy it sounded. New Orleans was an insane place. They had both seen and done it all, while working their jobs.

I told Hal that I thought I was going to have a problem with Beau, in the long run, and wanted him to check him out and see just how dangerous this situation was. He said he'd love to. This was going to be interesting to say the least.

We called Glenn and asked him over. He said yes. He was so nice. He and Hal hit it off right off the bat. When we got home Beau had left me a card, more flowers, a carton of my exotic smokes and a ticket to go on a dinner cruise in St. Augustine on my doorstep. He was not giving up.

We stayed in and had a really good night of laughter and story telling. We were still all tired from the night before. Glenn was great and we all made it an early night and said we'd all get together later that week, before New Year's. Little did I know Beau was closely watching me. He was trying to hide and avoid Gin. We got up the next day and I showed Hal the town after breakfast. We went out to lunch at the karaoke place on the beach.

Moanie called and declared that she liked Hal. She wanted to take him out and show him the other side of the tracks. He loved to investigate so he went to get the "poop" on Beau. She knew a lot and he could get it out of her. He's a detective for goodness sake. He is never on vacation in his line of work. He just acts like it to fit in. And it works out very well.

The next night we went to dinner at the nice place next to the cigar shop. They had the best duck on the menu. I grew up on duck. My mom shot ours fresh for years.

Moanie came out with us. Just Hal and Moanie and me for a nice quiet dinner out on the town. We were sitting outside at a table enjoying the warm front we were having.

The waitress just put our dinner on the table and we were having a wonderful time with Moanie telling me everywhere she took Hal on her "tour de jour," when Beau slid up and sat down with us in his work clothes.

Beau seemed nervous and paranoid. We were shocked. We all asked him how he knew we were there since we were in Moanie's car and we were parked way in the back of the place and our table was hidden on the patio. He said he had a fight with Gin and was pretending to be delivering printing up the coast. He thought he had John, his friend from the butcher shop, cover for him to help him hide from Gin. He said he had to see me.

Moanie was in shock! She knew nothing about his "amore" for me as of yet.

Just as Moanie asked about Gin, Gin came flying into the parking lot in a Chrysler 300, bottoming it out with sparks flying, at about 50 mph. She slammed on the brakes and jumped out of the car.

Gin left the car running with the door still open and the stereo blasting loud rap music.

She was screaming in her gravel deep voice, "I know you're here, you, 'Muthufucker'! I am going to find you and kill you, Beau!"

Moanie whispered, "OH SHIT! RUN BEAU!"

Beau ducked and shot through the hedge and ran as fast as he could through the two dark parking lots over behind the health food store. She was yelling and screaming. Beau ran as fast as he could and took off in his truck in the opposite direction. She ran around her car and up towards us screaming and swearing.

I ran into the men's room and hid. Hal and Moanie put my food in front of them to make it look like it was only the two of them. Gin raged by them and took a glance. She didn't even see or recognize Moanie. She flung open the door and almost hit the hostess. The bar was packed.

She ran around yelling, "Beau! I know you're here! I am going to find you and kill you!"

She rampaged the place with four small nice dining rooms. She then flung open the ladies room door.

I was watching through the cracked open door and then quickly locked the men's room door. Gin grabbed the handle and wiggled it.

She hollered, "Fuck! I know you're hiding in there, Beau."

The manager politely and aggressively asked her to vacate the premises, thank God!

She was yelling outside that she knew he was in there and that she'd find him and kill him.

After being escorted out by the owner, Gin did a burn out in the parking lot and left rubber one hundred feet or more in the parking lot, fish-tailing and almost hitting the high-end cars.

The parking lot was small and tight. It was filled with Mercedes and BMW's, and other high-end cars. The manager was trying to call the cops. After all, the police station was just across the street, for goodness sake. He could have just yelled out the door. It was true.

You could still hear her roaring down the streets with her still yelling out the window for at least four blocks. She flew past the police station going about 65 in a 35 mph limit. She was nuts and heavily self- medicated. For some reason she was invisible to the police.

We went over to the cigar shop just to see if Gin had dropped in there first before she rampaged the restaurant. She had made a huge scene there and Deuce had asked her to leave.

Hal was worried I was in real danger now. He thought this place was more whacko than New Orleans on a good day. Thank God he was staying a few more days and nights. I begged him to stay a week more. He had a heavy workload in New Orleans but, as usual, equipped me with all the information I would need. We had a strategy figured out. We always did.

Now that Moanie knew, maybe she could protect

me in some kooky way. She was a big help. Plus, she was enamored with Hal and would do anything to get some "coochie-coochie". Unfortunately, that was never going to happen. But one can dream. She was a nice, but desperate woman who was truly bored. She thought this was great, but dangerous for me. She was genuinely worried for me. Nobody liked Gin anymore. She was off the hook. Poor thing was whacked-out on '"Hillbilly Heroin" and who knows what else. We didn't try to guess anymore at this point.

Gin was dressed like a homeless person. It was so strange. Beyond grungy. And she smelled bad. What was that all about? Deuce said she had needle marks and sores all over her and was picking and scratching them in the shop. He said the next time she tried to come in, she would be asked to leave permanently. Beau too. Deuce had a lot to lose with folks like this drawing attention to his Speak-Easy. In fact he said that the whole group of crazies associated with 'Beau' were getting on his nerves and causing drama and drawing negative attention to his secret club. He could lose everything. And he didn't have that much left to lose at this point. He wanted peace in his oasis.

I was not affiliated with *that* group as far as he knew. He appreciated me more and more each week. I was favored as a client. I drew him good customers with my tiny Harley and was low key, mysterious, and quiet. He liked my presence more, turns out. Plus he still owed me money. He liked Hal and my ex-boyfriend, the mechanic, who bought cigars and was his pal. He liked the company I kept. Now I was safe there. How crazy is that? Who'd-a-thunk? We all knew we had a whacky week ahead of us now. It was inevitable. Times they were a changing. Not for the better as it turned out.

Chapter 27

Hal and I were plotting a strategy for my new year ahead. We were trying to enjoy the last days of this year too. We were trying to figure out how crazy Gin was. Did she pack a weapon or two? Was she capable of true violence? What was she on? Who and how much did she know about Beau's secrets?

We called up Red and Rave and asked how well they knew Beau and Gin since they were at their Christmas party. They were coming over to clean my pool so we asked quietly in my home.

Who were these folks? They pretended they were barely acquaintances and they had just run into Gin and Beau at bars with pool tables and shot pool occasionally. Hal asked a lot of important questions. Hal has a mild, calm manner with people that enables him to extract information without having them feel pressure.

Red and Rave thought that Gin probably packed a weapon or two and that she was dangerous. She was huge to start with and loud, but severely abrasive. Also, she was absolutely well connected somehow, to someone in power. And, why me?

They said that Gin had realized that Beau had moved

on, finally. They said that Gin had referred to me, the mystery girlfriend, as "fuck face".

Great! I had been called a lot of names in my life, but fuckface had never been one of them. My feelings were actually really hurt.

I asked Hal to tell Beau to "get lost!" This was too much! This was truly vile and nasty. I was too busy to have this kind of overwhelming drama. This was ridiculous. Now, I had the neighbors and Beau and Gin making my life difficult. Too many distractions were popping up.

All I wanted was my band, bike, hot rod club and peace. I liked Glenn. He was quiet and nice. And I liked Harry.

Harry my biker friend and no one else at this point. Why was this happening? What did I do to deserve this?

Hal tried to reason with Beau, but Beau said he loved me and wanted to marry me. Hal and I couldn't get through to him in any way the whole five days. He was like a tornado with too much testosterone. He followed us everywhere we went and Gin was on his tail constantly. No matter where we went, she would show up and make a scene. Gin could make the biggest scene that I have ever seen. She probably GPS'd his truck. Hal and I had to pretend to be lovers to cover it up. We tried to laugh, however it was insanely spinning out of control. Beau was obsessed. Gin was really obsessed. Insane. I had never had a man do this to me.

My previous ex's had all been normal. I am, to this

day, on speaking terms with most of them. No man has ever been insanely obsessed with me like this. Is this how American men had evolved? I was still so sad and broken hearted about Francisco. He truly loved and cherished me in a connected romantic way. Old fashioned love. I loved him for his honesty.

The minute I came off the stage in Mexico ten years ago, Francisco came up to me and asked me to marry him. On our first date six months later he was two hours early picking me up for our first date for lunch. He took me to a romantic island lunch with his best friends. We had a wonderful time on the beach with all of his dearest friends and had a huge picnic.

On the way home, he stopped at all of his families' homes to introduce me to his family and propose marriage to me with a custom made ring. This was the way the last man approached me, a man who was truly in love with me.

Unfortunately, Francisco was in an accident and died two months before our wedding, ten years ago. I have been alone ever since my old friend who was fixing my truck had gone down hill last year. He never played games with me. I was blessed with an honest true love. I thought I had suffered enough when he died suddenly. I mourned nearly a decade, so far.

Chapter 28

Beau was bouncing off the walls, obsessed with impressing me. Unfortunately for him, he was being followed by his ex. He followed me while she followed him. He owed her something.

This seemed nuts. They had lived under the same roof for eleven years. Why could she not resolve her issues in the privacy of his home, quietly? I had so much going on that him being interested in me seemed more like a pain in the butt to me, not love. His approach was undeniably bizarre. The lying, hiding, and whatever else he had up his sleeve was distracting me from my real mission. I hate distractions when I am involved in a serious project or two. I like to work undisturbed. My home is my studio and home, all in one. Personal space is the most important key to my life. Privacy.

Why me? Was I just a place for him to hide? It felt like that at the time. He was really trying to impress me all the time. Meanwhile on the other side of the tracks he was playing cat and mouse with Gin still, she seemed to always be in the picture.

It was like being in a bad B movie. Or living a re-occurring nightmare. While he, in his mind, thought it was exciting and romantic. I knew he was exhausting me, both physically and mentally. Too distracting in every aspect. Hal saw everything with his own eyes. He wondered what was he thinking? I was not in his league in any way what so ever. All he wanted was the new mystery girl in town. He told me he met Gin the first week she moved to town. I was a tomboy. She looked like one, but was not, deep down in her soul. She was a hairdresser and feminine but very catty when angry.

Chapter 29

Hal and I went to Harry's house on New Year's Day to goof around and hear the new addition to his already enormous stereo. It was full-bodied amazing. We told a bunch of jokes and then went to see Glenn at his friends girlfriends bar for champagne.

Hal and Glenn and I were trying to figure out what to do about Beau. Glenn and Hal agreed that he was obsessed beyond control. We had all of our photos taken for the New Year there at the hotel beach bar. Glenn and I looked so friendly and comfortable together. But Hal and I knew that Beau had done something threatening to Glenn. I could feel it. Glenn wouldn't say. But you could see it in his eyes.

I told Hal, "I can handle this."

Hal had to fly out at six o'clock p.m. for N.O. but I had a plan. Hal liked the plan.

Now, I was alone. Bait for the shark.

Chapter 30

Thank God I had band rehearsal and guitar lessons to get ready for Bike Week at the end of February. I was busy, busy!

Beau was calling me and saying he was in my driveway every day. No kidding. Twenty-four hours a day, seven days a week. It's strange how the pool cleaner, Red, would show up, and then so would Beau or the other way around. This was getting to be a regular occurrence. We would all sit out by the pool together. They would drink beer and talk about the latest things Gin had done and of my new nickname, Fuckface, and laugh.

I didn't really find humor in it at all. I was just trying to placate them. I was bored to tears. I couldn't ditch this guy. I was hoping that he and Red were having a "thing" so that they would get out of my life. I had to use finesse.

I was his new obsession. He was mesmerized with my independence and privacy and fame, all in one basket. Gin was hell-bent on keeping him and from losing her and gaining me, the "mystery woman".

Frankly, I was not interested in drama of any kind.

He and Gin lived for drama. This town was so dead and there was nothing else to do but make drama out of nothing. I avoided it at all costs. The folks were burned out old freaks with no teeth or life.

Plus, Glenn and I had a lot in common. I thought Glenn was the one for me. He was sweet and single and treated me with dignity and respect. Beau and his brothers must have paid him a visit because he all the sudden wouldn't touch me in a matter of four days. They were the "po po" after all. Police.

I was so happy. Now, trapped. Beau loved or was obsessed with me. He was full of drama, gifts and alcohol. Boring. Glenn was my object of affection. Beau knew he had lost my respect already by his endless games. He now had to make everything up to me and hide from Gin. It was not fun. He was causing me danger and stress. No man had ever made me so important in his life, as Beau. He was always at my home with gifts and flowers. He was stalking me. I was scared of Gin and Beau. It stunk. .

Chapter 31

Apparently Beau had stolen one of the keys that the previous owners had made for my home that was hanging on the wall above the door to the pool. One day, Red said I should give her one in case of an emergency. I never gave anyone a key to my home, ever.

I was obsessed with working out in my pool. Beau was trying to control me, and my lifestyle. I did my laps everyday so that I could keep on my crazy neighbor schedule for freedom. Remember, I had the hillbilly neighbor to deal with too.

I was practicing to sing as a guest singer with The Big Engine Band from Jacksonville. Tony, the lead singer, had invited me to sing at the next event. I was so excited. They were huge. They were the new Aerosmith or Journey. Amazing band. They were truly nice guys, with a perfect band and a huge following.

I lived for this kind of invitation. It was my highlight of the whole two weeks. Harry loved when they got me up on stage. We had a blast every time they played. Harry said that when I held the last note I broke headlights and windshields and folks took their tip out of the tip jar, as a joke.

I called them my "Lucky Charms". I say that because for some reason when I sang with them I felt like a huge beam of light, joy, and power. I would feel so happy that nothing could kill the feeling. Nothing could take it away from me. I owned the thrill completely. I felt blessed by God.

Since I was new in town from Europe, it was really great that they gave me my start here. They were the biggest in the state of Florida. I sang like a man, so it cracked them up. I do Jim Morrison of The Doors' song, "Roadhouse Blues". I have a huge voice for a small girl. They were so nice to me when I sang with them.

God gave me a huge voice packed into a tiny girl's body. It always shocked everyone, including the band and audience, when the first note left my mouth. We all got a kick out of their reactions. I loved it.

Afterwards, I would get on a huge old bike and kick-started it with one kick and do a burn out and leave. I did not drink or hang around after the gigs. I would just sing and leave. The performing was so powerful that I would be exhausted after I finished. It's the best drug in the galaxy. I couldn't stop smiling for at least a week. That's what makes me love my life. Making folks smile and laugh. The shock value was worth the months of practice and waiting.

Then for the next six months, folks started to recognize me here and there and compliment me. We would joke around about how heavy my voice was and we cracked up laughing. Joy. That's what life is about. Joy. Happiness. Doing the things you love to do. And being a blessing to others without drugs, alcohol, violence and deviation.

The band played at numerous bars during the event. Unfortunately, they played a lot at the bar that Beau and Gin used to work at, before being fired. Beau's half brother still worked as the garbage man there and he and parked bikes. It had a huge outdoor stage and had the best gyros in the world.

Since Beau said he was in love with me I had every courtesy. Beau carved, with his big buck knife, into the wood, "Beau loves Ruthie" to finalize it. And he wrote on the ceiling in the main bar, in black marker, "Beau loves Ruthie 2007". He did it at every event until 2008.

One of the women bartenders always gave me the "watch out" look. I gave her the "I know" look. She looked like one million miles of meth, cheap beer, and dead road – just like all of his buddies.

All of the biker men looked at me like I was from another planet. And they wondered how was I with Beau. I knew something was up. I only fit in with the bands, not the bikers here. Beau loved to brag that I was the best singer.

Everyone asked where Gin was when we were out. Beau always gave them the, "SHHHH" look.

They always asked, "Where in the hell did you come from?" It was spooky.

I'd say, "Spain." Then, I'd speak Spanish and say all kinds of funny things to freak them out.

They were all total rednecks. It was a funny game. It made Beau look strange amongst his clan of loser drunk locals. I dressed in a very European style. Not like Gin or the other local "chicks" - as they referred to them.

When I was bored, I spoke Spanish to complain. It

frustrated the hell out of Beau. Or I'd say, "Whatever!" Oh, He hated that one.

Wallpaper could peel off on its own when I said that. He obviously wanted to show the crappy, seedy town that he had upgraded to a smart and famous woman. While all the time I was trying to frustrate him and piss him off to get rid of him. So far, he was only allowed to come over by appointment during the middle of the day and for only for an hour or so. He was permitted to sit in the kitchen or outside in the backyard. No kissing and no nothing. After all, Gin still lived at his house.

Like my Dad told me: "If you can't beat' em, punk 'em." It always made us laugh.

If folks were cons, we would have the smarts of his to test them, to let them know before they did something really stupid. For example, grand larceny or lying about something huge. Time would heal all wounds and everything would eventually come out in the wash. Either that or they were a different kind of crazy altogether.

My Dad taught me street smarts since the age of four. He also taught me about boys and how different I was compared to the other girls. He told me why my Mom was the one who would try to make me insecure, not my brother and sister. I hung on my Dad's every word of advice since I was twelve years old. And I still stand by his advice. Plus, my Grandmothers advice always stuck with me: "Never trust a man."

Chapter 32

My car had to go into the shop for a few weeks and the truck was not titled in Florida yet. Beau had an extra Explorer, which was his "baby", sitting in the driveway. He let me borrow it. It had a Rebel flag front plate on it. It had WTF George Bush on the back and long, gross donkey balls hanging from the trailer hitch. It was hard to miss.

On Valentine's Day, a cold rainy afternoon, I went to a gourmet store in my neighborhood to buy some nuts and cheese. A very young guy was smiling at me and checking me out in the parking lot as I ran in from the rain. It was downstairs from a chic French restaurant that Beau promised to take me to. I bought some Spanish almonds and some wine.

As I was running out to Beau's SUV, the young good looking man ran up to me and knocked on the window. I wouldn't open it more than an inch. It was pouring rain outside. The young man told me I was gorgeous and asked me where I came from.

I said, "Why?"

He said he knew everyone in town and had never seen me.

I said, "I am too old for you, but thanks." And I smiled. I tried to roll-up the window and he knocked again as I was trying to back up.

I said, "What?" and smiled.

He asked me, "Where did you get this car?"

I said, "It's my boyfriend's car, why?" He said, "That's funny, my mom's boyfriend has the exact same car." He looked baffled.

Then he asked how long I have been seeing my boyfriend.

I told him we'd seen each other since October.

He said, "Hmmm! That's weird!" He asked if my boyfriends name was Beau.

I said I had to go.

I peeled out of there and up to the CVS and called Beau. I told him what happened, and he said that the boy is Gin's son and he works at the fancy French place upstairs. I was shaking.

Beau called and threatened him to not tell his Mom, Gin. Beau had raised this boy, turns out. Of all the young guys to hit on me on Valentine's Day, it was Gin's son. Here he was, keeping me trapped at home and never told me had raised a boy from age nine to twenty. No wonder he couldn't take me anywhere until Valentine's Day.

Beau showered me with gifts and flowers and cards and apologies and excuses. I have never had so much "I love you" crap given to me in one night. Beau couldn't stand the idea of anyone not liking him. He had invested a lot of time and money on me so far for insurance. I wanted to go to the café next to the cigar shop for duck. After all, the last time we were there, there was a lot of ducking in and out going on. It was the least he could do, he owed me for crashing my party and ruining my dinner with Moanie and Hal during the Christmas holidays.

Chapter 33

I made Beau take me to meet his mom. I had to know if I was just a big secret. I had to know exactly where he and we stood before Bike Week. We just showed up after dinner.

Mom opened the door and froze in shock. Her jaw hit the floor. She was genuinely flabbergasted.

I said, "Hi! Beau wants me to be his new girlfriend. What do you think?"

She burst into loud laughter. I loved her right there and then. We went in and talked and laughed. She collected mice of all sizes. She said she counted them and had over one million in her modest home. This was the home that she had lived in for fifty years. Beau grew up there and then bought a house one block down – he had lived on this street all of his life. He had never been anywhere but here.

She asked Beau how he was going to do that with "psycho Gin" hunting him?

He was in a jam now. I wanted to know too. Good one Mom! She asked me if I had had the pleasure of meeting the monster.

And I said, "Eh, not exactly 'meet'." I said that it was

more of a "drive by experience". I told her that Gin's son had hit on me in the parking lot earlier today.

She cracked up laughing. She said, Oh Shit!!" Shit was her favorite word that she often blurted out. She was eighty-six years old. She was cool. She asked how was it possible that we met.

I told her that he had been stalking me for over a year. Beau added, with a sincere tone, that he fell in love with me at first sight and that I was the woman of his dreams.

Beau's mom said, "Oh! That's why you broke up with Gin in front of all of our family last year at Christmas dinner?"

Beau said, "Yes Mom."

Now she really believed it. It was now a year and a half. I told her straight-up that I was not going to start anything with Beau until Gin moved out and on.

She said, "Good Luck with that."

I said, "That's what I think." It'll never happen!" We laughed and Beau got mad like a little boy, pouting.

She gave me a tour of all of her cool mice all over the house. She collected angels, too. I loved her right off the bat. I told her that I had a ton of collectables and that she should come over and see them some time.

She said, "Yes. I'd love to!"

We connected. Beau was frustrated. I was in with Mom already. Beau was a control freak as it seemed, but unfortunately for him we were out of his league. Inside, he secretly loved that his Mom loved me at first sight.

Apparently, Gin was going over to Beau's Mom's all the time and crying about him never being home. I told her he was never at my house overnight. In fact, he was never at my house past nine or ten PM, just talking in my kitchen. He must have been sleeping at another woman's house. It sure was not my bed or house ever. He never slept over at my house. I am very strict. He never swore or said "ain't" or anything ungentlemanly in front of me, which was rare for this town's usual redneck lingo. I had him walking on eggshells. He was noticeably changing, slowly, since he met me and everyone was aware of it in a very good way. People said he was acting totally different all of the sudden. I was fearful to see if he acted like a crazy monster, similar to Gin, before he met me.

Chapter 34

Gin didn't know, and neither did anyone else, that he had been fired from his job, as a printer, for stealing the companies machine and supplies to print for extra money at night. He was getting up, dressing in his work clothes, and then changing in his truck. He would come up to my house dressed normal and nice. Then, Beau would change at my house and say he had to go to work. He had everyone fooled. Even his Mom didn't know.

Whenever I asked Beau if we could go out to hear a happy hour band or get food, he would say, "Sorry my love, I have a printing job I have to do. The deadline is tomorrow. I'll be up all night after spending all my time here with you."

So I noticed that we had not had a second date yet. Bike Week was a week away. So I said, "You take me or you can never see me again." Uh-oh! Now Beau was in a fix. And I was a star. He had to think fast to pull this one off without a war.

The first thing Beau had to do was get Gin fired as a bartender. He also had to have her barred as a patron to protect me. She was taking months to move across the street, anyway. This move would hopefully get her out of there by April 1. This would start a war. And it was going to be a doozie.

All hell broke loose in Beau's secret world. I told him if I ever caught him doing drugs, lying or cheating, he'd meet my dad. That's why he couldn't be my boyfriend. I already caught him lying. He promised to never do it again.

Dad and Mom would say, "Once a liar, always a liar." The same goes for the two other rules.

He was undergoing endurance test that would change his life in meeting me. He said that this town was dangerous and he needed to protect me. He said something stupid like that to me. Uh, duh. Wrong answer.

I'd say, "Whatever," and go out alone.

He'd have a fit and show up wherever I went. Since I was new in town, the guys were all over me. Beau was jealous.

I asked Beau's mom about him. She said he was very private but psychotically jealous. I asked how someone could be private when living with a maniac, partying all the time. That wouldn't be easy to work with.

Now I knew what Beau did to Glenn, for sure. And Glenn would be at Bike Week, yay! Everybody who's anybody and people from all over the world went to Bike Week. One hundred thousand bikers from all over the USA and Canada came. It was huge. It was fun and crazy and louder than thunder. It was sleazy and hilarious. It was insane. I loved it. Without it, we all would've died of boredom there.

Now in public, Beau and I were officially dating since I couldn't get rid of him. He had to introduce me to his other brothers who showed up for four to five o'clock free beer. This would be fun.

I rode on the back of Beau's bike too. The shock on the brothers' faces was priceless. They were baffled. They asked me how we met and where.

I answered the same as I did to his Mom. I said he was stalking me for over a year. They were astonished at how tiny I was. I overheard them talking. Apparently, he preferred big girls. And I mean large.

My mind and mouth were big enough. I sure showed them when it came to talking about Harleys and engines and all the things that they thought girls shouldn't know anything about. They were in awe of me. Their dicks shrunk on the spot. I am a walking encyclopedia of antique bikes and cars. Their egos were BBQ'd by the end of their five gallons of beer consumption (in little over an hour).

Plus, I drank a little Crown and showed them how a woman can drink and blast rock 'n roll on stage with The Big Engine Band. I blew their minds! It was the best!

Then, I sauntered over and said, "Let's go downtown and party. I am just warming up!"

We all took off and went down to the main street and I sang with a friend's band after that. I was on a roll. Beau was really stunned like a deer in the headlights. He hadn't taken me anywhere in public yet. So he was in total shock now. He had no idea that I was such a handful. "Bad Ass" is what my friends who knew me called me. He didn't know what to do now. Seriously. He was scared. His brothers were speechless.

Chapter 35

My brothers showed up from Seattle the next day. My brothers told Beau that I used to deliver parts for the bike club in Amsterdam before Harley sold out and opened dealerships in Europe. I also brought used Levi's for extra tall men and sold them.

After that, Beau bent over backwards to wait on my brothers' hand and feet. They knew he had lied and was a bit of a shit, so they tested him. It was hilarious.

My brothers' wife and I have been friends since 1991. It was wonderful to see her and go out with her again. She is like me, only she is an expert on Nascar and muscle cars. I don't do Nascar. Only Indie 500 and Grand Prix Racing. We showed Beau that he didn't know that women had brains and that we often knew more than men. I think that Beau thought women were just sex toys with no brains. Beau was intimidated now.

Leather was my sister-in-law's name. I loved her. Now, Beau had all of us to deal with. One of my brothers built award winning rockstar bikes for rockstars and would win the awards every year at Sturgis. My other brother restored muscle cars. He was very famous in

Seattle. Beau and his brothers were small potatoes compared to these guys. Now what would he do?

Beau's brothers were in law enforcement and were avid bike enthusiasts. They were just connected with everyone because they grew up there and there was nothing else to do. They could never see a bigger picture in life. They were dull and bored to death.

Chapter 36

It was a long day of public appearances for Beau to introduce me all over town. First it was the antique bike show at the tattoo parlor with a thousand drunken bikers in the blazing sun. Then about twenty parties where he introduced me to everyone in the town. He was drinking like he was the happiest man in the world, he was in complete celebration mode. I was shocked he could hold all the varieties of liquors that he was consuming. He just got happier and more fun. The last stop was the Chamber of Commerce party where he introduced me to everyone who was anyone in town. It was a very long and overwhelming day for me. He was driving fine and especially safe on the bike with me. He was really taking care of me. We were starving by now.

He took me to Outback for dinner. It was cooling off and we were on the beach side of town where it was cooler at night. He was really trashed and bubbly by now. We went in and were sitting at the bar, warming up while waiting for a table. I got my B.G.S.T. and he got his beer.

Beau turned to me with the biggest smile on his face

and put his hand on mine, squeezing it gently. He stared into my eyes, soberly and seriously. He told me he had never met anyone like me. Tears of joy were in Beau's eyes. He was so sincere. He caught me completely off guard.

Beau then announced to everyone in the town that he loved me. Adored me. All day he had been proclaiming to this to everyone. He said he had never been so happy in his miserable, crappy life. He said he never thought anyone like me ever existed in the world. I was the perfect woman and the best girlfriend.

I was so stunned. After all the hell he had put me through the past months, I was really astounded and caught off guard.

And then he confessed, with tears of joy in his eyes, "I am so in love with you! I have never actually been in love before. I am really deeply in love with you. You are amazing. You make me so happy; I can't believe I met you. I want to spend the rest of my life making you happy. Will you marry me and let me make you happy?"

I almost fell off the barstool. I said, "My dad said, 'Never get married. It'll ruin everything'."

He froze and turned sheet-white.

Then, the new young bartender dumped my tall glass of whiskey all over my top and pants, drenching me. I jumped up and was soaked through to my skin with whiskey. It must have been a sign.

The evening went very downhill from there. They had no blow dryer in the ladies room nor did they have a dry towel in the place. I was drenched to my skin and it was in the fifties outside. I was soaked, cold and pissed-off. What a buzz kill.

We were on Beau's bike and had eight miles to ride to get me home, dry and warm. We were already cold and hungry when we arrived. This was a nightmare for me, and Beau's romantic plans to propose marriage were foiled. They gave us the wrong food and it was cold.

God really objects when he wants to. Beau sadly dropped me off and left full of rejection and loneliness. My brother's friends were staying at his house in Gin's old room. He had borrowed sheets from my guest room for them. It was early and they were watching a movie on TV when Beau got home around ten PM.

A few minutes later, Gin and a huge man came up to the door and pounded on it. Gin was wasted on whatever, and demanded to meet Fuck Face. She automatically assumed I was there because of the rental car with out of state plates in his driveway. She caused a huge scene on his front porch to the point that my brother's friends called me and asked me to call the police.

Gin was in Beau's driveway screaming at him, hitting and slapping him and the huge dark man with her was threatening to hurt Beau. My brother's friends were scared. It was so bad that after they called me, they packed up and left and drove up north to my house and slept on my couches. My brothers were disgusted.

Beau's problems had now ruined my own relationship with my whole family and their friends. Beau and Gin had cursed my nice happy holiday with my family. It was poisoned now. As a result of this night, complete with a marriage proposal and later a proposed death threat by Gin, my family and security were doubted. My family ended up leaving a day early, and they haven't spoken to me since because of Beau and Gin's drama. They weren't bikers anymore. They were coffee shop owners.

I called the sheriff's department to go to Beau's home. I knew that night, that Beau was connected to corrupt cops because they made me repeat his address one hundred times for fifteen minutes. He lives between three police stations and his brothers live in the same area and are cops too. Nobody wanted to come help. This was very suspicious to me, my brothers, and their friends. It was an exhausting nightmare. This would affect my life in some ridiculous way and it would get uglier before improving.

My dad said a man like Beau could F#$%ck up a wet dream. He knew about this kind of situation all too well, if anyone did. He had first hand experience fifty years ago with my mother. His situation was really ugly and unforgiveable and I, as a child, saw with my own eyes first hand.

Beau only had until April 1 to get Gin out of his house or I was out of his life.

I said, "You'd better get cracking!"

He whined, "I'm trying!"

Uh-oh! He promised he'd prove we should be married and that he would fully validate his love for me. He swore he would prove my dad was wrong about love.

News Flash: Ruthie hates whiners. Any guy I ever knew will attest to that policy. Absolutely NO WHINING!

Chapter 37

I decided that I would write a book. I started the next day. I really got into it. I was recounting funny stories about my dad and of growing up. It was really enjoyable and funny. Then, when Beau came over to visit every evening, I would read him the story of the day over a cocktail. He laughed his head off. He couldn't believe this was true. His dad was a bartender all of his life. He didn't have a fun dad. Too bad, but at least he had a cool Mom.

I had earned an editing and a publishing deal within a month. Beau got jealous. One late afternoon, he came over after I had written the funniest story about my dad doing LSD with us when we were about fifteen.

Beau snapped and said he didn't want to talk about my past or his past.

I jokingly said, "I'll just ask your mom when I go to take her to Wal-Mart."

He freaked out. His Mom was legally blind and couldn't drive anymore. And she lived alone. She loved Wal-Mart. I started offering to take her and help her read the packages and look at everything for hours. We had a great time. She was so funny. We would laugh and laugh about everything.

Now Beau was trying everything to keep me from becoming a writer. He was showing up uninvited during my designated writing time, buzzed, and would blame it all on Gin.

I said, "Get a hobby, already! Join a gym. Whatever. Help Gin move out! Whatever!"

Uh-oh. I said the trigger word, "whatever", again. Hearing this was like fingernails scratching loudly on a chalkboard to him. I told him I was not his life. I was a person with a life of my own. I did not depend on others for my happiness.

I said, "If you want to be with me, you have to be productive. I am." I followed with, "Go mow your mom's overgrown lawn or something. Take your mom to Wal-Mart, too."

He hated that I was not dependent on him. He was a control freak for sure. Just never in control of himself. Sad. I remember my dad saying that men love the hunt. The forbidden fruit. Well that is me. Like the Mick Jagger song too, "You can't always get what you want." Beau loved the chase, the scolding, and the works. The trick was to let him think he was in control.

What a job. What a joke. My brothers knew I could chew Beau up and spit him out like the Ginseng gum that tasted like dirt. The countdown was on. My birthday was in two weeks. Beau's favorite day of the year, St. Patrick' Day. Only two weeks away from us officially being a couple. Oh man, the pressure was on Beau now. He had to actually help Gin move out. He promised to keep this promise.

I actually had some space to write. I was so excited to have some free time alone to think. He was smothering me already. He was like a little naughty boy that had to be punished, otherwise he couldn't hold it together. I guess that after living with a drug addict and dealer for eleven years, he was in bad form.

I felt sorry for Beau at first but took mental notes of his behavior. Then folks started talking to me and telling me that Gin was the brains behind the whole operation. He pretended to have no idea that she was on drugs or a dealer. He promised me that he had never done a drug in his life. Bologny! I have seen and heard it all in my life. It's called being "codependent". Duh. He wanted me to think he was perfect and she was bad news.

This was a small town of seasons. I could find out anything in five minutes, and I found out more than enough. Turns out most the folks that I was talking to were involved with them in their secret dealings around town. Whatever those things were. I only knew my band members who are all straight and I hoped somebody would save me before I was in too deep. Druggies lie by nature. The locals all looked like bad road. How could I get the information I needed?

Chapter 38

It was one hundred degrees outside that day. And in a huge three hundred acre blacktop parking lot with three hundred Hot Rods and one hundred Elvis impersonators and bikes in the blazing heat. It was unbearable. Beau dressed like he was on *Hee Haw* or at a gay country bar, at the car show. He wore women's overalls with one strap hanging down and a shamrock green bowling shirt with the Joker from Batman printed all over it. So not funny. I was so embarrassed.

Beau was acting really strange and drinking heavily. His language was getting crude lately. He had never said "ain't" or "fuckin'" or any redneck slang before. Now he was talking like a real redneck all the time. He was embarrassing me. I noticed that he had lost some weight and his face was puffy and pink. He was acting totally different than when we first met and had started seeing each other.

I would ask him what was happening and he'd say, "Nothing."

I knew he had to have been acting this whole time just to win me over and now I was seeing the real Beau. He was not what I expected.

That's when I met my source of TRUTH. Thank You, GOD! We were walking around the huge Elvis impersonator contest finals, when a guy and his wife caught my eye. Beau knew them. They were not friendly to him, just cordial. They were giving me odd looks. I thought it was because of my blue leopard dress and crazy hair, but no.

I started talking to the couple about Colin Powell collecting this particular model of antique car. And Colin's relation to President Bush. Nobody knew who or what I was talking about. Beau had wandered off to look at some vintage Pintos. We were alone for five minutes.

The guy said, "We'll see you at the next meet next weekend, okay?" They said they had a whole barn full of classic cars at their place and wanted me to come over some time and see them. I felt like this guy had something important to tell me by the kind of secret way he was talking to me.

I just said "Nice to meet you," and smiled thankfully at them and went over to the Elvis show. I got an eerie feeling that this guy held information that I seriously needed to know ASAP. He seemed scared for me, as if he wanted to warn me about something bad before I got hurt.

The humongous owner of all the Harley dealerships was there, and was staring me up and down. He is deceased now. He was hitting on me in front of Beau. I asked who this gross blob was.

Beau rolled his eyes.

I said, "I'll take care of him." I snapped his eyes out like a crocodile. He was a bad man who weighed in at least five hundred and fifty pounds. Beau saw him give me the "hungry wolf" lip-lick. I gave him the "I'll kick you in the balls" stare right back, of course.

Then, Beau said his younger brother worked there and the man was an huge former drug dealer and he was a prick, amongst other things. I said he would have been the biggest loser on the Biggest Loser TV show. Beau said his baby brother had been screwed over by him. I didn't need his help. The owner was a disgusting pig.

When he gave me the "I own this empire. Wanna fuck?" look, I gave him the, "Not even in your wildest nightmares, loser" look right back.

I had huge platforms on and was ready and glad to open a can of whoop-ass on him. I can handle myself.

I said it was too hot and that we should go get rid of the truck and swap for our bikes in order to cool off. I pulled up next to the HUGE owner who was sitting at a table next to the curb.

I stomped my accelerator to the floor and left at least one hundred feet of rubber and wet, swampy black smoke to cover him and his big smelly stogie.

My truck had been through Hurricane Katrina so it still had nasty swamp sewer water in the exhaust that sprayed black muck all over the place. If Beau hadn't dressed like a freak from the Hee-Haw show, I would've let him take care of it, but I was the one in a blue French open back leopard halter dress with blonde hair down flowing to my butt. I had the power.

When I got home I called Harry and asked if we

could go on a ride the next day and have lunch up there at the Wing place. I showed him my burn-out marks I left and told him the story. He said he almost had a cardiac arrest laughing. He couldn't stand the owner, either. That's why Harry refused to work there. The black swamp water part was the best part because it sprays everything black all over. I knew because of the wall in my garage. Harry said that when he graduated from the Motorcycle Mechanics Institute the owner of the dealerships hired the students and worked them to death and never paid them. Glenn was working there as of late and I was worried.

I called him and warned him and his best friend Frank who had just come over from the west coast. They worked at the dealership downtown. Shortly after that, the same thing happened to them and they lost their homes and were in debt. Frank moved to the Bahamas with his wealthy girlfriend. Glenn's home was re possessed by the Bank and he moved to New Orleans to work at their new dealership. I told him I would visit him. I used to live there, but Katrina took out my old house. I had many other friends to visit there too. I figured a few days without Beau would help me breathe again. I booked a flight for late summer to go alone and have fun.

Chapter 39

Gin was finally out of Beau's house and on a quest to find out who Fuckface was. She was on a rampage. Beau and I started trying to go out to all of the normal parties and bars. Gin had her best friend out there looking for us. Her name was Lawanda.

Lawanda was in love with Beau secretly all these years. She wanted to cause trouble for us so she could get Beau to be her boyfriend. She was trashy and nasty looking. Many times when we would go to a street fair or some local fundraiser she would show up and Beau would try to hide me.

I said, "Why are you hiding me still? We are a legitimate couple, aren't we?" He said that all Gin's friends were druggies and liked to make scenes in public. We went to see Eddy Money and she was there with other freaks. We had to duck into the Harley shop and visit Glenn before he left. We had to hide until she left.

I said, "I am not dealing with all these games all the time after all you have put me through."

One night we went to the Mall and ate at a German Deli that had Beau printed the menus for in his garage.

As we were eating dinner and watching the musicians, Gin, Lawanda and another nasty looking woman came barging in and assaulted Beau at our table.

Pauline, who is a tall heavyset brunette woman, was sitting with us. Gin thought she was Fuckface. She didn't even look at me or acknowledge that I was even there. There was a huge fight between them. She was getting physical and throwing huge mugs filled with beer at him. She was punching and slapping and screaming as loud as she could, in a packed restaurant. It was a huge mess all over the place.

She soaked other customers too. Beau told me to go hide in the bathroom. The place was packed with German beer drinkers. It was a special event every Wednesday night at this place. Regulars came out and sang along and all of the regulars were passing around of the big beer jug. The owners and the crowd had to all get up and try to control her. She is six-foot –one and two hundred pounds and furious.

She was screaming, "Who is Fuckface? I am going to kill her!"

All the mall security had to come and drag her out. Lawanda just watched and laughed. You could tell she was playing both sides of her coin. It was a bad scene. Gin never suspected me. I was too small and blonde. He likes brunettes who are over weight.

Gin went out to Beau's truck and waited and yelled and screamed in the parking lot at him. I had to be taken out the front with Pauline and go in her car to a meeting place near by.

On the way home, I made him drive by her house on the way home to see. We did. She and her friends were out on her stoop smoking and trying to calm her down. They were very drunk, too. They looked like a bunch of skanky hookers. I asked him how could he be with somebody who spoke like that in public. He looked blankly and said he didn't know. He said he didn't realize how "fugly" she really was until that night. That was mean. After all I was being referred to as Fuckface.

I asked if this was going to happen everywhere we go. He said he didn't know. I asked where we could go, a place that was safe and fun.

Chapter 40

Easter Sunday family party at Mom's house was here. Beau's family get together was a huge, all-day Easter egg hunt for the kids complete with all the decorations and pot luck family dishes. Beau had me at the center of attention. His other brothers and sister had not met me yet.

My family always had formal parties so we had to dress up. When Beau came to get me I was all dressed up in white linen. He told me I looked too nice for his family.

I said, "Whatever. Deal with it. This is how I roll."

I told him I wanted to make a good first impression if he was so in love with me.

I witnessed the absolute funniest reaction I have ever experienced when we came through the door. Everyone was in the kitchen in the back of the house already. Mom's dog came running up to me and jumped into my arms. I walked behind Beau into the kitchen where his relatives, who had not met me yet, were drinking.

Beau introduced me and Mom hugged me. All of their jaws dropped and hit the floor with a loud boom.

I said, "Hi! I'm Ruthie."

Beau's Mom announced that I am Beau's new girlfriend. She had a gleaming smile on her face. She knew I'd freak them all out.

Two of Beau's brothers, his sister, and one of the brother's wives gasped. They couldn't even say, "Hi," because my appearance alone was so shocking to them.

I had my waist length platinum blonde hair with pink, purple and turquoise streaks in it. I had curled it very tastefully. I was very tan. I was wearing beautiful white linen tailored dress with nice white high heels. I was adorned with a lot of turquoise Navajo jewelry that matched my eyes.

They just stared at me in disbelief for a while. Baldy and Lottie, Beau's older half brother and his wife were both short and as round as they were tall. Baldy was a retired local cop who thought he knew everything. His wife had fried yellow nasty permed hair. They would barely say "Hello" to me. They looked at me like I was from Mars.

Beau's other half brother, Len, was the garbage man at the bar where I sang sometimes. You could tell he did drugs and drank a lot because of his prematurely-aged face and skinny, tall body. He had long, light blonde hair and leathery-dark, tanned skin. He was over six feet tall and hyper. He was power drinking beer in the garage with the other brother and Beau before lunch.

He boldly exclaimed, "Oh my God, Beau, where did you find this beauty?"

Beau said, "At the cigar shop." Beau was beaming.

Beau's sister looked exactly like Beau, in drag. She came right over to me and asked me to go into the dining room with her. Beau rolled his eyes and stayed in the kitchen and explained about me and answered all the family questions about what finally happened to Gin.

Beau's sister sat me down at the table and looked at me and then started interrogating me in a nice way. She asked where I was from. I said Spain. She asked how in the hell did I meet Beau. She thought this was a practical joke and I was hired to punk their family. I said that he had been basically following me everywhere like a puppy, for over a year. She asked what I did for a living. I told her I am a rock and blues singer and a seamstress and an artist and a filmmaker, photographer, etcetera.

She was silent for a long time. She just stared at me. Then, she asked me when I arrived here and what brought me here.

I said, "Because, I ride a Harley, drive a Hot Rod and sing with my own band and am a guest singer at all of the bike events."

She was speechless, yet again. She asked if I had been warned about Gin yet. I said I had had brief encounters with her but she never saw me for some reason. She said it's because Beau only dates big brunettes.

I said, in a whisper, "I am really a brunette. Ssshhhhhhhh, don't tell anyone," and, smiled and whispered, "I am not that thin either."

She loved me that moment. Beau was worried that his sister was going to tell me a secret, so he slid in and sat at the table with us to try to control the conversation. His sister and I were on the same page, on top of the great connection I had with his mother.

We decided to mess with Beau's head and say how Gin had been terrorizing me and calling me, F#$CK Face, etc. And that it hurts my feelings. He got all freaked out and panicked.

His sister said, "You'd better dump him now, before Gin finds out who you are and puts a hit on you."

His two Law Enforcement brothers were in shock at how pretty I was. They made comments about Gin secretly being a man, etc. His Mom always told me that they teased him all the time. Beau's sister took me outside and pointed down the street four houses and said that is where Gin lives now. I said I knew. I told her that I am not afraid of anything or anyone. She wasn't either. You could tell. She asked me what I was doing with him. I told her that he wouldn't leave me alone. He said I was the woman of his dreams.

She said, "That's for sure." She said he didn't even know anybody who wasn't a dirt bag. I had to be a dream.

I explained that he told me he is a printer. Printing is art. She told me that Beau was not an artist in any way and definitely not good enough or smart enough for me.

Then Beau's baby brother Jay came out and said, "Don't let Beau touch anything you have. Everything he touches turns to shit. He's a tool, but can't work with any tool."

Beau exploded. His Mom and family agreed with what was said and laughed. They were hillbillies, too. He was always trying to impress them. And he tried to impress me by saying he could fix anything. We all just laughed. The whole family laughed. Jay is Beau's favorite brother too. He looked almost exactly like him, except for eye color.

Beau said we had to leave right now.

I said, "Why? I am having a great time. I love your sister."

He said, "I hate my sister."

I said, "She looks just like you in drag!" I giggled.

He was in a snit now. He wanted to go have drinks some place. So, I went inside to thank everyone and to hug all of his family and thank them for such a nice party and then we left in my old truck. It was hilarious. I did a burn-out for his brothers. They were in shock. I laughed like Woody the Woodpecker at the top of my lungs. It was a classic moment.

Beau's Mom laughed really hard. She was like a child and loved cartoon characters. The rest of his family's jaws dropped just as before.

Beau said he didn't want to talk about it.

I said, "I think your family likes me."

Beau acknowledged that they did.

His fireman brother said, "What are you doing with him?"

I said, "He says he's in love with me." I later asked Beau what that meant.

He said he didn't know and didn't care. His brother thought I was crazy to go out with him, as did the rest of his family.

Beau was pouting now, so we went down to the beach to my karaoke place where I sang and he drank two huge pitchers of beer to drown his sorrows. I danced and sang with all of the crazy drunk women there. I had a blast.

Moanie was there and all over Beau, as usual. I couldn't stop laughing. Stormin and I were performing

Tom Petty and Stevie Nick's "Stop Draggin' My Heart Around" as well as some Sonny and Cher songs to get some laughs. It was fun.

Chapter 41

Gin was finally out of the picture and Beau's house was completely empty, except for his bed, dresser, clothes, and ironing board. It was amazing how he practically didn't own anything. Not one pot or pan in the house. He nuked everything he ate in a plastic bowl. He was particularly fond of corndogs and hot dogs.

I looked in his fridge for water and only to find tons of beer and at least fifty assorted flavors of jello shots. He had a back room with an old TV and a huge, fully loaded bar all decked out for parties. It was painted flamingo pink. He had a stereo system in there too. That's it, there was absolutely nothing else. In his mind, he was a bartender, just like his dad. I wondered why he didn't take a job as a bartender. I asked him, but he just shrugged it off.

We spent every weekend at furniture stores buying thousands of dollars worth of nice furnishings. He had me choose everything because he said I have great taste. He had wads of cash. Afterward, he would take me anywhere I desired for dinner and cocktails. Where did he get all this money? He was only printing business cards in the garage.

Beau was showing up at my home every night to take me out to dinner. When the weather was eighty degrees, it was perfect for me and we'd take his bike. His big "po po" looking bike was really comfortable and had a great stereo system. We went all over the place now. I felt free, finally. No more hiding from Gin.

Now I had a new worry. It was either D.W.I. or death on Beau's bike. We started to have a really good time and I had a group of friends that would all meet up and have a good laugh together. Our group consisted of about twenty people. It was nice after all I had been through. Beau treated me like a queen in public, but he would never let me go to his house after all the work I did decorating it. Something was up.

We still had not gone to St. Augustine for our romantic night. Our second Christmas was approaching and he had promised to take me to St. Augustine for just one night. He had not delivered on this overdue promise. It had been my only wish. We went to all the bike and music events, street fairs and outdoor concerts all over the place, except for St. Augustine. I had really nice, big dinner parties out by my pool with our friends. I was ready to go on a short trip alone with Beau. It was super hot and I was tired of all these folks. I wanted one night totally alone with Beau to see what he was like outside of his 'hood.

One day Beau came over to take me out and said he had booked us a romantic trip to St. Petersburg, and that we would then fly on a sea plane to Key West for a long weekend. He had even paid for it already. He demanded that he take me there, instead of where I wanted to go. St. Augustine.

I told him to call the travel agent and cancel it. He said there were no refunds.

I said, "Too bad."

I said, "You promised to take me to St. Augustine for one night, since last Christmas. We never got to go. Then you promised for Valentine's Day. We never got to go. We have not made love for three weeks since you helped move Pauline. I don't want to go to Key West in July. It will be sweltering hot and I'll melt."

He said with a whining voice, " I thought it would be so romantic."

I said, "No!"

He was determined to take me. I was angry and wanted to go just one hour north for one only, period. Was it really that difficult?

He had been acting very strangely lately. He seemed nervous and wouldn't look me in the eye. Also, it was evident that he was losing weight. Perhaps even stranger, he said he had a new, under-the-table paying, part-time job and he was on call all the time. He claimed he was doing file storage for law firms and the police department.

Beau was showing up late and expecting dinner to be on the table at my house. He'd then fall asleep a second after he had finished his meal. When he woke, he would pop up and say he had to leave immediately. He'd run right out the door. This was a total turn around from what I had been experienced and was expecting. Something was up.

Beau never let me go to his house either. He never once invited me over for lunch or dinner, not even to sleep there. I had just spent months decorating his house and I wasn't even allowed to spend any time there. What was he hiding? He must have had a whole other life going on.

One night we ran into some of Beau's buddies whom I had never met before. Well, they said they had a great time at his "after hours parties".

I asked why I was never invited and Beau said that the parties were always too late for me. No wonder he was falling asleep at my house. I was pissed.

Then one night we ran into Pauline and Tom when I was singing with The Big Engine Band at The Wreck on Main Street. The woman, Pauline, was acting really fun and crazy and said her husband wouldn't let her do anything without his permission.

Pauline was with us at the German place on that crazy night when Gin showed up. She was dressed sort of attractively, but she was a slurring drunk. She had more drama than Beau and Gin. Her husband seemed normal to me. Tom wanted Beau's little brother, Jay, to do some sheet rock at his house nearby, since he was a handyman. Jay reported that Pauline had a glass of pure vodka in her hand at nine in the morning and that she was coming on to him sexually while he was trying to tend to his job.

Pauline would call and invite us to join her for drinks all the time now. One time we were out and shooting pool at a local hellhole of a bar, near Beau's house. That evening, Pauline fell for Randy, our biker friend. She actually went to his trailer and did "the wild thing" with him. She was married and doing this. O.M.G!

Pauline and Randy had an affair for a long time. She told us she was leaving her husband and asked Beau to move her stuff for her into her new rental place. He did it. This was before the Key West trip. It was the third week in June. Our trip was for the sixth of July. After Beau had helped Pauline move her things, he carried this horribly guilty look. I was fairly certain that Pauline and her husband were swingers, too.

I knew that Pauline seduced him. They had it written all over their faces. A woman simply knows whenever her boyfriend cheats. He wouldn't touch me after that. He was always holding my hand and kissing me before all of this transpired. I was sick about it. I tried to pretend I didn't know, but she would call one of us every five minutes.

Also, Beau started drinking like a fish. And it was not beer anymore. It was straight Crown and tons of jello shots. And he, all of a sudden, was too tired to do anything with me. He started to blame everything on Prostate problems, blood pressure problems and colon problems. He was going to the doctor's office all the time. He said he was afraid if we made love, he would have a heart attack. Our love making used to be incredibly intense, lasting four hours everyday.

When we would be driving some place, Beau had extreme road rage. He was pulling his gun on old folks who were lost or simply driving too slow. He was acting like Yosemite Sam. He was scaring me half to death.

I said, "I want my Beau back! You're not Beau." Or, "Who are you? And what have you done with Beau?"

He said he was the same.

I said, "You are not the same in any way whatsoever. You used to be funny and sweet and romantic."

Even his hundred daily calls to me was diminished

down to ten. He was acting extremely suspicious. Even his Mom noticed. He started looking bad.

Chapter 42

The day we were leaving for St. Petersburg, I arrived in Beau's driveway in my big Beemer and he ran out nervously, in a cold sweat, shaking and freaking out. He told me to get my car out of his driveway and to park across the street and wait inside the car.

I was watching him have a melt down. He was in trouble with somebody or something, evidenced by the paranoia I was witnessing. I didn't want to go on this trip, anyway.

While I was waiting in the car, a big silver car with a huge, dark, bald man driving kept rolling back and forth in front of his house. The driver reminded me of Mr. T. He must have driven by fourteen times, slowly staring at Beau's house each time he passed.

It was as if Beau had to go on this trip just to hide. The trip was not about me, or romance, at all. He hid his cars and called a friend to check on his house. Beau reset his house alarm about seven times before we left. He was acting like he had a bounty out on his head. I didn't want to go anyway.

I said, "Let's just go to St. Augustine and drive back and stay at my house."

For some reason, he was hell-bent on preventing me from ever getting to St. Augustine. Something insane was happening right under my nose and he was trying to keep me out of it. He insisted on driving my car. His hands were shaking like he had just had the shit scared out of him. I said I wanted to drive.

He barked, "No!" in a very grumpy tone.

I asked who the guy driving the grey car was. Beau wouldn't answer me. He took every possible back road to the I-95.

I said, "You're in my car with black tinted windows. No one knows my car, Beau."

He wouldn't speak a word in the car for the full four and a half hours to St. Pete. He was still shaking and sweating all the way there. He had the trunk full of Crown and a cooler of beer. He was driving unusually slowly, as well, which is not like him at all. I was miserable. I told him he drove like old folks screw.

Beau was a different person now. Not a nice or fun one either. I wanted to turn around and go home but he was the one driving. The one in control. He was a nervous wreck. His eyes were glassy and he stared straight ahead, frantically checking the rearview mirror the whole way. He was clammy and distant. He missed the last turn off and backed up on the freeway. I honestly almost had a heart attack. That was it.

When we arrived to check in at the Hotel on the beach, Beau started guzzling Crown and beer.

I said, "Let's go eat and go for a walk and hear some music."

He was grumpy and non responsive. He was a different person now. Two nights here, then a Sea Plane ride to Key West. I asked about the Sea Plane. He said the travel agent screwed our reservation and now we had to drive nine and a half hours to Key West.

I said, "No! Let's just go home. I am not having a good time with you, including this heat."

He said we had to go.

I said, "No, cancel it. I want to go home. It's too hot and you're no fun."

He said he paid cash and couldn't get a refund. He promised to be fun. Another promise he wouldn't keep. He was boring and distant and wouldn't touch me or talk to me or dance. Nothing. He was paranoid and kept checking his phone. It was one hundred degrees outside and the same in humidity. Sweltering hot. We got up on the day to leave, after he had been drunk for the entirety of the two days we were there.

I said, "I am driving. You're still drunk."

Beau wouldn't let me eat breakfast for the past three mornings, so I pulled into a Waffle House for breakfast. He seemed edgy and in a hurry. After we ate and I started down the highway, a blinding torrential rainstorm was crawling through.

We were outside of Ft. Myers, when Beau asked if we could stop in and see my brother.

I said, "NO WAY!"

We had to get gas right away. Beau called information and got my brothers number while I was in the store paying and getting apple juice. He then, called my brother and asked where he lived and that we wanted to stop by and say, "Hi!" My brother lived, coincidentally, right down the street. Beau said he just had to meet him.

Glenn knew him, so it was probably a competition. He insisted that he had to meet him. My legendary crazy brother that Glenn was friend's with. This was all about me liking Glenn.

I said, "Whatever!"

I drove all three blocks and pulled into his driveway next to his Bentley. My enormous brother and my petite sister-in-law were standing outside waiting. We got out and I introduced Beau to them. We went inside for water and a short visit. My brothers home looked like a dungeon for a dominatrix film. Everything was black leather. Black painted walls in every room. We went out on the veranda. Beau asked about Glenn first. My brother, 'Swinger, loved to tell all kinds of crazy stories and exaggerate, too. I just stayed quiet. I had to use the ladies room. I do not know what 'Swinger' said to Beau while I was gone, but Beau was even more difficult after we left. I didn't care any more at this point. My brother had ruined every relationship I ever had when he had the chance. This was his final victory. It was so bad that I was sure he had paid Beau to ruin my life. My brother tried to curse me any chance he could. This was already a 'Bad Trip'. I drove and drove and drove. This was the worst trip I had ever been on. Beau refused to say a word to me. Nine and a half hours of silence. What was he up to? My Beemer is really fast. I was going the legal amount over, exactly. Beau scolded me. I got the feeling that he had something illegal in my trunk. I have never had a moving violation in my life. All he did, if he spoke to me, was criticize me. It stunk. Swinger must have told him to treat me like shit. Swinger is an evil S.O.B.

Finally, we arrive in Key West at dusk. He booked us

into a Bed & Breakfast. It was not very nice. We took our stuff upstairs. Then we changed for dinner.

It was a nice evening, but really hot. We ate at a place on the main drag. Beau was drinking like a fish. I only had one drink. We left to start walking around and suddenly I couldn't feel my legs. It was only nine o'clock by now. Beau nearly had to carry me to the B & B.

I got in bed and was out like a light. I woke up at nine AM to hear Beau on the phone with Pauline.

He said, "Pauline is on the phone. She wants to say, 'Hi' to you."

I said, "Hi! We are on our vacation. Can you please let us be?" sternly. And I hung up. They were definitely having an affair.

Pauline was still calling every couple of hours. She was obsessed. Beau had taken Gin here before, so he knew the town inside and out. He drank himself into oblivion and didn't touch me. It was one hundred degrees of humidity out and the heat was sweltering. I was miserable. I went shopping in the air-conditioned stores for relief. Beau just went from bar to bar, getting loaded and surly. I was taking loads of photos to show everyone how miserable he was.

We went into the lingerie shop for fun. I picked out a few very sexy things. He said he hated lingerie' and for me not to bother buying any. Anything I bought in Key West, he had a problem with. He didn't want me to have any fun at all. Then he made me walk in the extreme heat, all over the whole town. I was about to faint. He was trying to wear me out. We only had two nights there.

Then, suddenly, Beau received a mysterious phone

call. He was acting very uneasy and guzzled a glass of Crown straight. Then, he asked me if we could stay one more night and I would pay since he was tapped out. I was so tired so I agreed. My back and legs hurt so badly.

Beau said we had to go find this friend from the coastal town and give him a message. While he was looking for him, there was a Fair going on. There was a psychic there and I got a reading. The reader told me my boyfriend was very worried about something. She also told me he was not really my boyfriend and to be careful.

Beau had overheard the psychic. We started walking and I said, "Screw this! I am taking a cab."

We had a drink down by the ocean. Then, all of the sudden, again, I couldn't feel my legs again. Beau got us a cab and he took me home at six o'clock. I was out cold again. He must have gone out all night without me.

I woke up at eight a.m. and he had the car packed to leave. I had my tea. He was panicking that we had to hurry, now, to get back home by six o'clock. I was very drowsy still. I was thinking that he had slipped me a date rape drug. Rohypnol. That's the drug that completely numbs your legs.

I had been slipped this date rape drug three times in my life and I was previously saved by friends and taken to the emergency room. I knew the first effects of it. Beau was raping me physically by wearing me out and emotionally.

We got in the car at nine and I drove. He was passed out cold the whole ride to Miami. I know he was on a bender drinking and whatever else all night. It was bad.

He reeked of whiskey and sweat. He was snoring in the car very loudly for five hours. As we approached the crazy part of Miami I had to pull into a gas station and get out. I filled the car up and bought Beau two bottles of Five Hour Energy drink. He whined and guzzled them and gagged it down.

I said, "Wake up! You're driving the rest of the way." I told him that this was the worst trip I had ever had in my life. And that he was just a drunk. I then turned up the radio and sang along to every song until we got to the coastal town. I dropped him off and said, "Good –bye forever!"

Beau stood in his driveway and looked shocked.

I said, "Hurry –up and go see your new girlfriend!"

I did a burn out and went home and crawled into bed and watched a movie. My phone started ringing off the hook. I wouldn't answer. Beau came to my door and rang the bell. I wouldn't answer the door. I was done. He must have sat out there all night trying to get me to open the door. He tried again in the morning with no avail. I was pissed off.

The next day, I went to tell his Mom that it was over. I told her I would still take her to Wal-Mart whenever she needed to go or anywhere she needed to go. She was sad that Beau screwed everything up and had lost me already. I said he had been lying and cheating on me. She said he had made her miss five important doctors appointments in the past month. She knew I was not imagining that something was up. She said he was acting strangely towards her too. She hugged me and I wrote my number really big on the wall by her phone so that she could read it, despite her horrible vision. She told me I could call and talk anytime and that she loved me. She said I was the best thing that ever happened to Beau in his life. She said that she thought I was an angel sent from God to save him from the dark place he was in.

I said, "I tried."

She said, "I know, dear. He will be very sorry later for what he has done to you." She agreed that he looked like shit too.

Chapter 43

I went back to my life of guitar lessons and band rehearsals and trying to work out in my pool and hanging out with Harry. I would still go to the Karaoke place on the weekends. Beau started showing up and trying to make-up. I was done. He knew my schedule so he was showing up everywhere. He was bringing me cards and flowers and presents. I just didn't care anymore. I just ignored everything about him and concentrated on my book. It was so hot on the beach in August and September that you couldn't go outside until evening. Thank God my hillbilly neighbors were passed out drunk by dark.

Beau would come over and I'd say, "Why do you bother coming over and not saying a word to me, eating, passing out and leaving." I said, "Don't bother anymore." I told him he was boring me to death.

I started hanging out with my violin player, Rika. We played some music and went out to two places and danced and had a good time. Rika's husband was an asshole. He's a macho Italian, like Beau. He and Beau felt they had a sense of entitlement regarding women. Every time we went out, Beau would show up and try to smooth over the way he had treated me. He tried treating me the way he used to again in public, but unfortunately at home it was like Ground Hog Day everyday.

Beau would call me every morning at ten AM and say, "Good morning my love."

Rika insisted that I try to give him another chance.

I said, "Why? He lies and cheats and has not touched me since June and now it's October."

She said, "He is probably overwhelmed because he didn't know how famous you'd become after you started dating. He's probably intimidated and jealous."

I said, "Tough Shit! He needs to prove he cares. I worked so hard for my dreams to turn into reality. He was becoming a bothersome distraction. Talk is cheap. Actions speak louder than words."

She said, "Make him work for it."

She didn't have a nice husband. She had low self-esteem. Fonzo had punched it out of her for years. I called him Prick to his face. He and Beau bonded. They both smoked cigars and drank like fish and rode Harleys. I rode my own bike. I didn't need a boyfriend.

Beau went to Rika and gave her a huge sob story and she tried to talk me into giving him a second chance. I told her, "He's got a lot of explaining to do. And we have to start, honestly, from scratch."

Beau said, "I'll do anything to get you back. You have to have patience. I am sick. You can't kick me to the curb because I am sick. I'll be better soon."

I tried to believe him.

Rika said if I dumped him, I wouldn't have any friends. I asked what that meant?

She said, "Just don't dump him."

I was shocked that she said that to me. She knew something I didn't know. Little did I know, I was being trapped by something I didn't see or know or understand. Beau kept lying and saying he never cheated on me and never would. He said he's never loved anyone but me ever. And never would again. One night I yelled at him so hard that I strained my vocal cords and developed chronic Laryngitis. He tried to push me too hard with his lies that night and I snapped. Drama again. Oh Bullshit! The man lived for drama. He was The Drama Llama.

Beau still wouldn't touch me other than rub my knee when we were on his bike. He called about fifty times a day to see where I was and what I was doing. He always said, "I love you." I was always busy. He was showing up with more empty promises and lies. The arguing was escalating to a boiling point. I was taking notes in my head. I just played along with this nightmare. He really needed me to need him. He was wearing me out by a slow painful death of boredom and loneliness for me. Wild orgies and drinking and drug parties for him. I didn't want to be associated with Beau in public any longer. I was referred to, behind my back, as Fuckface and now that it was all over town that I was his personal private joke.

I really wanted to be single for Biketoberfest. I had a lot of musician friends now and wanted to hang out and sing with them. I didn't want to be stuck around a bunch of drunken bikers again. I had many different places and bands to sing with for ten days. Beau wanted to be by my side during the whole event. I was his arm candy. His trophy. He was so boring now that he had changed. His true color was boring gray. I would just leave him with his old biker drunk pals and tell him I was going to the powder room and be gone for as long as I could be before he found me talking to somebody.

Beau was so paranoid when we went to the bar where his brother worked because he knew that I might find something out about him from a local. I purposefully flirted with the bar manager who lived nearby me and ignored him to pay him back for what he had done to me. He wouldn't dance with me so I danced with Rika and all kinds of other folks. I just used him for a ride and to buy me drinks and dinner. I was done with the bullshit.

Then finally, one night, he surprised me. It actually would have been our one year anniversary if he was my boyfriend in reality. He brought me a card and flowers and a gift and took me to see the band we had seen on our first date. He actually danced with me for one song. He hugged and kissed me on the cheek during a slow song. That's it.

It had been over two years since he started following me. I liked him better when he was mysterious and I didn't know him, to be honest with you. Nothing about him was honest, sadly. I had no idea who this guy really was. Whoever he was, he sure didn't want me to get over him. He wouldn't let me break-up with him. He was incapable of telling the truth about anything. He showed up at my door every night no matter what and insisted on coming in to see me. He would come in and beg.

I was starting to feel sick physically. I would be tired

all the time for no reason. I had to really push myself to get my get up and go to work. I felt like I was drugged. I felt knocked out. No caffeine or tea would make me wake up normal. I was drowsy and dizzy and passing out on my couch and waking up in the middle of the night and trying to stand up and fall over and actually knock over stuff and then crawl to bed and wake up and fell on the floor. I couldn't feel my legs and just weave one direction and down I'd go boom. I would come to with bruises covering my entire body and scrapes and cuts in any position I fell to or on. It was bad and very painful and ugly. I was scared. I first had insomnia. I just couldn't sleep at all.

Now I was being drugged to sleep. I felt like a zombie all the days. It had to be something put into my Evian water. Probably the large Crown bottle, but I had quit drinking along time ago. He just had to poison me. Drowsy.

Chapter 44

Thanksgiving came along and I had gone over a week before and told his Mom that he said he has prostate cancer and had a colon problem and I still had never been asked to spend one night at his house yet, after over a year of dating. I asked if it would be okay if I went to Rika's house instead.

She said, "Good idea."

Well guess what Beau did when I told him I wasn't coming to Mom's? He asked Rika if he could come to her house too. Unbelievable. I needed a break. I couldn't hide anywhere.

Beau said he'd be better again and again. He still never touched me ever. The odd hug, with whining and begging and crying became far too familiar. It didn't work anymore. I went to see his mom. She said he never acted sick at all.

Now that Thanksgiving was over I tried to distance myself from Beau as often as possible. Red and Rave had some single male friends who wanted to meet me. They invited me out to dinner to meet a single friend of theirs one Friday night. Beau called and said he was in my driveway waiting to take me to dinner.

I said, "I am down south at a nice place with Red and Rave."

Beau had a fit. He asked where.

I said, "None of your business. They invited me, only, to go out with them".

He whined, "What am I supposed to do?"

I said, "What you have been doing all along. Ignoring me and not talking to me even if we are together."

He was pissed that he couldn't control me and keep me isolated twenty-three minutes north from his house. I couldn't drive at night so he was really angry that Red had picked me up. Their imaginary friend never showed up. After dinner Red took me to the deck and I sang with 'The Big Engine Band'. I had a blast. Red left. I stayed and then took a cab home. I felt so free. Beau didn't show up and ruin it for me, Thank God.

As usual the next morning he was at my door with flowers and a million questions.

I told him, "Your fault. You didn't ask me on a date. Somebody else did and was nice to me and I had a great time." I followed with, "You want to see me from now on? You call and ask me in advance for a proper date like a normal man would. I am tired of being taken advantage of."

He said he would. I made him. He tried. He was so boring and so drunk all the time. It was getting worse. He looked horrible. I started feeling as horrible as he looked. I felt exhausted all the time now. All these folks did was live for alcohol and nothing else. It was pathetic. I had secretly quit drinking. Beau wanted me to be a drunk. He was always buying me too many drinks. I suspected he was putting something in my drinks to make me tired. When he wasn't looking, I was pouring them out and adding water. I would go get a real Shirley Temple when he was busy talking to Fonzo or whoever. I pretended to be drunk.

I was on a diet and getting ready to start driving at night again. I didn't want him to know. If he was sneaking around, so could I. I started practicing every night. My eyesight was drastically improving too.

I guess one night when he was stalking me, Beau saw me. He had a key to my house. I felt that he was putting things in my drinks and water. He came over the next day and I had to run to the store for a few minutes. I came back, cooked dinner and then he did the same as usual: ate and passed out and then got up and left. I went out to my car to go for a practice drive to the gas station and back. As I was halfway to my destination, my headlights went out. I had to drive in the pitch black to get home. It was scary.

I went to my mechanic the next day and he said the fuse had been pulled out! My mechanic knew Beau had done it. Gin had a BMW when Beau met her. My mechanic was a man. He knew Beau was obsessed with me. We didn't appreciate how dangerous it was. Where I live there are no streetlights and it tends to be misty on the beach road at night. Beau was trying to keep me stuck at home for his own personal control. Now I was getting worried. What was he keeping me from? It's not like I'd bother going anywhere he hung out.

Chapter 45

Beau was persistent that I be his date on New Years Eve. My friends, who I sang with on Sundays at Nice Guys, were playing at a four star hotel. They asked me to come by and sing with them. Beau said he would take me anywhere I wanted for dinner, then there, after. He loved fireworks, like a child. Every Saturday night on the beach at ten o'clock p.m. there were fireworks all year around. After that we had to go down to the main street to view the party for an hour. My other friends' band was playing on the main street and they asked me to sing with them later on that evening. The main street was packed with partiers.

We went to find Rika at the Music Society. I had to go to the powder room so I had to fight through a crowd of wasted dancers. When I came out, Beau and Pauline were in a happy, laughter-filled conversation. He had bored me to death all night with no conversation.

I marched up to her and said, "Don't you have a husband and twelve lovers already? Leave my boyfriend alone. Have you not done enough damage to my life already?"

Beau was flabbergasted. I called them on their affair

right there and then. They knew I knew now. Even Gin knew before I did that night at the German Deli. I was pissed off.

Just then, as I was fuming, Glenn called and said he was across the street.

I said, "Oh Beau, Glenn is in town and he wants us to meet him for a drink across the street".

Oh Man, was Beau pissed. Paybacks. Glenn was like the "Duracell Bunny" with the batteries put in backwards. He just kept coming and coming and coming. He always showed up just as Beau was fucking up. How was this happening? It was great. Beau was busted and Glenn was Beau's worst threatening nightmare. Glenn was now a phantom threat to Beau. It made me giggle. It was as if Glenn was trying to get Beau back for me. I liked this trick.

I made us search for Glenn amongst the hundreds of sloshed partiers. We couldn't find him. Beau was even more threatened that he was here and not able to be seen. As soon as the clock stroke Midnight and everyone screamed "Happy New Year," Beau said he was drunk and had to take me home. He just dropped me off at twelve-thirty. I was awake because I had fake drinks all night. I wanted to have fun or make love and not be alone again like Beau had ruined it for me last year. I wanted to hang out with Glenn and laugh and be treated like I was pretty and funny.

I had Champagne and strawberries and whipped cream in the fridge. I was ready for fun. Beau said he was tired and would come over for breakfast and spend the day with me tomorrow. He could f@#$k-up a wet dream. What a loser. What kind of jerk does this to a woman two years in a row?

Happy New Ground Hog Day movie-on-repeat life, year to me. Not. He arrives at noon and greets me with a quick hug. I tried to unbutton his shirt and he freaked out. He wouldn't let me touch him anywhere. He acted like if I touched him, he would be burned by a match or be electrocuted. He was very jumpy since June. Then, he heads straight into my bedroom and lies down on my bed with all of his clothes and shoes on, passes out and starts snoring. Fun! What a loser. I knew for sure now that he had taken me home early and had a party all night with someone else.

Beau looked like he had been up all night. He looked like hell. He didn't say a word to me all day. I made an old fashioned breakfast of French toast, home fries, bacon and sausage for him. He shoveled it down and passed right out again, snoring. Then as usual, he popped up and said he had to go to his Mom's. I called Mom to wish her a happy New Year. She said he was not there. We both knew for sure now. This was all by three p.m. on new Years Day. Unbelievable.

Chapter 46

There was this nice old woman who was a psychic for all the judges and lawyers nearby my home. Her name was Alison. Her husband just died the year before at age one hundred and four. Her son was the boss at the State Attorney's office. She was probably almost ninety years old and sharp as a tack. She was recommended, by a nurse friend, who had been seeing her for twenty years. Apparently she was never wrong. I just had to find out what was going on in my life.

I called the psychic and made an appointment. I went over to her home. She had a tape recorder so that you could record the session and take it home and listen to it whenever you wanted to. I went in and gave her my name and birthday. She sat quietly for a while.

Then she told me I was in a lot of danger. She told me a man who was very dangerous was obsessed with me. He said he is a pathological liar and has a bad drug problem and is an alcoholic. He is also very jealous. She said he has many women. She said he is sick, in a sexual way. She said he had a sexual disease and to not let him touch me. She said he is hiding things. She said he was hiding his drugs some place in my home and to be careful. He has many secrets. He is very well connected with a very powerful group of sick corrupt police and judges. She said he has damaging dirt on many folks. That must have been how he never got caught with the drugs and drunk driving!

She continued to tell me to be very careful and that I had a high likelihood of going to jail because of him. I was shocked. I knew something "hinky" was going on. She also told me that I was very intuitive and that I knew some things already, but it was way worse than I thought.

She said, "He thinks he is the best lover in the world."

I almost fell off the chair laughing. She started cracking up too. I told her that he wouldn't touch me. She said I am lucky about that part but still in danger. I told her that I was trying to get him out of my life. She said he has been obsessed since the moment he saw me. I am the one he knows he can never get no matter what. He has been with loads of women and does not respect them. But she said I was special. He has me on a pedestal. He thinks of me as a possession. She said he is angry that I have stopped drinking. If he can't have me he will try to make sure no one else can. She also said that he has many people watching me, and everything I do, all the time. Then she said to watch out because he was watching me from my back yard.

I thought, "Oh no! He can't just be friends with the Hillbilly drunks, can he? OH NO! Oh shit!"

I asked if that was why my weirdo neighbor followed and watched me, She said everyone was watching me right now. She told me to watch and see who is watching me. She said Beau could control people with threats and drugs, but that I was too strong for him. He falsely thought he could conquer me. She said he was a real stinker.

I kept the tapes of her talking for years and they all make too much sense to me today. It all started happening just like she said.

I went back four more times until her son was in an accident and died. Her son could have helped him get arrested. But I was too late.

Shortly after that jolt she had a major stroke and couldn't read any longer. I used to go by and rub her back and hang out with her. She told me many more things before that. I listen again once in awhile just to hear her voice and it helps me to make sense of the chaos he wreaked. She was very religious and said Jesus would protect me with his angels. Just call on them. She said not to trust the police. She knew every Judge in town and did readings for them too. She told me who the corrupt Judges were. But Beau had bought off a few already. Beau's brothers, after all, are in law enforcement. God only knows who they had slept with to keep Beau out of trouble for forty-seven years.

Chapter 47

My Grandmother said that a man must be "crazy about you". Not crazy. Now my head was all knotted up. I had my Grandmothers and Dads voices in my head and the advice of Alison. My family values were basically to put a man through an endurance course to make him prove he loves you. You had to break up nine times before accepting any serious relationship with a man. She threw my Grandfather's engagement ring back in his face nine times to make sure he truly loved her.

To this day, I still have every pleading love letter my Grandfather ever wrote her. He begged for her hand in marriage like a gentleman should.

Now I have Alison telling me that Beau is no ordinary man he is a dangerous narcissistic sociopath. He was truly crazy. I really had a huge migraine coming on. Not to mention I had to worry about Rika's threats locally. I had a big problem. I didn't know who to talk to since the men in my family are all deceased. I was in a hole. I had nowhere to go but inside myself. I was alone and had to deal with everything myself.

I tried to put the puzzle pieces together, combining all the advice I had been given with my own common sense. Hopefully I could find a way out of this mess. This man was dangerous and highly connected. I used to be connected but not anymore on this turf. I had nowhere to run . I had no one to protect me but God this time. I was trapped. And it stunk.

Beau had built me up so high that I couldn't even reach my own pedestal. Jealousy is a very venomous emotion. It causes men to do insane things. They do things that never make sense to anyone except for their own jealous selves. It is a creepy disease like alcohol or drug addiction. It's when you don't have control of yourself but desperately try to control others. It's as scary as what they describe hell is in the Bible. To me jealousy is just an illusion. It is for people who can't grasp reality. They ruin your fun so they think they are having more fun than you automatically. As Beau's Mom told me, he was psychotically jealous. Folks like that are too lazy to do things for themselves and have a need to cling to others to heighten their self-esteem.

My family members were very strong people. I had phenomenal genes. They didn't have time for folks that wallow in self-pity. I grew up not being allowed the luxury of emotions, anything other than happiness. I would have been grounded for my life if I acted like a spoiled brat, not getting my way. Beau's whining repulsed me. I was never allowed to whine, so why should he? Especially if it was all just an act. We were never allowed to cry when we got hurt or anything. Bravery was our family's motto. Scottish folks are brave and tough as nails. We are not cry babies. I had enough of Beau's lying and excuses. He was a liar. Plain and simple. All of his bullshit was finally catching up to him and he was trapped in his own web of deceit, one that he had carefully woven now for three years.

Chapter 48

When I first moved onto my street, there was a really nice Café at the end on the ocean. I had to eat there everyday until my things arrived on the ship. The property owners were very greedy and decided to double the rent. The café owners were forced to relocate and they did. They were so popular that they re-opened two new cafes. The building sat empty for a year. It was so sad.

Then one beautiful day in September, when I was walking my tiny puppies around the block, I noticed that the abandoned café at the corner of my street had a few folks there working on it. There was an enormous, very hard-looking bleached blonde woman outside.

I said, "Hello. Are we finally going to have a cool place in the neighborhood to hang out, again?" She was sort of friendly and said she hoped to. I told her I was in a band and if she wanted live music we could play there for her. She said that it sounded like a great idea. She seemed pleasant at the time. I introduced myself to her and she said her name was Ness. I could see why. She looked a lot like the Lochness Monster.

I hoped the spot would open before Biketoberfest

and that we could play afternoons there. Well, it did open and my wish came true. We were hired and I invited the whole universe. And they came.

It was outside with a small gazebo for the stage. I could hear the music at my house twelve doors down the street. I sang and the place was packed. Everyone loved our bands. Our other lead singer was amazing. We both took turns singing to keep it really fun. The owner made more money than she ever anticipated. It became "the place to be" because of our music and friends. All the other folks in the neighborhood were old and retired and could walk up there. They only served beer and wine. It was so easy to just walk up my street and sing and eat and have a glass of red wine without having to drive four miles one direction or nine the other to go out. Since I was just getting used to driving in the dark, it was the best for me.

At the beginning, Beau would come with his brothers and their girlfriends. Turns out, Ness had a huge crush on Beau. Every time he came after the bike event, she would ask him to sit at "her table".

Ness drank like Beau. Pitcher after pitcher, for hours on end. Our band would play from five until ten when the sound curfew would be enforced. Ness had found the perfect drinking buddy. She flirted with him and gave him free everything. Ness had her office down below in the back. She had little "afterhours parties" with all the drunks down there through all hours of the night.

The folks that lived directly behind ran the City Newspaper. They were not thrilled, to say the least. They were peaceful Key West lovers. They had filed many complaints with the county. Ness was letting folks over drink and fight and drive after hours. The Sheriff was first there eating lunch and then later he was hauling off some drunken fighting at all hours of the night.

Now that Ness had the "hots" for Beau, she got him to do things for her with his connections to the dirty cops to keep her party going on. Our other singer was in an extremely bad car accident so I was the main singer for a few weeks. Beau was obsessed with me so Ness was trying to make my life difficult. She didn't want me there. She just wanted our band, and Beau. I could feel her bad vibes, they were overwhelming. Ness started booking another band in our place without telling us. We would show up and some other band had started at four o'clock and she'd say the manager made a mistake. We knew it was all because of her crush on Beau. He only went there for me and for her free food and beer. I just quit going there and we played downtown instead.

As a result of Ness' crush on Beau no one went to her bar anymore except for Gus and a few local drunks. The crowd that had spent the money and paid her rent were our friends. Loyal friends. They went with us. The place went downhill and the drunken fights got worse and more cops were called by all of the neighbors.

Ness caused all this drama to win the affections of Beau.

She could have him, I'd be glad to see him go. God knows I didn't want him. Little did she know he was only still hanging there so he could watch me, and my home. It was the perfect look out. I had to turn the corner to get to my house. It was in perfect plain view of my whole street and the main road so he could see me coming or going from a mile a way. I could see him watching for me too. Then he would hop on his bike and follow me to see where I was going. And he did. Ness was getting mad now. She was as obsessed with me as Gus and Beau now. She tried to figure out my allure. She thought she was the "queen bee" of the men with her free beer. Wrong.

Now the truth with Beau was going to get even uglier. Ness was starting to realize that the only reason she made any money was because of me. The band was sick of her jerking us around so even without me they didn't want to deal with her at all. As her business spiraled downward she realized that she really did desperately need us back. The fewer customers she had, the more alcohol she would consume and the meaner she got. I would walk my puppies around the block as usual, right before sunset everyday.

I had now lost a total of thirty pounds. Ness had gained my thirty back in beer and hot dogs and fries. As I walked by every evening I noticed less and less customers and now a Karaoke guy and a few old drunks singing. She had lost all of her customers but Beau. Beau has no visible friends and he was always alone on his bike. She would be sitting at her throne at "her table" holding court and giving me the "hairy eyeball" as I would walk by. Then, she'd say something mean about me and she would get the drunken hillbillies to laugh at me.

For instance, "Now she has nowhere to go and she can't drive at night. Ha ha!" Stuff like that. Ness, and all of her "court jesters", making fun of me. Little did she know I could walk five miles now.

Ness actually thought the world revolved around her place and that nowhere else existed. Delusional, drunk, mean, and horny was a nasty combination for her. I actually marched up to her and told her that she could have my problem (Beau) if she could afford him.

Oh man, she was pissed. She thought she was stealing my man. I told her I have been trying to get rid of this drunk, lying and cheating ass-hole forever. I told her to please take him and set me free from hell. That made her madder than all hell. I thanked her for keeping him occupied while I sang. I also thanked her for paying for his beer. I thanked her for everything she had been doing to help me get rid of him. She exploded! I saw a Hiroshima-sized mushroom cloud form over her when I said that.

She hoped she stole something from me. She saw me lose tons of weight.

I said, "He loves big girls. I am no longer big. He has lost interest in me completely. You are the woman of his dreams. I can't compete with you. Good luck and happy trails."

Ness was a ticking time bomb. She didn't see what was coming next. Beau dropped the bomb on her. The ultimate degradation: Roxy.

Uh oh. Competition for Ness.

Roxy was the same size as Ness, only shorter by one inch and nastier by a long shot. She was packing on the extra pounds with each subsequent beer she guzzled. With each shot. Greasy hot dogs, burgers and fries. Beau loved junk food.

At least Ness wore make up and did her nails and hair, aspiring to look like a hooker. Roxy looked like she was the reigning "Trailer Park Princess". It looked as if Roxy picked her clothes out of a dumpster behind a thrift store. Her yellow fried hair was like an old broom soaked in urine. Her face looked like it held a deep spider web of wrinkles. It was ridden with dry riverbeds of acne scars. You could tell by looking at her that she had never used moisturizer in her life.

To find fat women who were this unbelievably vile and nasty was a feat. Beau actually did meet her in the shittiest bar in town, for real. Now these fat monsters had to fight over him. Beau lived for control and drama.

And their language! Did these animals only know "hillbilly curse-lish"? They said "fuck" every other word and were big, vile, wasted, and desperate. The only thing she had going for her was that she was a swinger too. Apparently, that's how she met Beau.

He was bringing her into his other circle of swingers. This would be a huge mistake. He was building a "harem", or flock, of skanky, desperate old fried and dried up gals who nobody wanted. I had no idea. Nor did I care even if I did know. He was just a lying bore in my eyes now.

When Beau was around me he never cursed or did anything inappropriate. He was so well mannered. When he was with these folks, he was the biggest illiterate in the group, which was quite the achievement. Clearly, he had two lifestyles going on.

Now Beau had made his headquarters at Ness' place in my neighborhood. The whole three years I had lived there I had never seen him around there, other than to ask me out. He had to find friends as creepy as himself. He wanted them to keep an eye on me twenty-four seven. Little did he know that they all had a thing for Ruthie.

I was already busy dodging ass-holes daily as it was. I had my hands full. I was just trying to do what I wanted to do with no interruptions. I was living next to the center of a red-neck sex circus, as it turned out.

Chapter 49

I was singing on Sunday evening early when a female biker friend came into the Nice Guys bar and told me about Beau and Roxy at the bar Beau's brother worked at. She said he had been with her almost a year on Sundays making out with her in front of everyone. Rika was with me. I was so pissed that he was harassing me all the time that I needed a showdown. I called him at about seven thirty and left a message telling him that I knew what he has been doing.

I asked Rika to take me home since she was driving that night. We drove up to my home and I asked her to come in and have a drink. I wasn't drinking, but I made one for myself anyway. We sat and mulled around, discussing what was going on. I was fuming because Beau wouldn't let me get on with my life, but was living his own the whole time while keeping me as a prisoner.

At roughly nine-thirty, Beau rolled into my driveway – however I hardly recognized him. He flung my front door open and came waltzing into my house, bombed out of his mind and laughing satanically at me. An unbearable stench filled the room, he was rancid. He sat down.

Rika and I asked him what the hell was going on.

He was laughing at me like an insane person on glue. He started gloating about all the hell he'd put me through and how he planned everything to make my life miserable. He boasted that if he couldn't have me, he was going to make my life in his town a living hell and nightmare.

Beau asked me how I was enjoying his torment. He told me he had been with Roxy and everyone else in town, the whole time he had pretended to be with me! He said the other women would do anything sexually for him. He went on and on, saying disgusting things to me while Rika just stood there, blankly staring in disbelief.

Beau added, "I'm the king of this town. I can get away with anything. I've owned you since the moment I saw you. I will always own you. I'll kill you before I allow you to be with someone else. I'm going to take and destroy everything of yours."

I was wearing my blue leopard print dress that night. It was a halter-top dress.

Beau was so high and drunk that he was unusually strong, like a super human.

As he let out another ear-piercing, devilish laugh, he grabbed my shoulders and picked me up, gripping me as hard as he could. He hoisted me upwards and hurled me backwards across my living room. I flew. I flew over my glass coffee table, which was a tragedy waiting to happen. Lit candles, wine glasses and miscellaneous sharp objects were strewn across the table top, threatening to seriously injure me if I fell on them.

I continued to fly. Twelve feet backwards across the room and through the air, somehow clearing the candle flames by a foot, miraculously. It all happened in slow motion.

Rika was yelling, "Beau don't kill her!" She stood there on the sidelines watching a man try to kill me and couldn't do a thing about it because it happened so fast.

She screamed, "Jesus! Beau don't, she's fragile!"

All I could hear was Beau laughing really loudly while he hoped I would land on the coffee table and die. The options at this point seemed to be either death or become a quadriplegic or a burn victim... or all of the above.

Rika's plea to Jesus worked. Thank God! It all happened so fast but felt like slow motion at the same time. Rika later said she saw angels lift me over the table and set me gently on the loveseat unharmed without a mark on me. I had even cleared a light weight, wooden statue that was eight inches above the table. It didn't even jiggle a bit. I had just flown twelve feet! And yet my landing couldn't have been softer. I landed upright, utterly shocked but totally unharmed. I had been set down by angels.

Beau was still laughing hysterically but started toward me after watching my miraculous landing. He wasn't going to stop until he hurt or killed me.

I heard my dad's voice saying, "Punch him in the nuts as hard as you can!"

I was bare foot or I would've kicked him as hard

as I could. I suddenly felt the power of Xena, the warrior princess, come into my right arm and fist. I felt superhuman power for that brief moment. I went for it.

I slugged him so hard that he rose one and a half feet off the floor. He wasn't laughing now, at all. He was in extreme pain.

He was grabbing his balls with both hands with tears of agony shooting out of his eye sockets. His eyes were bulging out like he had been hit by lightning.

I said, "That was from my dad!"

Rika was screaming, "Thank God he didn't kill you!"

Beau was so angry that he had failed, that he started yelling at me even more. He admitted that he had done everything to purposely hurt me for three years. He was bragging!

He looked like a completely different person. He was acting like a different person. Talking like a different person. Who was this horrid monster? He said he would get me somehow or some way and that I will just have to wait and see what happens.

Rika demanded him to stop. He looked at her like she had betrayed him. That was creepy. All of a sudden, he just ran out to his truck. I ran out and grabbed him and slapped him and told him to never step on my property or near me again. I threw his phone into his truck cab so he'd have to leave before he could find it to call whomever he desired.

It must have been Fonzo he called because he called Rika and demanded her to come home right away. I was alone and freaked out completely. I had just been violently attacked in my own home. My only sanctuary left was violently violated and tarnished. It was disturbing for me to spend time there now. I couldn't feel anything for awhile after that. I was in shock.

All of the horrendous things he had said to me kept playing on repeat through my head. Why had he said he planned all those things to hurt me, poison me, make me sick all the time, and control me? He had added that he had just used me to get rid of Gin and to have a secret place to hide. He had just used and used and used. And unfortunately, I was the victim of all of it. All of this poisonous venom had shot out of his mouth, like harmful bullets. I never did anything bad to this guy. I just didn't want to date him. What a sad messed up "thrillbilly" he was.

I smiled up at my dad in Heaven and thanked him for the power of that punch.

My Dad would've laughed and exclaimed, "How about a nice Hawaiian Punch!" That became my new private joke from then on. It was about the only thing I had left to make me smile for a while.

Chapter 50

Hope has the potential of being a very dangerous thing. It can drive a man insane. Since Beau couldn't get me to buy any of his stories, he used fear as an insurance policy and as a way to majorly manipulate me. Fear was his vehicle to continue to live separate lives and get away with it, as usual. He decided to tell Ness and my creepy neighbors sob stories about how I abused him by ignoring him. He was trying to socially assassinate me. When he drank and his lips were loosened, he would blabber about all the tricks he was playing on me at the shithole bars around town to try to shut down the musical aspect of my life. Of course he would never remember the small things he said to the folks that actually liked me. They remembered and called and told me. Bartenders were not always his pals, as it turned out. A few of them liked me more than Beau - he would have never guessed it.

I was such a recluse since the sweltering summer had me trapped in my house for months on end this year. I would go out in my pool in the evenings and cool off and study music.

I started hearing a lot of voices that I recognized

while out in my pool. Every sound is amplified near the water. I thought I heard Red and Rave at one of Gus and Dodie's redneck cocktail parties one night. I thought I was imagining it. It seemed to go on forever that night.

After I got out of my pool and dried off, I decided to do a night driving lesson around the hood to get the skinny on the guest parking deal. I did it with my headlights off. My car was very quiet.

To my surprise, Red's little ragtop, with the Rebel flag plate, was parked on Gus and Dodie's lawn. I was not imagining it. Oh shit. My pool cleaners were swinging with the redneck neighbors. That meant Beau was pals with them too! They all had pretended to not know each other all of these years.

While I was putting these disgusting puzzle pieces together in my throbbing head, I realized that I was right. Beau and Gus were really stalking me together. I felt so sick that I had to pull over and get out of my car and barf on the side of the road. They were all in on this together. I had to drive around for a while to clear my head after that realization. I was in disbelief. This was really happening. A club. A freaky, swinger pervert club. Beau was always trying to cast suspicion on someone else. He was just using these folks for his alibis. Red and Rave were having problems in their marriage and Red wasn't working any longer. Rave was doing her pool routine. I guess he was selling his "home grown" to Gus and then they realized they all had something in common and that they were stoners and swingers as well.

Chapter 51

I was seeing a friend a couple of days after Beau threw me across the living room. My friend said I should get an injunction for protection from the Court House in order to keep me safe. Her son was a District Attorney in another state, but he had seen his father do it to her when he was a child. She was a real pro at writing the pleadings to the Judge.

She said I needed Rika as my witness to tell the court what had happened and to make the charges stick. I went over to Rika's place and asked her to write the judge a statement on my behalf. She did, and then she had it notarized at her bank.

Fonzo was out of town, luckily for me.

I took the papers down to the court and swore in the story and got a court date for the Protection Injunction. I was surprised at how many other women were there in the same predicament.

It took the Sheriff a week to find Beau and serve him the papers. They finally caught up with him at the disgusting bar where he met Roxy. He was stopped, with Roxy in his truck, while stumbling drunk out of the same sick bar they met at. It was a huge buzz kill for Beau. The court date was set for ten days later in May. My friend agreed to go with me as my support system.

We showed up and Beau didn't. I was automatically awarded the Protection Order that I was seeking.

Apparently at one p.m. later that day, Beau sauntered into the court and asked the Judge to forgive him for forgetting to show up and to just drop the Order. I received a copy of his request in the mail, which was written by an illiterate drunk person.

It was so bad that it was hilarious. He didn't spell one word correctly for saying he is a printer by trade. He acted like I was putting him out in some way and that I was a complete stranger. He was refused and blocked.

Well, to get me back, he did everything to terrorize me on God's Green Earth twenty four seven, from then on. He was in front of my home everyday just to see if he could scare me. I would take a time stamped photo and call the Sheriff. They would come and let him go. I kept calling and showing the photos to them. The injunction stated that he couldn't come five hundred feet from me at any time, no matter where, for an initial period of six months.

Chapter 52

I had Gus behind me now throwing parties and inviting Beau to watch me from behind through my fence and to follow me everywhere.

I had to keep going down to the Court House to file violations. It got to the point where it was consuming each of my days. The cops wouldn't help me. The order said they had to protect me anywhere in the state for six months until I got a permanent injunction for protection.

After two months of daily obsessive stalking and no cop help, I went and hired a woman lawyer. She told me to get a surveillance system put in so the cops would have to help me and that the evidence would stand up in court. I had a good one put in. It cost me a fortune.

Beau, Gus and Ness were watching me like a Hawk. I had tons of proof of Beau in front of my house. I gave it to the Cops and they blew me off every time. There was one Sheriff who knew Beau was stalking me and he even tried to help me get him jailed for violations, but he got bullied out of the department. He ended up leaving the Sheriff's department and joining the Army.

His reports are the only ones where action was taken on my behalf!

Beau's job and brothers had him sufficiently protected from jail time. I bought a stun-gun. My home had been broken into and ransacked. My bills, bank records, and other things were missing. My cars and my bike were booby-trapped to where I would be seriously hurt or killed. I tried to make police reports and was denied.

My neighbors were appalled. There had been no crime in this area in years. It all started when the Café on the corner opened. I was very good friends with all of my neighbors since I had moved there three years ago. They all knew it was from the seedy crowd at the Café that had gathered there recently. I had been walking around my block everyday for three years and never felt fear. Now I felt incredibly edgy.

Chapter 53

One night in July, my band was playing up at Ness's Café at the end of the street. I was celebrating a lucrative business deal. The band asked me and my friend to come up and celebrate with dinner and singing with the band. I had not been there since the end of May. We walked up to the end of the street and walked on to the patio and the waitress cleaned off our chairs and took our wine and beer orders. One of the girls that worked there was acting strangely towards me. She had always been cordial to me. She was acting nervous like she was waiting for something. Her demeanor was making me very suspicious.

Our drinks were set on the table and we wanted to order our food. We had our whole band sitting at the table eating already. It was early and the place was almost empty, besides a couple of local hardcore drinkers. We all made a toast and took a drink when, all of the sudden, a Sheriff cruiser pulled into the parking lot with the flashers on. This was normal for this place.

We all looked around to see "what now?" It was the same Sheriff who was always at my house. He was very rude and nasty to me, either that or he would ignore my calls.

He got out of the car and signaled with his finger for me to come outside of the patio. I instantly thought he had caught Beau breaking into my home or something to help me, finally. I smiled and tried to hope he had caught Beau at my house or anything to give me peace finally. Wrong.

Ness set me up to get arrested for trespassing. The only problem was that she wasn't there, firstly. Second of all, the waitress made the mistake of taking our order and bringing it to us.

The Sheriff made me get into the backseat and kept me there for one hour before Ness showed up, plenty mean and drunk. He asked her to take her huge sunglasses off since it was almost dark outside. She refused. He was getting angry, but he was acting suspicious about the whole set up. She bullied the cop into arresting me and demanded he put me in jail for trespassing. She wouldn't let up.

The sheriff was angry that Ness took an hour to show up. It was sweltering hot outside because it had just drizzled. He was losing patience, waiting for her to insist she could frame me for walking my dogs and to be invited in for dinner and drinks. He explained to her that I had not broken any laws and that I had been served alcohol and had walked there. When it came down to my past, I was fine. I was clean. I didn't even have one parking ticket in my whole life's worth of driving. He ran my everything and the results were the same as the other forty times I had called him for protection from Beau. He was in on it for sure.

Unfortunately, I had fifteen witnesses and hadn't done anything wrong. However, I was told not to walk on a public sidewalk with my dogs from now on.

The whole place emptied out and everyone came to my house except for Ness and the bartender who called Ness to alert her to call the "po po" on me. So Beau was obviously hanging out there so he wouldn't get a violation for being five hundred feet from my home. I could still drive by legally. I saw what was up after that night.

Everyone saw them all partying like maniacs from then on. My band quit playing there after that night and nobody went there anymore, which made Ness even angrier. She was trying to make me lose my band and friends and discredit me. Little did she know everyone was on my side except for her and the dirty Sheriffs. Now I was scared.

My security footage showed Ness in her Mercedes driving in and out of my driveway every night. It showed her employees parked in front of my house with their Rebel flags on the front, to give their cars away. I had tried to get an injunction for protection against her and Gus, too. I was rejected. I had tons of evidence. I even had witnesses testify.

They all still got off, regardless of all the evidence and witnesses. They were calling me with death threats and prank phone calls. It was out of control. I didn't have any peace.

We had a rainy season for quite some time. The Café Ness rented was completely outdoors, except for the bar, bathrooms and kitchen. When it rained she would have to close. She had a 'Speak-Easy' in her office at night for her regulars. Afterwards they would terrorize my home and keep me and my dogs up all night. I had the surveillance system running and recorded everything for the court. I had them live on DVD. But I was still ignored.

Chapter 54

Finally one of Beau's violations somehow slipped through the Sheriff's office and made it to the State's Attorney office. I was contacted by them and asked to go down to their office. I guess Beau had to go, too. I found out his appointment was before mine from the Sheriffs who were in charge of security at the entrance to the building.

As I was going through the metal detector, one of the Sheriffs made a comment about the photo I had of Beau. It was sitting on top of my stack of complaints as I put my belongings through the metal x-ray machine. They knew him. They knew he was dangerous. They told me to buy a gun as soon as possible. I told them that I have been terrorized and ignored and not protected by my restraining order. They shook their heads and said Beau was just there a few minutes ago and to be very afraid of him.

Then I went upstairs and the State's Attorney told me I would have to move away right away.

I said, "I just paid for my house one week ago in cash and the market is in the gutter."

They said to me, "Do you want to get killed in your

house? That's what's going to happen to you if you stay. We cannot protect you from someone like Beau because you live far from town where the police cannot get to you quickly enough."

I said, "The Sheriff has not lifted a finger to protect me with my Injunction for Protection since I got it. They keep letting him get away with every violation, every time." I told him the Sheriff parked at the end of my street at night. But they already knew and that's why they told me to move.

I very nearly had a heart attack in my car, as I felt my legs turn to wet noodles while unlocking the door in the one hundred degree heat. I felt lost. I just paid for my home and it was perfect in every way. I was so happy and now I had to find somewhere else to go, fast, with two dogs, three vehicles, and my house full of belongings . I didn't have a plan B.

Plan B had already expired as I had finally paid for the place. Oh shit. My head was going to explode. I was just down the street from Harry's house, so I headed over to ask him for help. I was so freaked out. He offered to go talk to Beau in attempt to get him to lay off of me. I told him he'd probably get killed or set up or beat up. I told him Beau's brothers were dirty cops and it wouldn't work. I didn't want Harry to ever have a problem in his life. Beau could ruin anyone's life just like his younger brother had said at Easter at Mom's house.

He said, "Well then, I'll protect you until you leave."

Thank God for him. Harry was so pissed off that Beau had done so many horrible things to me. He and all my friends were trying to think of where I could move to get safe. If the cops wouldn't help me in Florida, then I had to move to a new state for survival. My mind was blank and I was exhausted.

Chapter 55

Two days after that, around July tenth, Ness started terrorizing me on her own. She would drive in and out of my driveway in her gold Mercedes at all hours of the day and night. I would fling open the door and take a photo of her. She was also on my security footage, which was marked with the time and date. I had bought a huge calendar and was documenting all of this crap for the court.

Then the prank phone calls started coming in at all hours of the night and day. I had an unlisted, private number that was only given out to close friends. Beau must have given my numbers to every crackhead in town because the calls were always during the wee hours of the night. They were all from disposable phones with untraceable numbers. It was a nightmare and I couldn't sleep very well.

I was invited to be a guest DJ on a local radio station, so I was getting ready for my appointment the next day at noon. I washed my car in my driveway one evening and put it in my garage, but forgot to close the door and fell asleep on my couch.

When I awoke at five AM I bolted up and opened

the door to the garage to see that my wheels had been tampered with. I walked over to the truck and it looked o.k. I took it for a ride and found out he had cut the brake lines. I was unnerved to say the least.

My Harley had the seat removed and the clamps were unscrewed and jammed into the engine. My blue beach scooter was gone and all of my classic movies I had collected for twenty years that were stored in plastic tubs were gone too. I checked everything. I had been robbed.

I was so scared. I called Harry and my car mechanic. Harry said he'd come by after work and we could fix my bike. I got in my car to see what happened to it. I pulled it out of the driveway. It seemed a little off. My car mechanic said that someone has to use a special tool from Germany to get the wheels off.

I had the appointment to go about twelve miles up the coast to a tiny surfer town for the DJ job. I got ready and drove my car up there. It felt a little bit strange and there was a sound that wasn't there before. I was nervous and extra careful driving it.

The next morning I had to drive to Orlando with my Bass player for a doctor's appointment. I had to leave at eleven to get to Orlando by one o'clock. As I got to the end of my street on my way to the gas station, I saw Beau sitting outside with a pitcher of beer and Ness. His bike was right there by the side of the road. I hung a right and went a quarter of a mile down the road to the gas station. Who do you think was on my butt? Beau.

He hopped on his bike and came to the gas station to harass me. I froze in fear as I was trying to fill my tank up. He was hazing me. He peeled out and did a

U-turn and then came back and drove through the gas station trying to scare me. My heart was pounding. He committed road rage all the time to innocent folks and he carried a gun. I had experienced him pulling a gun on a poor guy with a baby in the car during Bike Week at a traffic light. I was the passenger on his bike that day. Terrifying.

He was drunk already at eleven a.m. I just prayed to God that I could ditch him and not be followed to Orlando. I pulled out my cell phone to call nine one-one and he took off. I took off and went down side streets to pick up my friend. My heart was pounding in my chest. I didn't have my camera with me that day. I would have to go to the Court House in the morning and file another violation. As I was driving along, my car started making a strange sound, even louder now. It was driving all right but I had a feeling something was done to it. My bass player was ready to go when I arrived.

We had called my violin player, Rika, and told her about all the crazy stuff happening. She acted shocked that Beau had gotten so obsessed. A few minutes later, we passed her going the opposite way on the road to Orlando. She sure got around. We called her back and told her she just passed us. That was funny. "Where was Fonzo?", I asked. They were inseparable. She said he was on his bicycle training for a race coming up.

Then we saw him flying down the road later that day. He really was fast for a bike rider. Rika told us that he rode to St. Augustine and back every day. Fonzo rode about one hundred and fifty miles a day on a bicycle. This was an unbelievable amount of exercise for a meth head and an alcoholic.

We got to Orlando safely and got back to town safely. I had to drive another half hour to get home. Harry was coming over to check my bike out and have dinner at my place. He fixed what Beau had done that was obvious, but the bike wouldn't start. Harry and I took it apart meticulously and couldn't figure out what it was, then, as I was sitting on the step side of my truck, I noticed something broken off inside of the kicker. Harry was lying on the garage floor and I saw what the "booby-trap" was. Man, Beau was good at his vandalisms. We got it fixed and then went riding as often as possible for the next few weeks until Hurricane Faye blew the daylights out of the beach areas and road.

We had to stay inside and board up our homes for four days, but it rained for weeks in August. It was ugly and blowing like the hubs of hell. Even the phone lines were out. Power lines were out too. It was extra spooky for me alone with a stalker. Nothing stopped Beau. Nothing. In fact the storm made it easier for him to kick my doors in.

After the storm, Rave, the pool cleaner had to come and clean all the pollen out of the pool. Red was pretending to have job interviews in Las Vegas at eyewear conventions to cheat on Rave. She was bored. When she was home at all, she made Rave buy her designer clothes at upscale stores. Just after that she'd stay in bed and whine and cry and tell him and everyone that she had cramps and migraines to avoid her husband. Rave had to clean all of her pools and his now. He was hydroponically growing pot and mushrooms at home to make their mortgage payments and buy her overpriced stuff. She was high maintenance. She never wanted to come over to my house, just as a friend anymore, either. When Rave came over, I told him all of the stuff that Beau was doing to me. He said he didn't want to hear about it.

I said, "You're my friend. Why can't I tell you?"

He said he had just listened to "the secret CD" and couldn't allow himself to hear anything negative. He just said he didn't want to know because he hated Beau and was not friends with him.

I said, "We all went to his house and their house many times together." He dismissed me completely. I knew that they were all doing things behind my back by that cheap answer.

I had to go to Orlando for a follow-up appointment on July thirtieth, with Harry as my bodyguard this time. I picked him up downtown in the morning. We were driving towards Orlando and I got the most painful zap in my neck that was so painful that I almost had to pull over. It was like a cattle prod. I had to grab my neck and hold it. It stopped then a really sharp pain for about ten minutes. It was agonizing pain. The car was making a loud moaning sound in the front.

We made it to the doctor's office alive, but saw a man get stabbed in front of a supermarket while we sat in a café and ate lunch next door. It was a crazy day so far. After lunch we were heading into a torrential rainstorm while driving seventy miles an hour in blinding black rain. The traffic flow was still seventy in all four lanes of highway. It was so bad. You could barely see the tail lights of the vehicle in front of you. My car was shaking at this point.

Harry and I were praying together. All the sudden we broke through the storm barrier and were in perfect Florida sunshine and dry road. It was insane. Relief. We made it almost all the way home so far without a calamity. I dropped Harry off so he could get his bike so we could go out for dinner and ride our Harley's up the coast to a fish taco joint we loved. I had to go to the chiropractor on the way home. I dropped in, got adjusted and told my doctor about my car noise. He was a car collector and knew my car well. He said to drop by the tire place on my way home and put it in the rack and see what's up with the noise.

The tire shop by the cigar shop was my regular tire place. I was driving down the street about three miles and as I turned into the tire place, right before it closed, both of my front wheels fell off right there. Boom. Clunk. The guys were in shock that I wasn't killed in the rainstorm in Orlando. So was I. I called Harry to pick me up. They had to keep the car, then, tow it down the street to my mechanic the next day. It was bad. It was definitely tampered with. The tire store and my mechanic wrote letters to the judge testifying I was in serious danger. I took the letters and made a report at the Courthouse the next day along with about ten more things that happened including when I arrived home and my side and back door were kicked in. I tried to make a police report and the usual happened. Nothing. The Sheriff was a dick to me as usual.

My detective friend from New Orleans though it was time to enlist the help of some professional services. He flew in to bodyguard me. I had filed so many cases that they stacked them all for one court date on August seventh. I idiotically thought I needed a lawyer at this point incase Beau was planting drugs in my home or vehicles to get me busted or something to cover his stuff and to get the Injunction for Protection dropped. He was doing everything in the world that he could come up with to make me scared and miserable, twenty-four seven.

Hal showed up in the middle of the afternoon so nobody saw him arrive. We went to the supermarket down the road and ran into a criminal defense lawyer friend of mine. We asked her what we should do. She recommended a woman lawyer. She knew who Beau was because he had been in trouble before. She told us to hire this particular woman because her husband is the head of the narcotics squad of the Sheriffs department. We called and got an appointment late that afternoon at five o'clock.

Her office was right behind Beau's house, coincidentally. Hal and I went up the steep stairs and she came out and met us. We showed her all our evidence and she asked for my financial records to see if I could afford her. I showed her. Hal told her that he had worked for me and been my friend since nineteen ninety-six. She asked if I was nuts because of my stress level and my chronic laryngitis. He told her no, I am very sane just exhausted. She whined that she had menopause and was in agony and bitchy and she apologized for her being curt with us.

I told her I understood her pain and that I had just finished twenty years early of it and had just lost sixty-five pounds in the last five months. She was angry I was so slim. First she called my witness Rika. Rika said she would testify at the hearing the next afternoon since she had witnessed me being thrown across my living room and written to the judge and had it notarized. Then, she called eleven other witnesses and they all agreed to show up on my behalf. She took my case with a five thousand dollar retainer. She bragged that her husband is the chief of the narcotic squad of the Sheriffs department and she could help me get Beau arrested for sure. She basically guaranteed it in front of Hal.

I was down to one hundred and ten pounds that day when I was weighed in at my doctor's office down the street before her appointment. He was scared and thought I had AIDS or was on drugs. I did a pee test and a blood test. All came out clean. The women in my doctor's office were nasty to me for no reason. It seemed like everyone was trying to find something wrong with me to make this all go away and Beau could go free. Since Beau grew up there his whole life and was a printer, everyone knew him it seemed like.

I was the victim. Why was I being treated like a criminal? The woman lawyer told me to have a camera security system put in my home a.s.a.p. in order to have proof that Beau was doing all this damage to me and my things. I called a security company and they were set to come at noon on Sunday undercover and dressed like 'red-necks' making it look like they were there to fix my truck in the garage.

It was late afternoon on Thursday when I retained her. Court was the next day, Friday, at one o'clock. Beau had twelve violations to deal with tomorrow. The female Judge had clustered them together for one appearance. I had just kept filing and filing and loading her down with violations. I had twelve witnesses. I was happy at that very moment. Twelve. What was his problem? Why wouldn't he let me be? I just wanted my quiet life back. He was truly obsessed. He was sick and sad and boring. He needed to draw all of this attention to himself in order to feel alive. How pathetic. He was wearing everyone out for himself, apparently. He was dragging everyone into this stupid drama he had created. Like I said earlier, "These folks love drama at any cost." These folks were as bored as he was.

I felt so drained. This was ridiculous and adolescent to say the least. It was a pathetic cry out for attention, since he was the second to youngest and best looking of six siblings. He was the loser of the family. He needed to have attention given to him anyway at any cost.

Hal and I went and had dinner, then went back to my house and did laundry and went to sleep early. It had been a very tiring day for both of us. My puppies were with us all day too and even they were tired from being in the car.

Beau came at four thirty a.m. with Ness and kicked my other doors in. Hal had just gone to bed and the dogs went nuts. I jumped up and flung open the front door and there they were laughing at me with a sledgehammer. I said, "Hal is here. Now I have a witness for court against you both." They just laughed and yelled, "Good luck with that 'Fuck Face.'" They ran down the street laughing. I could tell they were really drunk. Hal came out of his room and said he couldn't believe that just happened. I answered, "Welcome to my nightmare." He just hugged me and told me he would protect me and not to worry.

Chapter 56

Court was the next afternoon. I had twelve witnesses and Harry and Hal and a pile of evidence. Beau had Roxy, in one of my black dresses, which is ten sizes too small for her and her spanks. She weighed about two hundred and fifty pounds in my size eight cocktail dress he stole when they broke into my home another time. She had glasses exactly like my old ones on. Her hair was done like my old hairstyle. He was trying to make her into me. She was wearing my shoes too. I was standing at the end of the hall with my posse'. My nice neighbor was out by the elevator spying on Beau, Roxy and his pretend to be "alibi boss". Beau had hired a ghetto lawyer who looked like a drag queen. His group was looking for me, but didn't recognize me right in front of them. I had lost sixty- five pounds and cut and dyed my hair my natural color. I was wearing a beige pencil skirt with a white blouse. I was wearing white shoes and a matching bag and briefcase. I had brown simple glasses on and my hair up in a French twist with a nice brown hair comb holding it up in place.

Beau's pal/boss commented on how "HOT" I was, not knowing it was I. It was hilarious.

Roxy screamed at Beau, "Where's this bitch I'm supposed to look like?"

I said," I am right here." I waved and smiled.

My new female lawyer came out the court room and asked me which man Beau was. I told her he was the guy sitting at the end of the hall next to the Sheriff. Beau looked at her as she looked at him. They had some connection. Everyone saw it.

She said to me nervously, "That's the Beau you hired me to go against?"

I said, "Yes. Why? Is there a problem?" She looked upset.

Beau shot her a "how could you" look.

She whirled around and rolled her eyes like she was in deep trouble.

The hallway was packed with cases waiting to be tried. Her attitude towards all of us changed instantly like we were a pain in her butt. She took the wrong case and had to get out of it quick. We all noticed something fishy in her personality. It was as if she had been threatened.

The sheriff just happened to call my name and case up next and we all filed in and sat down. Beau was to my right slumped over the court table looking like he hadn't slept in weeks. His skin was all broken out in acne. He had not shaved in weeks. He had bags under his eyes that hung like hammocks down his cheeks. He smelled bad. The light green suit he threw on was not the dazzler he envisioned to impress the court. He acted like he won already. He sat hunched over like he was waiting for a beer and a shot in a bar, not court. He was blasé with the judge as if he had already had her paid off. All of my friends saw this. It was bad.

I had laryngitis still and could barely speak. My whole group of witnesses was waiting to be called up to testify against him. Beau's drag queen lawyer and my female lawyer went up front and spoke to the judge for a few moments. Beau glanced over and smiled mockingly at me like Satan was inside of his eyes. I didn't react at all. I looked straight ahead. Apparently, Roxy had taken the seat right behind me. She studied me, from what my friends told me later. She was obsessed now, too. Beau looked terrible because he was up all night breaking into my home and partying. Roxy was trying to act like I was ruining her life. She was so ugly and fat and miserable and stuck with Beau now.

I smiled at her and said, "You're next."

My friends shook their heads and looked at her like 'shame on you Roxy.'

I hoped my new lawyer had him by the balls, but I was disillusioned. She had the judge let him off on every charge. We were all in shock. None of us even got a chance to testify!

Thirteen witnesses. Beau really did have the judge and lawyers paid off. He got up and sauntered out like he owned the place.

The one clean sheriff was really angry. He knew this was a joke. He knew I was being victimized and in danger. My lawyer acted like she wanted nothing to do with me. Hal asked her what the hell was going on.

She, in a fit of mild rage, answered, "I can't do this."

Hal demanded an explanation starting with, "What? Explain please what just happened in there?"

She just shook her head and ran by Beau and his gang to the elevator and disappeared. We all just shook our heads and filed out of the court room.

Beau and his crew all laughed at all thirteen of us as we came out of the doors. While we were assembling to leave, Beau had his arm around Roxy's fat backside and he turned to look at me and in front of everyone including the Sheriff, he stuck his middle finger up Roxy's butt and she jumped and turned around and gave me a dirty look. We all almost threw up laughing.

My friends told them how disgusting they were and how they deserved each other. I couldn't stop laughing all the way down the elevator and outside, as we walked to our cars.

Next, we saw her alone and Beau leaving with his "fake boss" friend. He just left her there outside of the courthouse by herself, humiliated in my black cocktail dress. She looked like a hooker. He showed everyone that she liked it "prison style". We laughed at her and drove away. What else could we do? We went to my lawyer's office for an explanation of what had just happened in the courtroom. She coldly stated that I had to move.

Chapter 57

Beau had broken into my garage and stolen my beach scooter all my two hundred and fifty movies that I collected for fifteen years and the wheels off of my old truck. He also stole all of my banking and my complete records files of my whole life that I had hidden in my back guest room closet. He had my life. I had already filed in Small Claims court against him to return my things.

Hal and I told her, "No, you don't get out of this that easily. You are due in small claims court against him on my behalf next week."

She started to act like a real bitch to me. It was bad. Hal told her if she took the cases and the huge retainer she is obligated to represent me. It's the law. She got nastier and started personally attacking me. I saw her having a mental breakdown. She was greedy and now in trouble. Beau knew her personally and it was a conflict of interest problem for her.

It was Friday afternoon and we were all tired and upset. It was the middle of September now and Beau wouldn't let up.

Chapter 58

Back while I was in the Courthouse filing in the small claims for my movies, beach scooter and my truck wheels, a woman approached me and had my case in her stack of case files. She was looking for interesting cases for Judge Mathis and Judge Pirro shows for T.V. She chose me. It was hilarious.

I had a photo of all the things Beau had stolen. It was funny because everything he stole was all in just one photo. Since my Dad was a documentary photographer, I just naturally document everything like he did. I am lucky that art rubbed off on me, as it came in handy now, for court. They loved my cases. Beau was a "Grifter" and a con.

My problem was that I was dealing with a stalker and a thief and a rapist. I had to explain how dangerous this man was and that I'd have to decline. They said if I had any other cases, to call them and let them know. They said I'd be great on T.V. I made everyone in the Courthouse laugh so hard that day and everyday it was getting ridiculous. All the employees agreed that by now I should have my own T.V. series. The Sheriff's who are in charge of security at the Courthouse started calling me "Princess" from then on. I was there at least twice a week since May. They felt bad that they couldn't help me. They watched me lose about fifty pounds in four months. They always noticed and made a nice compliment to me as I went through the metal detector or walked me out to my car to keep me safe.

When Hal came with me to help me do paperwork and check Beau's background, they were happy to see that I had outside help. They knew what was happening to me. They had seen it before many times. They had seen Beau there on past charges many times, it turns out. But, they saw his brothers and the same female judge always get him out of whatever trouble it was and made sure he got off from the charges against him. They knew he was dangerous and connected as well. They knew someone in their courthouse was helping him get off. They referred to the Judge as the "Pig". While she was my judge, she made sure he got off. On his other cases we noticed she was the same Judge every time he got off 'Scott free' for drunk driving and once for plowing down a man with his car and excessive speeding.

I was lucky, suddenly, when I got assigned a new Judge that didn't let him off for my final plea for a permanent injunction for protection. Thank God for that miracle.

It seemed like a nightmare that was repeating itself weekly. Maybe he had slept with her. As Hal was finding out by his detective work, Beau was working hard to have things covered up to save his ass. Hal had been a Detective for twenty-three years and could piece corruption together like you wouldn't believe.

Now Beau was scared and knew I had a posse of DEA

and Feds as old pals of my uncle. He knew that my uncle who worked for the FBI making guns and special bullets was my guardian angel. He didn't know that my other best friend who I never divulged to him, was going to get him one way or the other and had higher rank than this Po-dunk town, full of skanky dirty Sheriffs. Time wounds all heels eventually.

After Hal's investigation, he discovered that Beau had grown up with all of these dirty cops and Sheriffs. He had dirt on all of them from the past. That explained why they couldn't help me. He could blackmail them. They owed him. As my Dad always said, "Information is power." We had the info, now. Beau didn't know. There were sealed records in the courthouse too.

The prank calls and late night vandalism escalated and no Sheriff's responded. The trips down to the Courthouse got more and more frequent. Beau was nuts. He was up all night creating mischief and destruction at my home on my surveillance system. I burned discs and gave them to the judge. Nothing was working. Beau had everyone lying for him and covering up his fun. The surveillance discs showed that he was in front of my home from two a.m. until five thirty a.m. How was he staying up all night and stalking me on his bike all day?

One night after Hal left, I was in my kitchen studying at about ten p.m. and I heard a huge crash in my front yard. I ran to my front door and flung it open to see Beau in his old black explorer plowing through my front yard with a bunch of friends and all of my recycling was hit and tipped over and my Evian bottles were strewn across my newly landscaped lawn and tire track marks destroying my grass and flowers. He was in the SUV drunk and yelling at how he was going to destroy my home and yard and pool and laughing like Satan. The truck was plowing through other neighbor yards too. They were driving all over the place crazy out of their minds. He almost hit Flynn, my neighbor and her dogs on their late night walk.

Twenty neighbors called the cops and it took them two hours to respond and all of our stories matched, yet, the lazy sheriff's took two hours to respond and the mean Sheriff was at my house interrogating me.

My yard was trashed. I photographed it all and all the witnesses told the cops it was Beau in his Explorer, high as a kite, creating all this destruction. We were all disregarded and ignored. The whole sleepy retired town was under attack and no help could be found. He was out of his mind. The video showed it. Neighbors saw it. The cops blew us all off. We were all very angry. We all started closing and locking everything up. Our peace has been compromised. Our lives were violated. This was bad.

Meanwhile there was another strange thing that started going on in our neighborhood as of lately. I lived six houses away from the river. One day while all these crazy things were happening to me, I started to see tons of Sheriffs driving around my neighborhood in the early evenings. I just walked my dogs regularly and tried to find out what was happening.

Apparently, there were decapitated and dismembered dead human bodies found in garbage bags floating up on the rich folks home docks all of the sudden. Most of the high end homes on the river had boats and docks. The locals were in a frenzy of fear and an uproar. The Sheriffs now really had to actually work. One of our very nice neighbors lived on the river for thirty years peacefully and was robbed, tortured and murdered in his home. He had a ton of money and the safe was cracked and everything was gone. The news in the paper and on the television reported that all these crimes were Methamphetamine related crimes. Everyone was in shock and fear in the area I lived in.

I never knew there was meth in our town the whole time I lived there. I only heard about pot and crack. What is Meth? I didn't have a computer or anyway to find out there. I had to ask Hal since he's seen everything in New Orleans. He told me it's very bad and folks have no feeling or conscience after they do it. It ruins a persons mind instantly. Our sleepy little town was under attack now.

A week later, I was driving to the supermarket which was exactly 4 miles from my house down the road. I saw two police cars and two sheriff cars.

I went to the supermarket and came back to the gas station to fill up my car.

I said, "Hey what's going on next door?" to the gas attendant.

He said he didn't know, but that we would find out on the local news that night.

The 10 o'clock news said that the first body was found in the river, totally decapitated and dismembered. Chainsaw style. Legs and fingers separated.

It was meth related. The town was buzzing with

chatter. All this was happening 3 miles from my house?! I was told there hadn't been crime in 40 years, why were all of these terrible things happening now? Was Beau involved?! I couldn't make sense of it.

Chapter 59

I had made friends with a couple of women I had met while riding my bike. One night they came up to my house and we went up north to another town for tacos. One of the women was my friend, Shawna, for three years. Her husband was friend's with Beau for ten years. She said Beau had her husband all wired out and hooked on Meth and it was about to cause them a divorce. She said her husband had been selling all their antique bikes on E-bay while she was at work and all the money was disappearing. She said he was acting abusive towards her to breaking point. She couldn't get him to quit. She told me what I was dealing with.

I almost had a heart attack, finding all of this out in two hours. She warned me he is extremely off the hook and dangerous. She cried as she told me in the café on the beach that evening. She feared for my life. I felt numb. She was in fear of her own life at this point as well but offered to help me in any way. She lives just down the street from him and has to pass his house to go to the supermarket. She told me she'd try to find out what was going on and call me. Neither Beau nor her husband knew we had bonded and were friends. Thank God.

The other woman was a recovered Meth addict. She said she did it for twenty years and she said it took twenty years to recover from the damage it did to her mind and body. She said Meth makes a person insane instantly and mean. She said if you do it, you barf and have diarrhea all the time and are sick as hell and want to kill everyone. She told me she stayed up for weeks at a time and didn't eat or sleep. Then she would gorge on pizza and garbage and sleep for a week then do it all over again. She said Meth is 'Satan.' I told them what Beau had been doing to me. Her friend told me that's why he shoveled my home cooking down and obsessively cleaned my toilet.

Now I was putting some of the missing odd pieces of part of the puzzle together. She said Gin and Beau were partners more than lovers all these years. He had to keep her close because she is a liability. Shawna said she had been to insane parties at Beau's house over the years where Gin ran around the party, wasted, in bikini underwear and a bra screaming, Where's all the coke?" in front of thirty or more people. He always acted like it was normal behavior and just ignored her as if he was numb.

She told me he needed me to need him, to make him look better. I made his life sane and clean. He told folks Ruthie is the best thing that ever happened to me.' She said he actually was better and looked normal when he was with me, but then he slipped back down the slope in to hell with Meth again. She said he actually was happy for a while with me, then, lost it again. She also said she saw him in the supermarket in the cold meat section, around the fourth of July, and he was sweating profusely, shaking and he acted paranoid and was very dirty and smelly. He said hello to her and then hurried to the check-out. I was shocked and sad and scared.

She told me he has a really old, big, fat girlfriend with a red convertible that is always in his driveway for over a year. This was a ton of information for me to process. He had me on the side for public appearance, and Roxy for whatever. An alibi and a drinking buddy is all I thought of Roxy. But Beau just kept coming after me. I had no idea he did Meth or sold it. I knew nothing until this night. I always wondered how he afforded all the mortgage payments and insurance for home and four vehicles and two other properties he made no money from by just illegally printing in his Mom's garage at night. They both said that Meth makes people obsessed with other people. It heightens jealousy and every other bad mental problem a person may have. My friend had seen Beau and Gin fight at parties and bars for ten years and it was violent, ugly and sometimes bloody. They both told me he would never let me move on and be with another man ever. I was implanted in his psycho mind forever.

I had to move away no matter what. I just sold my other house and would have the money soon. I would be free. Where to go was the problem. My head was about to explode into a million pieces. I felt so sick.

The crazy thing was that Beau had a D.U.I. and was not permitted to drink or drive for six months. Hal had found that information out when he checked Beau's records. He was supposed to get pee tested once a week for six months. Hal contacted his parole officer and found out what he had to deal with. He informed her that Beau had become unhinged and was on a streak of terror.

She asked if he was dangerous and an alcoholic and Hal said, "Definitely." We thought that might help, but no. He was taking his old Mom's pee and putting it in a rubber glove on Wednesday mornings and strapping it to his leg to pass the test and come out with a clean report. After I met him he told me the trick when he was drunk one night. He said he and his brothers did it for them as favors for 'the old, you owe me for saving your butt, etc, type of blackmail favor, since forever to keep their important friends out of trouble and definitely out of jail. We read the court reports that showed he had been in trouble in the past and now he was listed for all the times he had harassed me, but no action was taken because he had the same Judge every time who was letting him off on every violation. Hal was disgusted. Hal recommended me to go away after Labor Day and have a breather to be able to sleep and think. Hal said he would fly back in mid-September and help me arrange to move and get me a gun.

The next evening I was driving down the street and Gus was walking his dog at the end of the street. I slowed to a stop so he and the dog could cross in front of me. I said, "Hello", just to keep peace. He then ran up to my window and reached in and tried to punch me in the face. He called me a "fucking bitch" and I was jerked my head over and punched my accelerator to get away.

I was shaking like a leaf in a hurricane. I called the cops and they actually came and made a report. They only came since it wasn't about Beau for once. I got the other dimwit Sheriff who kept trying to tell me my Injunction was not valid against Beau, in the past. He liked Gus for this one since Gus had a five-page rap sheet.

This report made it to the States Attorney's office for some miracle. Apparently, Dodie was really angry with Gus because he was having a three-some with Red and Rave and took off for a few nights and stayed down south at their house. He was on a week long bender that consisted of drinking, crack smoking and sex.

This was a huge reality check for Dodie. She had to give in to them. She was screaming that she couldn't believe they were really swingers. It was okay for her to be bi-sexual with other women but for Gus to have a party like this pissed her off completely. He had just arrived home to be thrown out with all his belongings and I got physically attacked for it. All I could hear was Gus peel out as the Sheriff tried to catch him. It took the Sheriff ten days to find and serve him. He finally came home and it started all over again. It was a never-ending nightmare.

Chapter 60

Well, Labor Day weekend came along with even more harassment towards me. Dodie let Gus come back because she "loved him". Codependent.

Gus and Dodie had started a whole weekend of insane hillbilly drunken parties all day and night. They had their music and screaming start on Friday afternoon. They had Red and Rave and Beau and other swingers over. They were all screaming laughing and bragging about all the bad things they have done to me and gotten away with.

I was devastated to think I was trapped and had to get out of my home before I went nuts and died of lack of sleep. Since they lived directly behind me, it was like they were in my backyard. My bedroom opens out to the pool. They were ten feet away. I put earplugs in and tried to get to bed and ignore them. They purposefully were trying to hurt me. At about midnight, I drove around the block and saw ten cars parked in front of their house. Beau was there. I went home and went back into my house.

Finally I got so angry that I walked through my

neighbors yard and yelled, "I can hear every word you are saying about me."

They laughed like magpies and yelled, "Hey Fuck Face" and other nasty words back about what a frigid bitch I am and how stupid I am. They laughed that I didn't realize that they were all in on this sexual harassment the whole three years. It was all a plan to get me to be a drunk and a swinger and how I wouldn't have anything to do with them. They were furious and acting out because they couldn't get me in any way whatsoever. They yelled that they would make my life a living hell from now on. They already won that one. I just went in to my home and closed my self off for the weekend and just listened and learned what they were planning for me next. I was truly scared and called a travel agent to get out of there with the puppies on Labor Day.

Since Beau had always promised to take me to St. Augustine and never did, I thought that's where we would go. You can drive on the beach and take your dogs on the beach and swim and do everything fun. It was an ideal place to rest. I never touched a computer in my life and was planning to buy one but I had to buy the security system first and that wiped me out financially for a while, but worth every penny.

Chapter 61

The most amazing thing happened to me at the gas station one evening. The bartender and the bouncer pulled in on their Harleys. I had not seen him since March at Bike Week when I sang and was last seen with Beau. I had lost a total of sixty-five pounds, cut my hair just below shoulder length and had dyed it darker.

I had new white shorts and white tank top on and I was very fit and tan from walking my puppies up to five miles now, a night. The only way he recognized me was because of my car and because I ran up and hugged him. He was stunned like a deer in the headlights. He and the bouncer took a minute to stare at me in amazement and compliment me so very kindly.

They told me to wait outside and they wanted to talk to me about Beau. I was shaking while I finished gassing up my big car. I was so excited to find out what was the real deal on this psycho. I had to know the truth. Nobody had said one word to me about Beau. It was like a "secret society of creepy secrets". The bartender thought I knew and that's why he assumed I wasn't going to that bar anymore. I informed him that I knew nothing and was being terrorized by Beau and that he had come to my home after being at his bar and threw me across my living room with super human strength and tried to kill me.

He said that Beau was the biggest Methamphetamine dealer in this county for eighteen years and he was a junkie and that Beau fucked every disgusting bar whore and stripper in town. I almost collapsed. I couldn't feel my legs. I was in shock.

He said Beau has been with Roxy for over a year and they drink from ten a.m. until about nine p.m. every Sunday. He said they were just business partners in the drug business. He said they announced their engagement on March fourth and everyone laughed at them. Beau was a notorious liar so everything was a joke that he said to folks who knew him.

I told him Beau had brought me a three hundred dollar rose bouquet for my birthday and taken me out for dinner on my birthday which is a week after that and begged me not to break up with him. He said I was "Beau's Trophy". He said Beau bragged to everyone that I had no clue and I was perfect arm piece because I only went out to sing and it made him look good in this shit hole of a town. He said he'd never give me up. He asked people to watch me and tell him where I was all the time and follow me and I was even being photographed. He was obsessed.

He said that he heard Beau tell a man that if he couldn't have me he'd have me killed and asked the man to do it in trade for 'Meth.' I told the bartender and bouncer that I had to get a stun gun and mace and a security system and the Sheriff wouldn't help me at all. He said Beau had grown up with all the cops all over town and had them all paid off and he was untouchable. He said I was in serious danger. He said to get the hell out here as fast as I could. He said I was a huge threat to Beau's creepy life, now and he was paranoid as all hell. It turns out the reason why Beau never let me into his house was because he had all night Meth/swinger parties with whores and trash.

He had been to one party at Beau's house and he said his house smelled really toxic and he didn't want me to see or smell the parties since I was so straight. I told him that Beau never let me spend one night there after I redecorated it for him after Gin moved out. The bar keeper told me Beau is the biggest scumbag in the world.

I told him I was leaving the next day to think because I couldn't get any sleep. He said Beau told someone he was using his key and going into my home and putting drugs in my Evian water bottle and drugging my other drinks. I told him I started feeling sick to my stomach.

He told me he was putting anti-freeze in my drinks. I also told him I was tired or felt like I was on speed when I woke up and took a drink of water in the middle of the night and I was cleaning out my closet and stuff. He said he puts meth in your water so you can't sleep to wear you out. He said he saw him put the poison in my drink at Bike Week to make me tired so that he could take me home and come back to see other women. He thought it was the date rape drug. I asked when all this started with the cheating and he said end of June, last year.

I told him Beau wouldn't even kiss me since then, but wouldn't let me break up with him either.

He said, "At least he didn't give you what he has now.

He's stuck with a sex disease and wouldn't give it to you." That's all the respect I got.

He said Beau is really sick mentally and now physically. He said Beau looked great when he dated me and now looks like just what he is. It all caught up with him. Instant Karma. He said one time Beau was so drunk that he told him he ruined the best thing in his life, me, but couldn't make it right no matter what. And that he just couldn't let me go. He said he couldn't stand to think of me with another man. He had to kill me if that happened. He was causing me hell so I couldn't get on with my dreams.

This was a boatload of information to handle. Roxy and Beau were partners in the meth business and swingers with everyone! He had everyone owing him favors. They all had the same cooties, now so they could only sleep with each other. I was Beau's perfect angel and he blew it. Every man in town told him he blew it daily and rubbed it in.

But now, the bartender and bouncer were still looking at me and saying how they couldn't get over how amazing I looked now and how Beau blew it and how they would rub his face in it forever. They said everyone asked where I was everyday and night everyday already and in front of the sleazy Meth-headwomen he was with. They told me I was the prettiest and coolest woman in town and Beau would never live it down and this size of a "fuck up" was huge in a town this dead.

They had nothing else to talk about. The other guys told Beau what a loser he was everyday while I was just trying to have a nice quiet life while all this was going on behind my back. He said Beau stayed up for a week at a time and looked and smelled disgusting and acted revolting. Meth. He was in charge of a huge Meth lab in the boondocks and used his Mom's garage for a cover fake business. He always used Mom as a cover and alibi for is absence. His Mom said he was never home to help her. The bar manager told me he worked in a huge chemical warehouse manufacturing Meth all day everyday and that was why he showered five times a day.

That's how they all were able to do this to me. He had been blackmailing all these regular folks and Government officials who he got hooked on Meth and downers and had them all doing sexual favors and illegal errands, for him, for nearly two decades. He made folks do horrible and nasty things and got them hooked so they would gladly do his dirty work. He was truly a narcissistic sociopath. I was so happy someone told me, finally.

The two of them thought that I knew about this loser all this time. What was going on? I told them I was busy working and didn't have the luxury of time, to contemplate any idea or the ability to psycho analyze Beau's adolescent games. I lived in an intellectual world, not a party world.

Beau was trying to live a double life. They said he even dressed, talked and acted differently when he was with me. He was clean and polite when he was with me, to the surprise of everyone, I might add. But now he was the way he was before he met me. He appeared as sleazy, dirty and vile. He was acting like 'Tony Montana' again. He studied me for over a year and thought I was upper class and he just had to 'act' and study me to learn to be with a woman like me. They said he really tried, but couldn't hold it together, with his past constantly crawling up his ass to bite him. It turns out Meth was his bread and butter for almost twenty years. "How pathetic," I thought to myself. He was stuck between the world he wanted to live in, and the actual world he did live in. He didn't know any other trade. He only had the business card printing in his Mom's garage for a cover, but he prints for the police department, lawyer's offices, and Courthouse.

Beau was afraid Gin would report him to the city for his illegal printing business or his neighbors on account of the loud noise late at night. He really was trapped by being well connected at the same time. They told me how he had cheated on Gin daily and treated her like shit. Now he had her living four doors down from his mom's house so he could keep an eye on her. Everything had a purpose for Beau. Everything in his insanely complicated mind of control.

Chapter 62

He was looking worse and worse every time we had to go to court. It was disturbing to watch a man lose his grip , health and hygiene after he had been perfect with me for almost seven months. He had dragged the relationship out obsessively for five years in total and this was the visible aftermath. He was an ugly monster. I felt sorry for the guy. He looked like hell. If I ever saw him like this before, I would have never spoken to him. He was dirty and rude and ignorantly repulsive. He was the 'King of his Hillbilly Meth Empire'.

I thought he would have finally grown up by age forty-eight. I told them I would have to move to another state in a few weeks for my safety. They told me to call the bar on Sunday so I could be free to move about town in order to relax on my Harley and get a breather without him in tow. I was thrilled to pieces for a few measured hours of safety on my Harley. I rode longer, and with purpose.

Some locals decided they respected me for no apparent reason, and really helped me a lot that night. I am truly grateful to this day for their kindness. They said Beau was so far gone that his number would be up real soon. They said he would take his own life before he got busted, or "be taken care of".

I was excited about my trip now. I went home and loaded the car and threw out all my liquids and food. I packed all nice new clothes that fit me perfectly, as well as all my documents that were left that he had not stolen. I took all my extra keys and jewelry and medication to my neighbors' house in a box and had them hide it for me. They said they'd watch my home for me and check the pool and all while I was gone. I love these folks. I was so happy I had help. I was scared and had to think about too much. This was going to be a nightmare. A hard, tiring, expensive nightmare to ensure my safety.

Beau had told me it was a two hour drive, but truly it was only an hour up the beach, and a pretty drive at that. I booked a cheap motel and packed us up for ten days of peace. We took off, out of my garage, and traveled the nature route way up to the next town and then hit the beach road.

It was a perfect day. I watched my rearview mirror the whole time. I was grateful to Red and Rave for the camera and printer they gave me for Christmas. It was coming in handier than I thought. I arrived at about two p.m. and the motel was not on the beach.

I parked in the very back and hid my car. My room opened to my car. I took a drive downtown with the dogs to get food and go for a walk around the old town. It was only a ten-minute drive. There were no tourists because the holiday was over. It was like a ghost town.

We ate at an outdoor café and then a huge rainstorm hit. We ran back to the car and headed to the 'No Tell

Motel' near the beach. I went to bed and watched TV, drifting in and out of sleep from the stress, and then woke up with a bad flu. Everyone in town had the flu before I left. I must've touched something in a store and got it. The woman who worked for Ness called me, on speakerphone, to see what I was up to. I told her I had the flu and I was in bed, with my house all boarded up and locked. Just a tiny white lie, in order to placate both her and Ness. I told her I had to go out on the patio for cell phone reception, as did our other neighbors. Truth. But in God's eyes, I was lying to save my sanity. I was really in St. Augustine in a motel.

The storm and flu lasted the entire first week of my trip. I was really sick and miserable. However, it did give time to unwind and start to plan my escape, the search for my new place.

Hal was flying in on the seventeenth to help for two weeks. I was walking the puppies across the road on the second night, and noticed a Holiday Inn on the beach down the road. I inquired into moving when the rain stopped.

The Holiday Inn was practically empty so I got a deal and a dog-friendly room that opened out to the pool and beach. It was effortless. I now thought that everything would be all right. I thought that I could hide my car here too. Now I could finally relax.

Chapter 63

Well, I woke up the next day and my car was blown up in the parking lot! Thank God a friend of mine from the Hot Rod club worked as a mechanic in St. Augustine. I gave him a ring and he towed my car immediately and hid it in his shop.

Thank God. Now I had to rent a car. Shoot. There was one rental car available in the whole town. Golfers reserved all of them as there was a week-long tournament going on a couple towns over.

Now I had a tiny clown car. My car had been blown up. Dead. Done. My baby. How evil.

Beau had followed me to vacation and made sure I couldn't have it without it costing me a complete fortune. My mechanic said the car couldn't be fixed. I had to junk it and buy a new car. I was so pissed off. I wanted to call the antique Volvo guy to tow it down to town and dump it on Beau's front lawn. He had tons of dead machines all over and it would've just made his property look more upscale.

I was never so mad in my life. Just when you thought it was safe to go take a quiet holiday with your dogs for their first birthday in the ocean. Now we checked for the GPS. It wasn't there. We were all baffled at the time. He was personally on my trail.

I started noticing an old, beat up redneck truck following me around here and there. There were three nasty looking men in it.

I had my stun gun and mace in my beach bag. I was being watched closely and I could feel it. How did they know where I was at all times? I was scared.

I called my female lawyer. She had zero advice other than to bail and leave the state. She knew something I didn't know. She was a waste of money and time. She had a huge problem: conflict of interest. She had been greedy and had not done her homework. She put my life in jeopardy.

Then I got a new housekeeper, one that was total white trash. She lacked front teeth. She just happened to start working there the morning after I checked in. I would come back to my room and it would be left open. This was not acceptable. Anyone could have stolen my stuff. I called the desk and complained. The general manager lived one block away from me back in my town and commuted. So did the man who ran the housekeeping. They were nice folks. They gave me a new room on a different floor and housekeeper and apologized.

I just had to make it until Hal came in the next week. I knew something was up in the hotel, too. I was too tired to move again and just kept my things with me everywhere I went from now on. The night clerk was always really rude to me for no reason. He went out of his way to insult me and make me feel uncomfortable. He followed me around. It was a 'tell-tale' sign he knew

Beau. He was too obvious. He didn't know Hal was coming to watch him and everyone. Dumb bunny. The general manager was going on vacation soon and then he would be in charge. He had Meth teeth too. Which means no front teeth at all, bad skin zits along with a bad attitude.

I drove back to town to see my doctor and I went back up to the hotel and tried to stay safe. I could feel someone following me closely.

I started taking a lot of what looked like tourist photos. But they were of everyone around me. I made it a fun game. Whoever was following me got a photo taken of them. When Hal came with his laptop we could see what was going on. I knew nothing about computers or sites. Nothing. Hal is a detective and can find out who anyone is. I picked Hal up at the airport in Jacksonville and we discussed all the terror and my beautiful dead car situation. I traded the clown car for a trashed brand new Toyota mini van, which was a great vehicle. It must've been broken in, in a swamp. It was comfy and fast and dirty and dented. We had dogs and luggage to haul around now that I was living in a hotel room and safe with Hal as a Bodyguard. We got a dog room for Hal and I got an upstairs elegant room two floors above so we could talk by balcony if needed. We stayed the weekend and hung out on the beach and ate in the old town. We checked out of the hotel on Tuesday to go back to my beach house. I was ready to start packing up my house and leave that crazy town.

Chapter 64

I had arranged to move to another state the following Wednesday. I had the movers lined up to move me really fast. As we arrived home that evening, the neighbors said the Sheriff had come by all week and left his card in my door. Hal called. Nothing happened. The next day he came and I was at the store. I missed him, again. After breakfast we went to buy me my gun at a pawnshop. We were in there paying and they were looking up my record to see if I had any arrests when suddenly a short nasty Sheriff came barging in and announced my name and I busted into laughter.

I answered, "What now?" and I kept cracking up laughing. The owners started laughing. He said, "You can't sell her a gun. She is being served with an Injunction to not be able to enter her home or go within five hundred feet of her home indefinitely. No gun for her." The lady owner, who waited on me, and I, couldn't stop laughing. The short Sheriff was pissed that I didn't care. He threatened to arrest us for laughing. Hal pulled out his cop laws and rights, to giggle, and chewed the Sheriff out for how rude the cop was to me.

Hal was a cop eighteen years in N.O. and then States

Attorney detective for eleven years. Now he is a private eye and Bodyguard. He's thorough. He knows how to do it by the book. Laughing, while being served, is not a crime. I knew some shit was going to hit the fan and here it was. Hal was at least two feet taller and two hundred pounds bigger than the tiny cop. The cop kept trying to hang in there with nothing and just to try and intimidate me. I wouldn't stop laughing no matter what. The owners asked the little cop to leave because his business was over with. He was an asshole.

Hal and I read the Injunction. The same female Judge buddy of Beau's had granted it. The same one that kept letting him off was now making me homeless indefinitely. Unbelievable. We had to go to the Courthouse, the States Attorney's office and to no avail could we get it so I could go into my home and get my clothes and toothbrush and my doggies. Thank God Hal was there to save me.

We went to the Sheriffs department to make a police report about my home being broken into while I was gone and they physically pushed me backwards out of the building. Hal was in the car and the dirty cops thought I was alone. Hal got out and stood up and showed his badge and card.

They backed off. They were for sure, in on this ruse. I called the movers and they were available to work that day. I told the manager to meet us at my house. My elderly neighbor lived exactly five hundred feet from my home and let me stay at her house for the three nights it took to watch and pack the house up and put all my stuff in storage.

I went to the Courthouse and tried to find out when I could enter my home. They said not until court in late October. I wrote the judge. She denied me access. Hal supervised the packing, but it was very hot and stressful for everyone. I had to stand down the street with binoculars and watch them hurl my whole world into a truck. Gus and Ness and Dodie all drove by in shock that I had movers come that fast. They didn't know I had planned to move the next Wednesday. "Foiled again Batman."

We re-checked into the same hotel in St. Augustine and put the puppies in a kennel nearby, while I tried to get a lawyer retained to sue the Sheriff's department and Beau and Dodie and Gus and Ness and Red and Rave. I got the biggest prick in town. The lawyer made me give a huge retainer and then made me get psycho analyzed because nobody believed how bad this all was. I had no problem with it. I did it and passed. We got back to the hotel, exhausted and crashed. I woke up to see Beau, in my room, ransacking my purse and stealing my credit card at one thirty a.m. I screamed. I called the desk and Hal downstairs in his room. Hal went to the front desk and called the cops from there. It took the cops until almost noon to respond.

The housekeeping department went up to my room and determined by the computer key card, that my room was entered at one thirty a.m. Beau was given a key card, from the toothless housekeeper, who had been fired the day before for stealing. The night manager never called the police. He waited until his shift was over and the day manager arrived to escape his letting Beau in and he made the security footage disappear. I have the same system in my home.

The night manager was a meth addict with rotten

teeth too and Beau was his supplier, turns out. Hal showed Beau's photo to all the employees and they said he had been bringing skanky women there all the time late at night. So this is why Beau would never bring me to St. Augustine for a romantic night. It was all coming together now. At this point nothing shocked me, anymore.

Chapter 65

The cop finally showed up at eleven in the morning the next day to make the theft report. He was the biggest pock marked faced ugly 'mother-fucker' I had ever seen in my life. Hal had packed his stuff to check out and I was packed and ready to leave after I did the report. The nasty cop was trying to harass me, not help. Hal came up and I pretended to have lost my voice so Hal could get him to stop intimidating me. Hal told him we already alerted the Sheriffs in my town just to see if he was in on it. He exploded and made a call. My card had already been used to rent a car seventy miles away at Enterprise Rental car. I had a Budget rental at the same time. It was impossible for me to be two places at the same time. The cop tried to cover everything up in his report. House keeping told him my room was entered at exactly one-thirty two a.m. with a master key. He acted as though he didn't make a report, but he did, and it said I was making trouble in the hotel and was asked to leave by management, when we went to the police station to check later, when he wasn't there.

This was eerie as all hell. Hal had seen a lot in his experience, but nothing this devious and corrupt. We went into town and checked into the Hilton on the river. It was beautiful. Then I collapsed and checked into the hospital. I thought I was having a heart attack. We though I'd be safe there for a few days until we left to get up north. We had to drive back and forth every day to the lawyer's office and Courthouse until October first. It was wearing me out. Hal checked the photos I took of the folks following me and found them all on My Space as Beau's friends. We noticed that Beau had been buying illegal guns from his lesbian pal, Pistol from the health food store and cigar shop, on her MySpace site. He also showed his photo around and found out that he was literally following me within minutes and just feet behind me all over St. Augustine.

It was the exotic tobacco shop that gave Beau, Fonzo and Rika away. They were in on it too. They were the ones using my credit card. Rika looked like me. They rented the car in town and spent twenty-nine thousand dollars in five days on my visa. Unbelievable. Who else was going to pop up next? A lot of the folks I thought were my friends were just being used by Beau to hurt and spy on me and rob me.

After being in the hospital they weighed me and took my blood pressure. My blood pressure was through the roof. I had also lost eleven more pounds in one week. I was there eight and a half hours being checked out from head to toe. I even had them drug test me to see if I was still being drugged. Nothing. I was just worn out and dehydrated from all this stress. The doctors were so kind and thorough. They told me to rest and I told them I couldn't and the predicament I was in. They gave me some medications and released me at eight-thirty in the evening. Hal and I went out to dinner and called our best friend, Quinn, in New Orleans for help. I explained everything and he was at our hotel within three hours. How he does this, we'll never know. Hal had to go back for his son's birthday. His time was up and he was worn out too.

This was not a small problem anymore. I was in serious danger. I needed 'Quinn Help' and had it pronto by a single phone call. Thank God.

He was just born a handsome, charismatic 'bad-ass'. When Quinn appears, he's ready for thunder. I am not kidding. Put your seatbelt on and lock it down. Quinn is not an easy man to describe. He is the calmest and most serious help you could ever have on your side in your life. He is like a phantom. He appears and flashes his all access I.D. and all your fears disappear instantly. He comes locked and loaded and dressed to kill in hand tailored Chinese silk suits. When he smiles it's amazing. When he doesn't, you better get ready to run. You never want to piss him off. He is as serious as a heart attack and as dangerous and as tricky as James Bond. He is connected to a higher source. He never sleeps or gets tired and if he did it would never show on his face or in his actions. He is inexhaustible.

It scares me a little bit sometimes. When he is not working he is funnier than anybody. He is also an amazing artist on his free time, whenever that is. He knows where the line is at all times and lives honestly and fairly on both sides of that line. I am so lucky to know him and have him as my friend. He is one of those people that there is only one in ten million, if the world is lucky enough to even have that many gifted men. He has a terrific gorgeous wife, who is a genius, too. He's got it all going on.

Chapter 66

We had only two days to tie up loose ends and figure out which city would be safest. I prayed to God for a sign. While Quinn was securing my safety in the late evening, I ran next door to an old historic Martini bar to see it and listen to what folks had to say. The place was buzzing with rich folks with live jazz music out on the patio. I went in to take photos of all the antique Italian fat people on the walls, when I overheard three people bragging about Charleston, South Carolina and that one of the men's son was a realtor up there. Apparently it was the new cool place to live.

I politely butted in and asked a few questions about rentals. He gladly called his son and booked Quinn and I in a very cool cheaper hotel than we had booked up there. We now had a connection. Relief. We chatted and made a plan to meet up there in a couple of days. We had to get out of here and switch cars first, outside of town. It just started to change from ninety-five degrees to in the sixties over night. I had been living out of the same suitcase since Labor Day and now was sick of my same clothes and was cold.

We went to an outlet store late the last night and got

me some tiny new warm clothes since I was moving up north now. I was still in an exhausted state and in disbelief that Beau had orchestrated all these bad things to happen to me. The bartender wasn't joking at the gas station, in August that evening. Beau really was trying to destroy my life if he couldn't control me or have me be his girlfriend. Nobody ever noticed me before, let alone stalked and put an all-state harassment on me. I was completely bewildered, homeless, identity thefted and worn out. He was obsessed and insane and unstoppable. WTF? Why boring old me?

Quinn didn't have an answer either, yet. He just flew in and hadn't had enough time to evaluate all this cluster of weird bullshit. It wasn't even believable to be honest. I didn't even believe it was happening to me. It seemed like a crazy game when Hal was there. But when Quinn got on the job it became a serious reality. I was terrified. Quinn won't even show up unless someone is in grave danger. This meant I was doomed without his help. I was trying not to crack. He was trying to keep me from falling apart. It was the most straining two days of my entire life.

Quinn and I tried told accomplish about thirty things the second to last day. I also had arranged my going away party for that evening. A few friends came up to our hotel and we went to the small café around the corner. Apparently, Hal had called them all and cancelled my party thinking I would still be in the hospital. I had to call them all back and they came up. I was so exhausted that when we went on the horse and carriage tour I fell asleep on Quinn's shoulder. I was finally felt safe. We had a wonderful party. These friends had no connection with Beau.

The next day we would be driving up north to my new state of sanity. Neither Quinn nor I had ever been there. We had to leave where we were immediately. Now we had a place to go and a hotel reference too. Quinn was relieved because he was on a very tight schedule and had to fly out to Washington D.C. because he is first line of the Secret Service and the President was calling him to go on a trip with him. I told him to get to bed because he had to drive me out of the state safely in the early morning and we had to drop off his rental car somewhere on the way out of town. We noticed that were definitely being watched, by the dirty local cops. They were sitting in their cars outside of our rooms in the middle of the night.

I had insomnia and needed a smoke, so I was on the balcony watching them watch us. I had my camera and was taking photos of everyone and everything. Beau's girlfriend Roxy had been following me around up there for three days before. I had photos of her looking right at me, and she not realizing it was I. I took tons of photos of Beau's buddies watching me. Quinn checked Beau's My Space and they all matched and were from seventy miles away. He was in disbelief. As long as Quinn has known me, He has never heard me lie. He also has never seen me date or have a boyfriend or stalker, for that matter. He also knows I have never touched a computer in my life, so how would I know unless Hal opened up Beau's creepy world.

Beau was counting on it that I would never put

the pieces together. He was so busy thinking he was connected while I was the connected one.

We were told it was a four and a half hour drive to the town we chose in S.C. I went to the cash machine to check my balance and saw that I had been wiped out of my checking account. I had been a victim of Identity theft, again. Now my normal checking account was empty. It was wiped out and overdrawn too.

I was in a state of panic. How could Beau keep doing all this to me when I had bought extra identity protection on all my accounts to keep safe? I was so upset. Quinn was upset too. We went to the store and the creepy 'red-necks' in the beat-up red pick-up were following us and parked in the parking lot. Quinn saw them and knew they were following me. He could see how scared I was. He was very quiet and deep in thought.

We returned the rental car at the small airport and he took over, to drive me safely out of the creepy state of insanity. He wanted to make sure a dirty cop couldn't pull me over and plant drugs on my car. I had stayed up half the night packing all my stuff into my tiny rental car, so I had hurt my back a little. Quinn was dying to drive this cool car I got because all the economy rental cars were taken by the golfers. We got on the highway and drove and Quinn was not in a talkative mood. If you even think you can talk to him you're dreaming. He prefers to drive while you sleep. I couldn't sleep in such a tiny car. Plus I wanted to see where in the heck we were going because I would have to drive back to get my puppies out of the kennel in a few weeks.

Quinn was thinking so hard that I could almost read his mind. I was trying to think happy thoughts about my new life in a few hours. It seemed like we were driving forever and ever. We had to stop for gas in Georgia. I had to get out of the car and stretch and have a smoke. Quinn hates smoke with a passion. He was tired and cranky now and wouldn't let me drive the rest of the way. We were in another state and he still thought we were too close to not be followed and hassled. He is very good at what he does. We asked how much further to the cashier of the service station. They said two more hours.

I bought some funny junk to make Quinn laugh and lighten up. It worked. I got him in a fun mood. We bombed up the highway and got off and stopped at a cider house on the side of the road that you have to turn into, to get to the area of South Carolina we had chosen by fate. We had good cider and I bought some grits and jams and homemade stuff for my hotel room.

We got back in to the car and drove what seemed like three more hours in slow motion. The old highway was beautiful, but the speed limit was forty-five m.p.h. An hour later we were technically there, but took the wrong turn downtown because the hotel guy told us to turn left instead of right. So we saw the whole ghetto part of town first, then the really old gorgeous mansions, then finally found the hotel tucked into a secret corner of the center of the city.

I couldn't wait to get out of the car at this point. Getting lost with Quinn in the car is not fun. He hates to get lost and have wrong directions given to him, turns out. Neither of us knew where we were. We only knew we were safe now. It was seven p.m. by the time we checked in. Quinn flashed his magic I.D. and we had excellent treatment. He asked the desk clerk for a flight out to D.C. She got him one by the time we unpacked the car and collapsed in our rooms with wine and cheese and other treats thy offered in the tiny elegant lobby. Turns out she was just working there until she finished her term studying at Quantico, Virginia.

We were in good hands. It was beautiful. They gave us a discount on our rooms since the hotel owner is a politician in S.C. I would be staying for a few weeks until I found the rental of my dreams.

After we freshened up, Quinn wanted to take me to the nicest restaurant for dinner around the corner. I was too tired for fancy and not dressed for it either. I made us eat at a dive across from the nice place. The other had an hour wait anyway.

We sat down and just looked at each other in disbelief that we had been in three states in one afternoon and had not had a fight yet. We are like brother and sister where we like to squabble like kids in the back seat of our parent's station wagon when we spend too much time together. We were very tired people now.

Quinn had to be on a four a.m. flight. He was on a whirlwind tour this time. I will never know how he does all this work for the good of mankind. His heart is huge. He almost had to carry me back to the hotel because my legs were frozen up from all of the hours sitting in the car. We said good night and good luck and went to our rooms and collapsed. I woke up at six a.m. and went across the beautiful outdoor atrium. There I found the owner of the hotel at the front desk trying to figure out who I was and how important I was to have Quinn deliver me there.

The owner was darling to me. I told him I wasn't feeling too well. He called his private doctor and got me an appointment that afternoon for a check up. He told me everything I needed to know and then welcomed me and disappeared. Apparently he never checked in on the hotel because his younger brother ran it for the family. Nicest folks on earth. I felt at home right away. I had my little boom box and played my quiet soft blues and relaxed in the atrium on their antique comfy furniture. They had everything I needed and nothing more or less.

Later that day I got a check up. I was dehydrated and exhausted. The fancy private practice doctor gave me sedatives to sleep off the moving nightmare. I went back down the street to the hotel and slept like I had jet lag on and off for four days. The hotel moved me to a larger room with a couch, a room where I could also smoke. They really tried to help me in every way.

The real estate guy and his Dad came to talk to me about where I should live. We made an appointment for the next day to look at places. The homes behind the hotel were in the million dollar range. He wanted to show me just so I could see some of the historical homes. Dream homes. I liked his friend's home. It was amazing. We made an appointment for the following week to tour and see it. I already met the owner and she unofficially showed me most of it. She had a very old Chow dog. I had one like him when I was a child. The dog liked me. I petted it when I met the owner while we drove around the neighborhood the next day.

The wife was the owner, liked me, and wanted me to buy her home. She told me tons of stories about her family and that they had owned it since eighteen-twelve. She told me she was sick of it and wanted a small quaint beach house. Her kids were all grown and gone and she wanted a divorce form her jerk lawyer husband. She wanted out of all of it. It had a guesthouse that had five bedrooms. It was huge. I could've rented it out and made my mortgage payment easily.

This whole city was very expensive like Paris or New York. This city only invited rich people or people who worked for them. Nothing in-between. I told the realtor I couldn't afford the place until I sold my home on the beach in Florida that I had to vacate in twenty-four hours only two weeks before. Two weeks felt like three months at this point. Beau could really run a girl into the ground when he wanted to.

The realtor said he'd find me a beach house to rent since the season just ended for tourists on the Island nearby where he lived. He called me the next day and I drove fifteen minutes to a tiny remote island and met him in a hotel parking lot. We drove around in my convertible on a beautiful warm October afternoon and looked at hidden beach homes on the island. We found one furnished that was O.K., but it was not perfect. I would be able to get an unfurnished one in December from an agency and arrange for my belongings to be shipped up by the moving and storage place in Florida. The beach places were monthly, but in the winter you can get year leases and a cheaper deal.

The temperature dropped down to the low sixties during the day and the fifties at night. It was cool compared to the sweltering heat of Florida. I had to buy warmer clothes. I was down to one hundred and eleven pounds from anxiety and stress. This place was a cold paradise. Dogs were allowed on the beach. It was gorgeous and so quiet. They had these crazy bars in the center of town that had theme nights almost every night. It was bad shit crazy for a quiet island. I was like a little mouse the first two weeks. I snuck around checking the places out.

Chapter 67

A place downtown where I first stayed was elegant. This island was a red neck drinking white trash paradise in the winter, the time when locals waited on the rich tourists to leave so they could get their crazy on. It was now their vacation place. I decided to try and be invisible and chill out. I was still very confused, tired, scared, and alone. Beau could still find me and kill me here. Reality check.

I walked the beach everyday. Rain or shine I walked as far as I could. I had to walk my stress off. I never tired from walking. I loved the beach and the sound of the ocean cleaning my mind and healing my hurting heart. I had to drive down to St. Augustine to pick up my puppies. I was scared to go alone. I didn't know anyone in this place yet to take with me for support. I just prayed I could slide in and out unnoticed if I could. I got in the car and drove down to Jacksonville. It was really cold in S.C. when I left and I was just planning to run down and back in one day. However, I took the wrong exit outside of town and ended up driving the long way down the beach; taking an extra two hours.

It was really hot and I had to strip down layers of my clothing to be comfortable.

I had nothing extra in the car with me. I got there too late and the kennel was closed. I was so tired and scared. I just checked into the same Hilton so I could hide my car in their underground parking for safety reasons. They gave me my same room I had stayed in before. They asked about Quinn. I called him to say, "Hi". They all said hello to him. They treated me like a princess. After that I snuck over to the Church to pray.

Hal and I had been going there everyday for two weeks praying for a miracle. It was just behind the hotel and I could go through the alley and sneak into the Greek café and grab a Spanakopita and a Greek salad for supper. No more driving today. I forgot about the creepy night manager who didn't fit in with the Europeans that ran the desk in the daytime. He asked me if I was hooker one night when we first checked in. I had made a complaint to the management about him when Quinn was there last month. He was up to something and I knew he knew Beau. I got a glass of wine in the bar and walked through the lobby towards my room.

There he was alone at the front desk. I was still angry at his comment so I decided to tell him just what I thought of his rudeness, since today I was dressed like a road warrior not just in a skirt or t-shirt anymore. I had also just dyed my hair black in S.C. for a big change along with my skinny new appearance. He didn't see me coming this time. I slid up to the desk and asked him how it was going. He looked at me like he saw a ghost. I looked up at the security camera, waved and smiled. I asked him if he remembered me. He froze like I had a shotgun aimed at his head. I asked him how Beau was doing. I swear he pooped his pants.

I smiled and said, "Watch out jerk-off. You never know who is watching you".

Then I turned and walked away to my room. I had a sinking feeling in my stomach that he already knew I was here and had alerted someone or did something in my room to scare me.

I took a shower and crawled into bed with only my water and my glass of wine. I passed out immediately. I awoke at three AM choking and sat up quickly to gasp for breath. I had a nightmare about Beau again. I had no medication with me to sleep so I drank my wine slowly. I went out on the balcony to get some air.

It was not two minutes out on the balcony when a local creepy cop pulled up and parked outside on the street just below me. He just sat there and watched me. I waved then ducked into my room to grab my camera to take a photo of him to scare him away. I found out that this really works to get rid of cops.

It worked as I said, "Smile officer. Tourist shot".

He fired his black and white up and took off as though he had gotten an emergency call on his radio. I laughed more out of disbelief and lit another smoke.

My nerves were shredded. I knew that the jerky night manager had arranged this to try and instill fear in my only night there. My hands were shaking so much that I accidentally tipped my wine over and now had no way to get relief to sleep. I kept smoking and drank Chamomile tea and photographed the sky above the river.

Chapter 68

A month before, one afternoon there was a school of dolphins that swam by and I had taken photos of them. They were so happy, elegant, and free. The way I used to be. It was so pretty at night from this spot as long as no cops dirtied up the view. I sat and thought of all the encouraging things my Dad had told me for self-preservation before he died. Anything to ease my fears and to help make me feel sleepy and safe. I could feel something was wrong but couldn't put my finger on it.

By about four a.m. I was still wide awake. I went into the bathroom to use the mouthwash and as soon as I put the little hotel bottle up to my lips and went to swig some to swish around my mouth, I felt it in my mouth. I quickly spat it out. It was in my mouthwash. Just like back in my home, months before, when I couldn't sleep. Meth was in the mouthwash.

Now I was feeling like before. Speedy and wide awake. Oh my gosh. Now I knew I wasn't imagining that the night manager had been in on it and was helping Beau all this time. I was freaking out by now. The sun would be coming up soon and I would have to drive and get the puppies and then drive up to S.C. on no sleep and on Meth. I had to think quickly. Breakfast was at seven in the lobby. I took a hot bath and laid down for a while and prayed.

Then I thought, "Why not go to the hospital for a check-up before the kennel opens and get a drug test right after breakfast?"

I was still shaking from the effects of the drug and my anger. I prayed it all away.

I was the first person in the dining area. I was ready to eat and run before anyone noticed I was gone. I got my car up out of the underground and blasted across the bridge to the hospital. It is on the safe side of the bridge away from the dirty police department. I walked right in and was seen by the same nice doctors as before. I told them what I thought happened. They wanted to protect me in every way. I was so relieved. I did a pee-test and blood work. They told me it was great that I ate. They told me Meth wears off in about seven hours max and because I had food, it would wear off faster.

By the time they discharged me I was clear. I zoomed across the other bridge and kept watch for the dirty cop. The kennel was almost across the street from the police station. I had called ahead and the dogs were ready to go. Poor little things were stuck there for over a month. I was just as scared when I dropped them off, as I was when I picked them up. They felt fear instead of kisses like they should've felt and which they deserved. I put them in the car and we blasted off out of the creepy town as fast as we could.

We saw the bad cop in traffic but thankfully he didn't see us. We put the top down and cruised out of hell as fast as we legally could. I was relieved to cross the

Georgia border safely. It's funny how you never realize how bad something is until you leave and have to come back. It wasn't over yet. I still had to come back for my Permanent Injunction for Protection in December. It was not that far away. I had to get in good mental and physical shape. This problem was far from over.

I also had to wait for my beach house to sell before I had any money to be secure. I still lived in a temporary house until I could have my things brought up by the movers before I could live in an unfurnished rental house. The weather was taking a turn for the worse and the Autumn rain was here.

No matter the weather, we still walked and played ball on the beach. The dogs deserved time to be made up to them for suffering in a kennel for over a month. I diligently walked them and let them run. We had the beach to ourselves. The rental was terrible. Finally on Thanksgiving we got a tip for an unfurnished house at the other end of the island. It was beautiful and cheap for a rental there. We arranged to move in on December tenth. It was across from the Mayors home and the opening to the beach. It was on stilts so it was a lot of daily exercise. We loved it. It was big, all wood, quiet, and only twelve blocks from the mad wild local drunks.

I was scheduled for court on December tenth, but Beau got into a bar fight, broke his ribs, and the court rescheduled for January ninth. He wrote his own excuse and got out of court. No doctor's letter or anything. That was more than proof he was connected to the corrupt female Judge. The same Judge letting him go free was putting me through all this bullshit. I received a letter saying I would be appointed a new Judge. A male Judge. I was afraid at first that he'd be a good old boy, then I prayed for a miracle that I would be appointed a clean Judge that Beau couldn't pay off. I had to wait for the movers to come with my stuff on December fifteenth anyway.

My friends helped me get the first load of stuff and moved me over to the new place fifteen blocks west. I cheerily awaited the movers to find my tiny Island. They showed up at noon on the fifteenth. I was so happy, like a kid on Christmas. They backed the truck into my driveway and opened the big back door. I was so excited. Then as it opened I was devastated to see all my things destroyed as they literally fell out of the truck in broken pieces. My family's antiques were in broken pieces. All I had ever owned and cherished was destroyed. I was devastated. I called the company for an explanation. They said someone broke into the warehouse and trashed my stuff. I asked why they didn't call and tell me. They were acting suspicious and avoiding an answer.

I asked where they stored my things and they told me. It was next to where Beau's fake job was situated. Why am I not surprised. Now I could barely contain myself. Anger. My family had these things for eight generations. Beau managed to destroy my family memories too. As the truck was being unloaded, I saw my whole past in shambles torn and hacked up and broken into millions of fragments. Irreparable damage. My heart broke into a million pieces that afternoon. Two thirds of my life would be in a dumpster by the end of the day. I was devastated. This was all I had left of my family since they were all dead and gone. These lovely things were all trashed and soon to be gone. They were all I had. My clothes, jewelry, china, were missing and the rest broken or missing. I hardly had anything left. He knew what I loved, and it was missing. He knew I loved my bed and it was broken beyond repair. It was a new nightmare. He was unstoppable. I was furious.

I had to get him back in some obscure way. I called my friend who has two degrees in Criminal Psychology. She had had her mother do a similar thing to her. She was pissed off too. We put our heads together and I came up with a brilliant idea to get Beau back with her computer help, since I still didn't have one yet. She is a whiz. I went to meet her and gave her a list of things I thought I needed. She thought it would be fun and we planned to do something legal. I was never so ready to mess with him legally.

He destroyed everything my family and I worked for, for hundreds of years. I knew my uncle and Dad would approve. Even my Mom would love this idea. My Mom is a huge believer in revenge. I usually am not. This was more like a huge punk than any actual harm. My friend found out everything about Beau that she could and printed a hundred pages of info out on him and his douche bag buddies. Then, after a careful study and the putting together of pieces, we could connect the dots to this man with a lie as a life. "Information is power," would work with this and he would have the shit scared out of him.

Paranoia. That's what he needed. A huge dose of his own medicine would cause him to live in fear. I called in a few friends to do a few drive by's. I had three left in town. All they had to do was drive by his home or have a beer at one of his regular crap hole bars on their way home and text me to tell me what he was doing at a certain time every week and who he was talking to and what about. What he was wearing and which vehicle he was driving. And to tell me what condition his house and yard were in just to let him think I was still there. Harmless paranoia. He was always high and drunk so it would work.

Hilarious was the first thing that came to mind. I have always been slow to anger like my Dad. My Mom, on the other hand is quick and furious to anger. She is a volcano waiting to blow at all times. I decided to combine my Dad's sense of humor and my Mom's anger to get the best results. Beau said something to me one time when we actually dated three years ago when someone hurt my feelings when they were drunk and I didn't know they were drunk. He saw me hurt, not angry.

He said, "People only hurt you because you have a heart of gold and they know you will forgive them".

I remember throwing him out of my house that moment and getting really angry with him for thinking and saying that to me. I have always had a memory like an elephant. Now memories of all the lies and deceit were welling up in my in my mind.

Chapter 69

I was beyond pissed off having Beau and his weasels on Meth destroy my life and everything in it that crossed my line of comfort and joy. I was over my breaking point line by miles. My friend and I decided on an innocent plan that was cheap and fun. All I had to do was what Beau and his buddies did to me in reverse. It reminded me of the movie *Reversal of Fortune* with Bette Midler and Shelly Long. My friend and I figured out a fool-proof plan to make his whole gang of idiots paranoid. It was beautiful. She handled the MySpace part, and I handled the non-traceable disposable cell phone bought with cash in another state that we registered in his name and address. After all, that's how they harassed me and scared me months ago day after day, even in my own home. Time to play cat and mouse.

Beau still thought I didn't have any computer experience and that was a good thing. He knew he had broken me financially as well as my heart attached to all of my belongings. Between the two of us, we thought up a way to make Beau very confused and broke. It turned out between the information I already had, the new, and daily combined Beau could be made paranoid;

easily. I had about three weeks to make Beau scared enough to mess with me in court. I had to make him think that the Fed's were watching him every second of everyday.

The first rule was Dad's rule that information is power. Since I was three states away from Beau and using local spies, I had the trump card now. My friends were great to me. They went out of their way to help keep an eye on him and inform me on my other safe disposable phone. They would text me at the moment Beau did something. Then I would text Beau and ask him about whatever situation he was in at that moment and warn him he was being watched and listened to. I made him think that when he was out, someone was at his house. He had this thing about moving his vehicles obsessively behind his house and switching back and forth all day and night between his new truck, old SUV, and his beloved cop-style Harley. My friends would tell me which he was driving and which he was hiding and where and when. That was a fun start. That made him scared. I knew because he did it every date we had at the beginning because of Gin. I noticed that he had always done it as his regular routine of paranoia.

His bar buddies were easy. My old neighbor was a regular at happy hour at the shit-hole bar within walking distance of his house twice a week. My friend was sitting next to him half the time while texting me his exact words. I would then text him and repeat his buffoon conversation as if he had a bug planted on him. My friend thought it was hilarious because he got to sit and watch him squirm when he checked every fifty-word text that cost Beau loads of dough. I would jam up his phone and make him pay the bill, therefore making it a task to clear his texts in order to be able to receive his drug deal texts. His phone bill must have been enormous.

I pretty much knew his whole schedule within a week. I loved the times when my friend told me Beau would take Meth-whores out to his truck for sex/drug-trade blow-jobs. I'd text and ask how it was, ruining poor folks lives getting them hooked on Meth, making them waste their lives in prostitution with a dirt bag like him. And did he not have one ounce of respect for anyone on earth.

I harassed him by asking him how many women and men did he give AIDS to. I asked how Roxy would feel about his cheating on her and did she know he could have Syphilis and so could she? I reamed him. He was trapped and couldn't alter it or his cronies would be suspicious that they were in jeopardy. He couldn't risk breaking his pattern. I was throwing buckets of icy-cold water on his "Happy Hours" making him not so happy anymore. Then I started adding information about what he did to me and Gin, to give him the impression that someone was keeping score of his failures. I just kept jamming him up as best as I could with what I had to work with. Plus, we had all of his criminal buddies on MySpace freaking out. We would read their messages and slide that info through the texts on the phone. Eventually we had all these freaks scared and doubting Beau. We just had to plant the seed of doubt that Beau could be a "Narc" on MySpace.

He was buying and organizing illegal weapons with a girl named Pistol from the health food and cigar shop.

I was scared that she did that as her other income. He, with the first Injunction for Protection, was not allowed to own a fire-arm, and all 12 that were registered to him were confiscated by the Sheriff when he was served in May. I told the Judge and Sheriff at the Court House that he had tons of weapons that he loved and used in road rage on innocent lost tourists.

He was buying street weapons now. I had to win the Permanent Injunction in January or I would be dead soon for sure. By Christmas, my friends said he was partying and getting into fight after fight in bars regularly. He didn't suspect me. He was paranoid that someone local turned on him. He was on weeklong benders at a time and looked like crap. His yard and house looked like a junkyard.

I would make comments about how crappy his place looked and why didn't he mow his Mom's lawn while he did his. That kind of thing. It was funny to do that. Then my other friend who lives on his street would see him at the supermarket and she would go as far as to tell me what was in his basket. I would get him so freaked out. He thought he was being watched everywhere he went.

The crazy parties at his house came to a screeching halt. He loved his parties. No more fun at "Beau's House of Orgies". I had a few of his friends phone numbers and did the same to them as I did to Beau. Now they all doubted one another. By New Years he had been on such a downward spiral that he was really trashed. He had been partying with broken ribs all this time. That had to hurt. I looked up Meth on the Internet and it says you throw up a lot when you do it. Well, that explained him cleaning my bathroom fanatically in the past. If he was barfing with broken ribs now; he was in trouble. Broken ribs take months to heal. I asked a few local guys who worked roofing and they told me how bad it is. A little pain wouldn't kill Beau. I just wanted the Judge to see how skanky he really is. By the ninth of January it would show for sure. I finally had him by the balls.

He was so scared and paranoid by January that he had a nasty female cop friend call "The Phone" and leave a message asking if I, "Ruthie", was leaving these messages. She left her number for whomever to call back to verify. I laughed my butt-off. Then she called again a few days later and stated she didn't think it was "Ruthie" and apologized to whoever the phone belonged to. It was on-line registered to him at his address. I couldn't wipe the smile off of my face. All they had to do was look it up and it was one of his paid cash drug dealing disposable phones. If he showed the messages to the dirty cops they would assume the Fed's finally got him. They would be paranoid too now. Everyone was dirty. What a sick town.

I arranged to pay a six foot six, solid muscle body-guard to drive down with me to get the Injunction for Protection and pick-up my poor car that Beau had blown-up, that he had hidden from my mechanic for four months. It was raining and cold in S.C. so Jake, the body guard, gladly took the job. Not only was he massive muscle but he was also gorgeous with straight auburn hair down to his butt. He had a huge and perfect "Tom Selleck" mustache and goatee. He was funny, nice, and very protective. He owned his own plumbing business and knew everyone in S.C. Now I had more than one friend in S.C. I had his friends too. They all wanted to protect me from Beau in their state.

Right before we took off for Florida, the phone was drained and fried. It wouldn't charge anymore. I took this as God saying, "You've made your point, Ruthie". I agreed with God. He let me leave one last message before the phone died. The last message on January fifth was texted as this: "You will pay with you heart, mind, spirit, soul, and wallet for what you have done to destroy the lives of innocent people Beau. You will, pay!" Then the phone went black and I duct-taped all the broken parts separately to a truck heading for Florida.

He had victimized poor folks who had no money and lead them into a sour life of crime and degradation. It was the ugly truth and he was freaking out having it on his phone. I embarrassed him to the point that he couldn't share the messages with anyone without showing guilt.

I had him trapped in his own bed made in hell. If he showed Roxy, she'd be upset. If he showed anyone else, it showed he exploited anyone and everyone who he encountered. I had chosen every word very carefully to condemn him no matter what. Now everything was his fault. He couldn't use this as evidence no matter what. "Suspension of disbelief" was what Beau wanted. He could invent more games than Milton Bradley. I prayed he couldn't sleep before court. The other times he hadn't slept he looked like hell and we had a new Judge now who wasn't used to his disheveled outdated appearance.

Chapter 70

Jake and I got in the car a day before the court date. I made reservations at the only four star hotel in town with security underground parking. We picked-up my old car and Jake drove it around town while I relaxed in the hotel. My car has a special license plate and that made it easy for Beau and his creepy friends to find and mess with it. We used "her" as a decoy. We prayed Beau would try something before Court the next day. He always did in the past.

My car had black tinted windows so that Jake could drive around town and see, but not be seen. I sent him out to spy on Beau's "state of mind". Jake had been to my town before and knew it like the back of his hand. I, the same as Beau, couldn't be within five hundred feet of one another according to the Order of the Court. Jake could be my eyes and ears in my blown-up vanished car.

He saw Beau in the same bar on a major bender the night before Court. This was great for me. I was clean of alcohol and everything since the St. Augustine trip. I worked out and looked young and healthy and professional. I tried on my outfit and I looked like a Lawyer not a victim. I knew I would win.

My neighbor was going to show up to testify on my behalf, even though his wife had cancer treatment the same morning. They were my family and were angry I was driven from my home and Beau had destroyed my life. Del was coming to save me like a knight in shining armor no matter what. He saw Beau in front of my home many times and had written to the corrupt Judge and was ignored. Now he could face a new Judge and be a respected witness.

We were all to be at the Court House at eight-thirty in the morning. Beau was a no-show so far. We were called in to the courtroom. It was full this time. Del was on his way. We sat to the right. The Judge called the first case. It was short. Then, the second case, which was a long and petty argument. Beau breezed in like he didn't care about respecting the Court. The Judge took note of his tardiness and hygiene. He slid into the only seat on the left side. The Judge noticed that I was from out of state so he called us up next. Del walked in two minutes beforehand and it was perfect. Beau didn't see him coming to help me.

We were called up to the front and sworn in. Beau was grinding his teeth and chewing the inside of his cheek. He smelled and looked like a thousand miles of bad road. He was dressed in old crappy preppy clothes from the eighties that he bought at the Junior League thrift store next to his shitty bar. He looked ridiculous for his age. He was lazy and arrogant to the Judge. He acted toward the Judge with a persona like, "Don't you know who I am?" The Judge was very serious and had no idea who Beau was other than the one hundred pages of violations he had on record, the court reports proving that he didn't bother appearing for the first Injunction, and all of his pages of illiterate written excuses. Beau couldn't pay-off this Judge.

And since the court date was changed at the last minute three times, the Judge had to review my case three times and was very familiar with Beau's getting off on all of his violations in the past. This Judge was from up north, like me. Oh Thank God. Del got up and testified against Beau and it worked. Del was a retired Navy officer and was about the same age as the Judge.

Beau acted carefree and flippant as he sauntered lazily into the Courtroom one hour late. Beau angered the Judge. He asked for Beau's alibi. Beau had nobody to help him this time. He was alone. I had three credible witnesses. He announced that he was engaged and showed a ring he was wearing. The judge didn't believe him. Where was Roxy today? He was a wreck and alone. He had burned his witness bridges and Roxy.

Beau told the Judge in one angry sentence what he wanted like a spoiled little boy. He said, "I want my weapons permit back so I can get my guns back and I want to drive teenagers around town in a van". The Judge almost slammed his gavel on Beau's head to knock sense into him. Wham! Denied. The Judge boldly stated in front of the packed Courtroom that Beau had to get a new hobby immediately and to take his focus off of me permanently.

I then was awarded a Permanent Order of Protection for every state, forever. He also stated that Beau was unstable and dangerous. That Judge saved my life that day. We did a huge burn-out when Beau was marching to his truck while cursing up a storm. As we passed him and his truck, I did my famous "Woody Woodpecker" laugh at the top of my lungs and peeled out laughing with the top down and spirits high.

Beau was screwed now, forever. He looked terrible and not anything like the man who proposed to me two years prior. No resemblance in any way what so ever. Who was Beau? Who was this man? He didn't even resemble the Beau I thought I knew, loved and trusted before, in any way. Since he threw me across my living room last April, he was a totally different person physically and personally. He had vacant eyes with no heart or soul behind them. Beau had no conscience by the way he acted. All Jake, Del, and I saw was a psychotic child-like tantrum and a pouting man about to blow. He was a ticking bomb and I was his target. He looked like an ugly stand in for the man I had loved. He stared at me with blank eye sockets.

Jake and I went to my favorite Thai restaurant for lunch and celebrated my safety and victory. We went next door to see a friend of mine to say hello and tell of my victory. We went to see all three of my friends who Beau had not paid off with Meth, to thank them for their help. We planned to split in the morning after check out and drive back to safety three states away. I was so happy to leave this place and have a new Order for Protection good in all states permanently. Thanks Judge.

Chapter 71

Jake and I drove out of town and were glad that the stress was over for now. I still had to return one last time to pay for my new used car at the airport in a month. When I got back to my rental house on the island, I picked up my mail at the tiny post office. The island only had P.O. boxes, not street addresses. It made it easier for all of the rental property owners and renters to vacation in peace. I opened mine and had five Identity Theft reports waiting for me. I rolled my eyes and thought, 'Now what is Beau up to?' I just couldn't get him to stop. He tried to apply for a Black card, which has no credit limit, in my name. He also tried to get an L.L. Bean card in my name. I spent days on the phone trying to fix my credit. Beau was trying to bury me in banking "bull-shit" now. I had to cancel all of my cards again. I was trying to pay cash for everything anyway since September to fix the last Identity Theft that he and his pals had done to me when I was in St. Augustine. I was in disbelief. The Judge had added four extra clauses to my Order for Protection. One was prohibiting him and anyone he is associated with to do any more mischief to me in any way. No calls, no e-mails, no nothing to harm me anymore. Beau obviously couldn't read or didn't do so when the Judge gave him the stamped and signed document.

Now I had to write the court and send copies of the credit alerts. He would make my life a living hell no matter what. He was having a ball screwing-up what was left of what was my life, which wasn't much anymore. I cancelled everything I had left and closed all of my accounts. I alerted all of my banks and warned them in advance. I went to small "Mom and Pop" banks and opened small accounts and told them of my situation and put Theft Alerts on all of them and waited. It was a nightmare. I had to call every bank I had automatic-payments with and change passwords and everything. It was exhausting.

I contacted Washington, D.C. to file against the movers. I photographed all the damage and sent it to them. They investigated and found out Beau was friends with one of the movers and he let him in to destroy all my stuff. Beau did fifty-thousand dollars damage to my furniture alone. So far over one-hundred thousand in Identity theft. My car was still messed-up and didn't start every time. The toll on my house in Florida was around twenty-thousand dollars so far. My health was non-repairable damage.

The economy was worsening in Florida and I knew I would lose more than half of my life savings on my house if it ever sold. Beau had a plan to deconstruct my hard earned life at lightening speed. I knew it would get worse before better if it ever improved at this point. I was running out of options and money. It seemed like every day he had a new nightmare in store for me. I prayed for sleep and dreaded waking up in the morning. It seemed like I'd never get out of this wasps nest. He was breaking me in everyway.

I had collected enough evidence against Beau to have him put in jail in any other state permanently. I put it all in a file and had it ready to submit to the Judge for violations, as well as for the police department to report Identity Theft. I had to drive down to buy my rental car and fire my lawyer for not showing up in court for the Injunction a month before. Did I have to do everything by myself? I guess so. First buy the car. Next fire the crooked lawyer. Then, on the way out of town, stop at the police department to report the Identity Theft. I called the police department and asked which one I should go to because I was on my way out of town, forever. All I had left to do was to file the report. I told them I was on way. I had all of the banks papers and proof of Beau's crimes.

The new police station was on the way to the main highway. I had it all timed so I would be back in S.C. by dark that evening. On my way from the bank to the cop-shop, I was ready for an ending that would free me from Beau forever. I arrived at the new police station with a black under-cover car in my rearview mirror. We pulled into the parking lot at the same time. I parked near the main entrance.

It was ninety-nine degrees outside. I had my top up on my car and the air conditioning on full blast. It was sweltering humid that day in Florida. I was headed to a cold home up north. I just wanted the case to be investigated like a normal person. The other folks were treated nicely in there with courtesy and kindness, I listened and waited. I had a positive outlook that day when I arrived with the proper documentation.

I walked into the main station and sat down in the waiting room with my folder packed full with evidence. There were two cases in line before me. I was ready for a long drive so I did my exercises while I waited my turn. One hour and forty-seven minutes. Then when the others were gone, the female cop came up to me. I said my name and went to hand her my file. She was rude, mean, said she wouldn't allow me to file my report, and told me to leave after I waited over one hour for my turn. She wouldn't allow me to speak or drop off my evidence and went behind a door and slammed it. Then, all the folks in the glass protected area disappeared and I had no one to file my complaint to. The place evacuated in two seconds flat. It was the worst feeling I have ever experienced in my life. I actually felt fear.

I went calmly out to my car and headed towards the highway. I noticed the same black car that followed me earlier following me to the highway. I was so discouraged and knew Beau and his brothers had blocked me from getting him arrested. I drove out of there angry and victimized. I checked my mirrors all the way to the Georgia border to make sure I was safe. I must have lost five pounds sweating with the fear of corruption every inch of every mile. I tried to get home as fast as possible. I felt so sick that Beau had even paid off my two attorneys and the local cops. In fact, I was disgusted. I was saddened to think my tax dollars were spent on ruining folks lives and supporting crooks, rapists, etc.

Meanwhile, back on the tiny island, I spent my days playing with my puppies on the beach. We were tireless in order to wear off the stress. We swam in the ocean and played Frisbee and soccer from sun-up to sunset. Then it was winter and it got cold on the first of December.

My friend from college was coming to do a film of the island for me the first week of December and to have a fun reunion. We were both from Ohio and spent tons of time at College making fun, cool films together. I wanted to document this crazy event. He showed up and we had a blast. The fourth day, when he was doing some personal work on his web page, I ran to the post office to get my mail. I was just getting used to walking around and not looking over my shoulder after fighting for the last five years. I thought I was safe now.

We had a cute family joke that went like this, "Just when you thought it was safe...." Well that popped into my head when I opened my post office box that moment. There was a package slip in my box. I went around the corner and asked the lady clerk at the counter if I had a package. She took the slip and went into the back of the room and returned with a medium size green gift package. I froze in fear as I looked at it and backed away. I told her to hold it for me. She realized my fear. I told her I would be right back. I drove twelve blocks home and I told my friend and the mayor's wife. She told me to put rubber gloves on and go get it and give it to the police. I did what she said.

The only cop on duty was the fat, dumb one. I was having an anxiety attack. He took the parcel and I showed him the Injunction for Protection. He was so lazy and slow. The package was sent to my street address, not my post box number. I was registered under a fake name with my lease, post office box, and my bills. Only the police knew who I really was. How did Beau find me? Who told him? I was petrified. The fat cop took the package and said he would put in safekeeping in the evidence locker. I told him the police have to open it and send it to the Judge in my town in Florida. Normal protocol.

He told me to wait for the Chief of police to see it and they would call me and tell me what was it was. I thought it was drugs or a bomb. The next day my house was broken into. The door was jimmied open with a knife and the screen was cut open. I called the police and got the same fat dumb lazy cop. The next day I got five death threats on my phone. As usual, I got the same lazy cop. I was so used to dumb lazy cops by now that I insisted to the Mayor that he help. This was getting ridiculous.

Chapter 72

My nephew and sister-in-law were coming for Christmas and I was trying to get my old car painted and drivable to give to her as a gift. My mechanic was a dear friend and was working day and night to make sure it was really repaired this time. She always wanted a BMW. They were to drive it back to the west coast of Florida safely the day after Christmas. I was so stressed that I couldn't eat or sleep. I kept getting death threat messages on my disposable phone. I took the phone down to the police department. They acted like I was nuts. The calls were from my old area code. I called the tracking company and talked to the owner. He said no one has ever traced one of his phones.

My nephew and sister-in-law were coming for Christmas and I was trying to get my old car painted and drivable to give to her as a gift. My mechanic was a dear friend and was working day and night to make sure it was really repaired this time. She always wanted a BMW. They were to drive it back to the west coast of Florida safely the day after Christmas. I was so stressed that I couldn't eat or sleep. I kept getting death threat messages on my disposable phone. I took the phone down to the police department. They acted like I was nuts. The calls were from my old area code. I called the tracking company and talked to the owner. He said no one has ever traced one of his phones. He saw the hacked calls. apologized, and sent me a new untraceable phone over night; guaranteeing I would be safe from now on.

I was in danger now anyway. My safety was completely compromised. Within ten days I had too much of a scare. I lost ten more pounds. I was a nervous wreck and it was Christmas Eve. My family showed up and I tried to act like everything was normal but they knew something was wrong with Beau and that I was scared to death. He had found me. Now I would have to move again. My family was wonderful to me and they loved my car as a surprise gift. That made me very happy. On Christmas night my perfect car was tampered with in my driveway. My mechanic couldn't believe it. We figured out what it was and fixed it quickly.

How was Beau doing this? Was he here? Now we were all paranoid. Everything was getting broken into just like back home. Booby-trapped cars, house break-ins, and death threats, etc. A repeated pattern. Beau's signature was all over it. Prank calls, death threats, and all of the typical crap he knew how to drop on me. Someone had to be on the island from Florida. We all decided that I should go and check into the hotel downtown when my family checked out for a while until the local police investigated. I threw all my winter things in my car and put my dogs in a kennel again indefinitely. My stress level was at boiling point. It was only fifteen minutes from downtown but somebody was on the island watching me. I tried to figure it all out.

My dear friend happened to be working at this hotel instead of the one I met her at when Quinn dropped me off a year ago. I was so happy she was there. I had no one after my family left. It was the coldest winter on record in thirty years. My electric bill on the island would have been the same as the hotel bill. I just pretended to be on a vacation downtown until the Mayor told me it was safe to go home. He lived directly across the street from me. His wife was my only friend on the island. The Mayor promised me that the police would protect me and investigate the recent crimes. I waited in the hotel for a month. I called and got no information. The cops were lazy and didn't care. In fact the fat one threw away my evidence. They all had to cover up for that somehow.

While I was in the hotel thinking the cops sent the evidence to the Judge in my old town, they were tying to cover up their screw-up. And it was huge. They didn't know that I had already sent the Judge, back home, a letter telling him of all that had happened and photos of the package so he knew the cops on the island had it in the evidence locker. I had sent it the day before New Years Eve. I finally hired a lawyer who was my friend's brother to look into it. It was definitely a cover up. By February, the cops had no answer and I had to go to my rental house sometime. I couldn't afford a hotel anymore. We made an appointment with the Chief of police to discuss all of the reports I had made. The chief looked like Mr. Clean from the T.V. commercials. The locals referred to him as 'Chief Buttwipe.' They all had lied their faces off and tried to cover up every mistake they made. I asked to see what was in the package. They said was a "love book" with all the pages torn out of it. I asked to see it. They said they threw it away. I said it was evidence and it was sent to me and I had a right to see it. They didn't realize that I had studied my rights in law books and knew my limits to the law. They had destroyed evidence. I called them on it.

My lawyer told them of my rights. They treated him as badly as they treated me. He was sickened by their corruption. They messed up royally and my life was in danger because of them. I told them I would sue the police department for not protecting me. After all, it was their job and responsibility. The place was dead in winter. The only crime on the whole tiny island was committed on me. They had my restraining order filed there since the day I arrived. They were the only ones who knew I was Ruthie and they were the only ones that knew my fake name and why I was there hiding in fear for my life. Idiots.

Chapter 73

I was in fear of my life now because of dirty cops, again. They were dumber than a bag of wet hammers. They could mess up a wet dream, as my Dad would say. I was screwed, again, and out of another home and unsafe. I deserved respect and safety. I had done nothing to deserve this ugly treatment. I went to the Judge, who was my friend, and he said I would have to move again because of the lazy cop. He told me the Downtown cops would be taking over soon because of their incompetence. I got an offer on my house in Florida and I had to take it. It was two thirds less than I was asking. I had to take it. I was desperate and had to roll.

Since I didn't know who was watching me yet, I was paranoid and watching my butt all the time. It was an extremely cold and rainy winter on the beach. The wind was fierce. My dogs loved the beach and I was packing my things at night so I could be outside on the beach with them in the afternoons. The weather was volatile and the wind calmed down in the afternoon for a few hours. There wasn't anyone on the beach when it was like this, but an unknown man appeared with a pit bull dog one day when it was mild outside. I had bundled up to take the dogs to play Frisbee and the man appeared, came up to me, and tried to strike up conversation with me. He had a heavy New York accent. He said his name was David. He flirted with me and asked too many questions for a stranger. I had been so guarded for so long that I only answered his questions with a question back. Then I would excuse myself and leave.

From that day on, every time I went over to the beach the first week I got back, this man would appear with his dog at the same time I did. I had everyone memorized on the tiny island, but this guy was new and didn't fit in at all. Around the first week I was back on the island the man was coincidentally almost everywhere I went. He wore a long black leather jacket, jeans with a studded belt, and black turtleneck. He always wore a baseball cap and sunglasses. He had shoulder length black hair beneath the cap. He was always trying to talk to me wherever and whenever he saw me with my dogs on the beach. I tried to leave when he got there, but he was getting there just a minute after I arrived. He had a very gentle dog that wanted to play with my dogs, the balls, and Frisbee. However, he wouldn't let it play with my dogs at all. In fact he acted like it wasn't his dog. He never petted it or anything. It just walked along with him like a movie prop. I felt sorry for that dog. My dogs were so happy and carefree and friendly to every dog. They had a blast swimming and playing everyday at our beach. It was our paradise; before David showed up.

Now there was a stranger who creeped me out, and my dogs could feel it too. He would come towards me and my stomach would get in knots. The stranger had now contaminated our paradise. It was the only place I had felt free and safe for over a year. I felt like, if I was alone on the beach with this man, he would hurt me physically and no one would find my broken body washed up on the beach and my dogs would go to doggy jail. He would show up and out came his cell phone and he would take a photo of me with his phone camera and then text someone quickly and glance up at me on the beach. He had that phone in his hand at all times. Then he would approach me and try to ask me questions. I knew he was texting Beau and telling him his perception of me and how I was living. I was not in a band. I was not singing. I was just wandering on the beach with my dogs like a ghost all bundled up in a windbreaker and knit hat and big sunglasses so that the sand wouldn't blow in my eyes. I was hiding. Some locals knew and were helping me stay safe. I always had my camera in my pocket. I took photos of him following and texting me manically on his phone.

My neighbors behind me had a huge pond and a wildlife reserve. They saw the man watching me and following me a few too many times so they invited me and my dogs to go on their private property safely to play. For us, I had a three-hour playtime minimum. It was the only way to clear my head of anxiety. I was walking three miles a day to the pier and back, but it was too cold now. We needed walks. They calmed my nerves. The mayor's wife informed me that this man mysteriously showed up in the middle of dead winter and rented a couch at the meanest drunk lady on the island's house across the street from me. He was sneaking around and watching me whenever I went out, because from her house he could see up into my house and porch and carport. He was watching everything I did.

I was paranoid already, but now he was showing up when I went to the local dive to eat for a break from packing. He continued to badger me with questions and I continued to ignore him. He was rude to everyone he encountered on the island. The local folks were very tight and I was in with some of the nice ones that had lived there forever. They didn't like him one bit. They could see through him right off the bat. He rubbed them the wrong way too. I wasn't imagining anything at all.

Folks on the island had to go to the mainland to the supermarket about five miles across the bridge and wetlands to make their purchases. Every time I went to the store he was right behind me. First he followed me in his car, then on foot in person. Everyone on the mainland noticed too. He had the same car as my old one that I had given to my sister–in–law for Christmas and he had Florida plates too. When he followed me home everyday, he would back his car into the bushes across the street, and then put a cover on it and lock the cover so you couldn't see the plate on the back.

I refused to speak to him or answer any questions as he hazed me everywhere I went. I pretended to be deaf, basically. He then started acting more aggressively towards me in public, trying to and embarrass me in front of folks. It didn't work. The locals liked me more than I knew and saw him as a square peg in a round hole. He didn't fit in no matter what he did or said.

Chapter 74

The mayor had a re-election party at a local restaurant shortly after I got back on the island. He showed up, sat next to me, and bullied me while I was trying to eat. He even tried to buy me food and a drink but I wouldn't accept anything from him. He acted like a jilted lover as Beau had acted towards Glenn on Christmas Eve years before. He was demanding a reason why I wouldn't talk to him. He was trying to put me on the spot in front of folks. I just ignored him. It was driving him nuts. What did he want? He was bringing a lot of attention to himself, which was a strange thing to do. He was making a spectacle of himself everywhere he went. Who acts like this?

I just wanted to be off the island as soon as possible because the stupid cops had put my life in jeopardy there. I knew this man was sent from Beau to mess me up. I could feel it in my gut. I got a call from my friends in my old town and they said Ness had lost everything and was now living out of her car. Wow, her Karma came back quick. They also told me Gus left Dodie. Rika and Fonzo lost their house and all their junk. Beau had used all these folks and they were all losing everything they owned by being his friend. He was ruthless. He was even jealous of my nickname. What an insecure jerk. He didn't care who he used up.

I had two of my vehicles hidden in mechanic shops on the mainland for storage and preparation for the night move I had planned. I was very good friends with these folks now and they were trying to help me get out of there safely by April 1st. I had already given notice with my rental company that I would be gone by May 1st, incase anyone was asking them questions about me or if anything went wrong. I had to cover myself from every angle. You never know who knows who on an island like this and I was trying to do about 50 things a day to dodge this jerk that was following me all over the place. He had nothing else to do but follow me around and harass me. He obviously didn't have a real job.

I had so much to do and I didn't have time for all this nonsense. Time was racing. I was exhausted and didn't need this guy stressing me out. The police were a joke and so I was nervous. If this man had been sent to hurt me, by Beau, I had nobody to protect me but the locals; and my stun gun. The locals were mostly alcoholics with nothing much to do, so they offered to help me pack and move. I slipped them a few bucks to help me get my stuff packed and lift heavy things for me. They were wonderful. They saw the guy watching me all the time. The old drunk lady, Tipsy, he was staying with, was very unpopular on the island. Nobody thought it strange that the creepy man was camping on her couch with the dog. She had no friends anymore.

They tried to make David uncomfortable and unwelcome. Southern folks are very territorial and you can trust me on this point. This island was their home and they were in charge. They saw me as a woman with enough on my plate and they disliked the dirty cops plenty. That's the only good luck I had going for me at this point. They were furious at the lazy incompetent Mayor who said he'd help me and didn't bother. My neighbor who let us use his yard was the retired Mayor. They all had their own axes to hack about the present Mayor. They thought he was a jerk.

I started staying up until four a.m. packing and separating all of my things. I made a pile of things I didn't need anymore for the poor locals. My friend Dan traded me help for giving stuff to his neighbors. I needed all the help I could get. Time was running out. My sister-in-law was on the Internet trying to find me a safe place to live far away from the island. I had just bought my first computer and I didn't really know how to work it yet. I was on the phone with my family while they were trying to find me the perfect new Utopia.

The guy who was following me had the audacity to march up to my front porch, twenty-five steps daily, pound on my door, and look into my windows to see what I was up to. I always hid in the bathroom. I mean, he did it every day and pounded hard. I felt completely violated like back home. It was a nerve wracking thing to endure this all the time. What ever happened to privacy and my 'No Trespassing' sign that I had posted at the bottom of my stairs that lead up to my porch and front door?

The weather started to clear up and it warmed up a little bit for a week or two in early March. The mean drunk lady, Tipsy, across the street, started following me around and taking photos of me and my dogs with a huge camera with a telephoto lens. What was she up to now? What a nut job. We were entering the beach way down from the street on another part of the island. All we wanted to do was throw the ball on the water and swim before we left. She was going out of her way to follow me. What was her interest in me after ignoring me and going out of her way to be rude to me everyday for a year? It seemed like I was trapped with her on one side of me, and David the creepy guy on the other. I think he was taking photos of me with his phone and then texting a lot while he followed me. This caused me more anxiety.

I resorted back to the huge yard for a refuge until we left to play with my dogs. I could sneak out of my back door and out the back and hardly be seen. I could watch my house completely from the back of that place. I loved all of the sculptures the man had made out of junk and plants. The pond had fish and the local friends would fish and BBQ everyday. It always smelled really good out on my back porch. They invited me to all of their parties but I had no energy left to have any fun unfortunately. The kind local folks made me feel safe. Thank God for them being on my three sides of my house.

I hired a local guy to help me move in a U-Haul for the two last days in March. I had everything packed and the other stuff given away. A realtor called and told me of the perfect, safe, house in a gated community that my sister–in–law had found. She sent me the photos on the Internet. It looked too nice for me to live in and double the price of the great deal I had on the island. I was fortunate. The other houses on the island were five thousand a week and mine was only 15 hundred a month. I had been blessed for a year and four months.

The moving company from the last move sent a couple thousand dollars for the damage that Beau's buddy movers had done to my family things. They owed me 50 thousand dollars, but I bankrupted them, putting them out of business when I had contacted the D.O.T. I needed all the money I could get back for all the moving and destruction I had been through in just one year. Beau had done a great job deconstructing my whole life so far. Now I had to pay double for another new life.

My best friend from college told me to move to where she lives. It was a new place I had never been. She bragged to me about how beautiful it was. That is how my sister-in-law was able to help relocate me so easily. The place was very safe and that is the reason the rent was so high. The police in the new state and town take Injunctions for Protection very seriously it turned out. My friend assured me that I would be completely safe there and the high rent was worth the trouble. The realtor said the same thing. I read up on the place and it looked very nice. I had to jump into the unknown again because of Beau.

Chapter 75

It was a small beach town where everything was five to ten minutes away from all the conveniences a person needed. That is my kind of town. Now I had to send the lease, money, and run back and forth from the island to downtown once a day for a week, while also taking care of other things in between. I was lucky because I had to pass by all the car places and my bike place on the way to the city and back. There was only one road to the island from downtown. I had to call a car carrier to arrange for all my vehicles to be picked up in the nighttime a week before I left. This meant that I wouldn't have a car for a week and I was at the mercy of my backyard and the front nut job stalkers across the street. I had my stun gun, Louisville slugger, wasp spray, mace, and an FBI registered eighteen-foot stun-gun ready to use. I just kept cleaning and talking to my sister-in-law on the phone in order not to have a meltdown from exhaustion.

A few days before my cars were being picked up, I had one last doctor appointment. The weather unfortunately had taken a turn for the worst. It just happened to be the day before my birthday. It was 26 degrees outside and raining so hard that you couldn't see a foot in front of you. The streets were flooded deep with water. I had to drive 45 minutes away to a Hand Specialist's office for my hands to have injections for arthritis pain management. It is a very painful procedure and difficult to drive with this kind of weather. But, I am tough and have had this for years and am used to it. I used to have it a week before "Bike Week" twice every year. I didn't tell anyone I had an appointment until one o'clock that day. I left at twelve o'clock to give myself a little extra time on account of the bad weather. I arrived on time. I was the first patient after lunch. My procedure only takes ten minutes. It basically numbs your thumbs and helps with the chronic pain. My hands were worn out from packing and walking my dogs on the leash. My car was parked directly outside of the clear glass wall looking out at the parking lot. Somehow with the weather, loud thunder, loud hard rain, and foggy windows, someone took a knife to my front tire. Strangely enough, nobody saw anything from the other side of the glass window in the Doctor's office, which faced my car.

I got in my car and headed towards my chiropractor down the road. The car was fine for about three miles to my last appointment. I got there fine. I went in, got adjusted, then thanked him and his assistant for helping me so much the past year and said good-bye. I got back into my car and drove up the road to take my U-turn and head home. As I was stopped to wait for the massive traffic to pass and the huge blinding waves of water spraying at me, a huge white utility truck with three men in it facing me caught my attention. These men were waving frantically and flashing their headlights at me to not go. They were pointing at my front right tire and doing the hand across their throat, sign language. I put the flashers on and put my car in park. I got out and walked around the front of my car and my tire was slashed and flat on the rim. I waved a big 'thank you' to the men and gave them the sign of the cross and a peace sign. I got back in my car and they blocked the oncoming traffic so I could limp my car across into the Mount Olive Church parking lot. I was directly across from triple A as well. Thank God.

I called them and they came right over. It was almost five o'clock. The tow truck took me three blocks to the tire place right before closing. They miraculously had my rare size tires and had just finished a rush. They were about to close in a few minutes. I had my tire analyzed and photographed for the police. The tire guys said it was slashed with a deer hunting size knife across the name brand name just enough so that when I took off at fifty miles per hour it would have exploded and I would've been in a terrible wreck. They were shocked and I was mortified. I called the lawyer and told him. He was in over his head this time and couldn't believe it was getting this bad for me. He told the cops. They refused to make a report as usual. Typical.

I was blessed that day. I still got home by six o'clock. I was watching over my shoulder for David or Tipsy to be following me as usual. Neither were following me. They must've followed me to the hand doctor then split and went home. When I got back neither David's BMW nor Tipsy's car were in her driveway. Hymn? This was strange.

I took all my stuff up to my house in the pouring rain

and was so happy to see my puppies alive. While driving home all kinds of thoughts entered my head. I prayed them away. I changed into my pajamas and hugged my dogs. I peeked out my secret window to see if the bad guys were home yet, now and then, until I went to sleep. There was no BMW in her driveway by ten p.m. Tipsy's old car did arrive at some point, but I didn't see when. I went to bed and woke up on my birthday alive. I got a phone call from my insurance agent in Florida who was out with the flu for two weeks. She called to tell me that while she was home sick, someone had called pretending to be me, two weeks before, and had cancelled my car insurance and bike insurance. She knew my situation and knew that Beau and Roxy did it. She reinstated me instantly. I almost had a heart attack on my birthday before breakfast. I told her what had happened the day before. She knew my stalker was behind this caper. I told her of the weird guy who showed up bothering me all the time. We agreed it was all related.

I gave my Fed friend a call and told her I had eleven incidences happen since the beginning of December and now I was really scared and had to move no matter what. She told me to get as far away as fast as I could as soon as I could. She also told me the cops where I was were very dirty and connected to the cops in my old town. She said not to be intimidated by them in any way. She told me to act like I wasn't scared of anything when I was around them while I was preparing to leave. She told me since they screwed up they would try to intimidate me and not to worry because they were in trouble on record now. She told me she had it all under control and just to get out of where I was safely and quickly. I told her it was already a done deal.

I looked out the window to see if the BMW was back and it wasn't parked across the street. I was thinking he did it for sure and left town thinking the worst had happened to me and he was victorious with his mission. He was arrogant as hell.

I had to go and deliver all of my vehicles to a certain safe parking lot to be picked up by the carrier later that night. I had to go see my BMW mechanic to say thanks and ask a question about my old car and get smokes next door. As I pulled into his shop parking lot, I saw David's BMW in his lot. I asked my mechanic what was going on and why that car was there and when it came in. He told me some jerk had it towed in yesterday around two o'clock. He said the guy was acting like a Mobster towards him and demanded him to fix his car immediately. My mechanic had fifteen cars ahead of his. I asked what was wrong with it. Mark said that the oil pan and all the seals and gaskets had blown. He said it was about nine thousand dollars or more in damage. Oil was pouring out of the car like Niagara Falls. The engine was blown. He said it should be at the dealership, but the guy refused and only wanted it repaired at this shop. He insisted on flying under the radar. David badgered my mechanic friend until he had angered him. No matter what, my friend wouldn't fix his car.

I told Mark the mechanic about David following me for months and harassing me. I also told him about what happened to my car yesterday and the call I got from my insurance company this morning. He said he had actually seen him annoying me at the dive bar on the island one time and was suspicious about this guy being there too. He said he had heard the buzz from other folks about how rude and nasty this guy was to all of our friends and that he had been around the island asking questions about me. Nobody knew a thing about me personally or my real name because they were always hammered and just plain didn't care about anything during their winter vacation. Thank God. I thought to myself, 'I almost had a new life', but Beau somehow had found me and won again. I wondered how much he paid this guy to find me. Then I realized that my first gut reaction was exact. Beau was like Cancer. Moving was like Chemotherapy. You had it and you tried to get rid of it but there was no guarantee of a total successful recovery and the chance that it could come back would always haunt you.

Mark used to be a bartender at the most popular bar on the island for years. Therefore, he heard tons of gossip all the time. Turns out everyone wanted to know what this jerk was doing on the tiny friendly island now and why he was staying with Tipsy. Mark said he'd get to the bottom of this and see if he could find out if this guy had anything to do with all the recent mischief done to me. In our heart of hearts we knew it could be no one else by David's suspicious behavior.

While I was being told of this, David appeared, in the drunken woman's car, which was an old beat up Toyota. I wasn't surprised to see him at all but very disappointed he had found me so fast. The parking lot was full so he had to park way at the end about five hundred feet away and then walk through dozens of cars to get to me. I was right between the smoke shop and Mark's car shop.

I quickly asked Mark if he could delay the diagnosis of David's car because I was almost sure he was the one 'booby-trapping' my old car and that is why Mark had to keep on fixing it in December. That was when David came onto the island to stay at Tipsy's house across the street from me. It was all starting to make sense to us now.

I told him I had given notice and was moving in a week because I was so scared. I was close to tears at this point. That made Mark and his wife angry. They were my friends and they knew my circumstances. They somehow knew this new guy was responsible for all my problems. They asked to help. Help, like beat the living crap out of him kind of help. I pleaded gladly to just keep the guy's car there until I could get off the island safely on April first. They offered any help if I asked at emergency speed. I thanked them with all my heart. I was just getting into my truck getting ready to back out when David approached me aggressively. He smiled smugly and asked me where my car was, sarcastically. I didn't answer him. Mark heard him and could see by the way he acted that he knew exactly what happened to my car. He was bragging more than asking. I wanted to punch him in the nuts. Luckily for him a car backed out just around the corner in front of the smoke shop so I backed into the spot and left my motor running for a minute and ran into to get my special smokes for the long journey ahead of me.

I was changing vehicles all the time, anyway, to keep him off my back. My other car was hidden now, for good.

Nobody messed with my truck to where I couldn't fix it myself with a screwdriver and a wrench in a jiffy. Plus, nobody has ever touched my truck negatively. Not even Hurricane Katrina could hurt it. I would make it disappear, forever, next. Poof.

Mark, with his slow heavy Georgia accent, explained to David that it was the end of the day and he hadn't had time to look at his car just yet. David exploded, with zero New Yorker patience, and demanded him to do it right then and there. Mark just said if he wanted any help with his car he had better be nicer and have patience or tow it to the dealership. David stayed and followed Mark around badgering him. The other mechanics came out and told him to take off and that he wasn't getting any closer to having his car fixed by delaying them from finishing their other work ahead of his car. They wanted to beat his ass.

I was just coming out of the tobacco shop next door when he intercepted me and blurted out, right in front of Mark, "Where's your convertible?" I said, "Bye Mark. Thanks so much. See you later". He replied, "Thanks for all of the referrals, Frank." David spun around so fast that his cap almost flew off. I hopped into my old truck, fired it up, blasted off in reverse, then threw it into drive, and did a burn out to get out of there. I watched David run to the little car in the outer parking lot and get into it and try to catch me. Mark saw that too. I caught a yellow light and he caught a red and I was gone. I could see him in my rearview mirror slapping the steering wheel in anger. I was laughing my nervous head off as I flew over the big bridge into town for one last hug good-bye and to share and celebrate my birthday with a dear friend of mine who had been there for me the whole year.

The realtor in the new town where I was moving had to send the lease, by Fed Ex, to my bank so I could sign it and send the certified check along with it back the same way. It was about a 15 minute ride each way and the waiting and all, made the trip about an hour extra out of my already hectic day. It was already the last week of March and I was stressed out with David watching me all the time. I was speedily arranging my things, the U-Haul, and men to pack the truck. My vehicles were disappearing.

I had to get money to pay everyone in cash and certified checks for the car carriers and the U-Haul truck. My credit was a disaster from undergoing Identity Theft so many times by Beau and Roxy. They had buggered up my perfect credit really well, to where I had no credit at this point. I had taken all the cash I had left and stashed every penny in a secret savings account. I had been living on pennies just to be able to move away to a safe place in case this situation happened. I only had one day left to do way too much. I had everything arranged perfectly and timed down to the last second until I got on the plane with my dogs and we disappeared forever.

Chapter 76

The real estate lady spaced out and forgot about the Fed Ex and my lease that day. Apparently she was too busy riding her horse and up in the mountains or getting Botox injections in her face. I waited at the bank all day the third to last day and tried to call her on her cell phone. The bank closed and I felt like I had no safe place to go. I was so tired and discouraged with her. It was too late to change realtors. After all, I was getting on a plane headed to a place I have never been and I was a little scared and very suspicious at why she spaced me out. I had explained my circumstances to her. You'd think she would have one compassionate bone in her greedy, lying body. The rent was a huge amount of money for me at this point in time.

Safety first, worry later is what I thought. I anxiously left her a message asking if she cancelled my lease. She finally called me back later that night and casually said to do it again tomorrow. I told her I was down to the minute and running out of time. I was angry and told her off. I told her my vehicles were on the truck already on the way there and I had no ride available on or off of the island after tomorrow because I would have a house full of strangers packing my things. I told her I was very uncomfortable with this problem. She pretended to care and assured me that she would pick me up at the airport when I arrived next week and everything would be fine. She said the rental house was safe in a gated community and all redone really nice with fresh paint and landscaping. She told me to relax and not to worry. I knew something was strange after her call. She treated me with very little respect for the money I was putting up. It was a lot of money for a year rental. I felt uncomfortable but trapped and would have to get to the bottom of her arrogant attitude after I arrived there. Right now I had no time left for any sudden changes. I had to get out of where I was immediately and stick to my plan because I was in serious danger.

Miraculously, the car carrier company called and said they would be there at my secret place the next night but would still have my vehicles at my new rental exactly when I arrived at my new place. They were reassuring and definite. I had a little bit of extra time to get ready. Whew. I needed all the extra help and time I could get at this point. It was all a matter of whom I could trust.

The next morning, my island friend Dan asked me who was moving me, when he picked up the last of my "give away" things. I told him it was Bill. He shook his head discouragingly and said Bill is a thief and a friend of Tipsy's across the street. Oh no! Too late now. Why didn't anybody say anything before now?

The U-Haul truck rental place manager had referred Bill to me. He gave him an excellent reference. The U-Haul guy was also my Harley mechanic. Oh great. Now

I was confused and scared. I was ready to be ripped off again. Beau was involved, as usual. How could he get to everyone in the universe to help him mess me up? It's funny how you can think you are safe and find out it's all an illusion at the last minute. I truly believed that all bad people were connected somehow, now. My worst nightmare was probably about to come true. As my friend John always quoted from a country song to me, "If it wasn't for bad luck, I'd have no luck at all". Years ago it was about my health, not danger. And because my Fiancé's death before our wedding.

This time I called my bank manager to set up the Fed Ex and to sign for me so I could buy some time to get as much accomplished as possible with my car the last day that I had one. Everything was falling into place for the day nicely, other than David following me in the drunken woman's car, all day. I had to go to the bank for the last time, again. Faith was all I had to keep me from cracking up. I signed the lease and sent the check back to the realtor.

Chapter 77

I got back to my house by noon. The packers were waiting on my porch. It felt better having anybody there, at this point. I had stayed up and finished packing my very important things and taping the lids shut and marking them in my secret code. I had reserved the largest truck U-Haul available, but it still looked too small compared to all of my stuff. I knew all my things wouldn't fit in it. I gave away more things as we worked. Anything I hadn't used or touched was out of my hands now, and given away. I was down to just my family things and my precious things. I still had too much. Bill assured me it would all fit in the truck. He said he'd work his magic and not to worry. The vehicles would leave tonight and the U-Haul would appear in the early morning and take two days to pack with four men working. I would escape and disappear out the back with the dogs into a taxi to an airport hotel to unwind. I would fly out the next morning free and safe and happy by April Fool's Day.

I would be stuck with only my dogs and a house filled with boxes for three days and two nights. I had to think of everything and my head was about to explode. First, everything my Dad ever said popped into my head. One thing he always said, with a big smile, whenever I was scared of lightening was, "Oh ye of little faith. God will never let lightening strike an angel like you". But in a way it had already struck me many a time since I met Beau. My quiet sweet life was a nightmare now. I felt like a gypsy running from town to town being shooed out by the dirty cops. I had two nights to reflect on what he had accomplished lately. I had all of my doors barricaded with loud door alarms installed as well. I had left the curtains up until the last minute. I left the T.V. on low sound in the living room. I was armed in my bedroom with all of my legal weapons of mass destruction and a cell phone ready to dial the real cops. I couldn't sleep or eat. I just smoked cigarettes and drank herbal tea and waited to get killed.

My dogs were really good guard dogs. They would go nuts when David would try to break in again and again. I know my bigger puppy bit him because I heard a really loud noise on the back stairs one night. The back porch door that had been broken into and repaired was the easy one to get into before I "booby-trapped" it. I did a good job. Good luck next time.

Everything I had been through, for three years, was running like a ticker tape through my brain. I couldn't believe I had to live like this, and why? I never hurt anyone. Beau was so narcissistic because I dumped him. He couldn't let go of my rejection. I studied the mental effects it has on a person, after I got my computer. They are serious. He was a ticking bomb and on Meth which accelerates paranoia. He would never get over me and my rejecting him, ever. I ruined his ego so he ruined my life and my future. And then I thought about how he ran me out of my home and I had to live in hotels, motels, and now rental homes in multiple states for three years.

The new State's attorney was elected and he said I was always allowed to be in my home. He said the others were corrupt and forced me out of my home as a joke because they could lie. The real law gave me more rights than the "red-necks" who lived behind me. He tried to kill me by physical force, poison, his drinking while driving, and whatever else he did. He had broken in and raped me and got away with it all. Beau and Roxy and Rika were "Identity Thefting" me all the time and never seemed to be stopping anytime soon. They were on a joy ride at my expense. He destroyed my perfect credit while he had fun with other women while using my hard earned money.

In the meantime, as I tried to move away and get a new life, he was breaking into my storage and breaking and stealing my whole life's treasures. All those days in court with lawyers robbing me while the Judges were protecting him, for bribes. I had to ask myself, 'How in the world could this happen to me?' This was insane. I just wanted a normal life and a nice fun boyfriend who I had a lot in common with. Normal, quiet, fun, romantic, and simple was all I wished for. That's all. I never even got it, but it was taken away from me anyway before I thought I might have a chance at having it. Now I was homeless and scared. He took my hard earned life away. For what?

I was so incredibly sad. I didn't mind moving in the past. But now I was broke from moving seven times.

Plus most of my things were broken or stolen. He was trying to break my spirit. He had touched and broken everything I cared about, from the littlest thing to my bed, cars, and bike. He stole my clothes for his big fat girlfriend to wear in court in order to upset me. I have to admit he could focus on his prey like a cheetah. He was a true hunter and killer.

Then, to top it all off, Beau insisted on meeting my brother and ruining my vacation on purpose. His lying, cheating, and being an embarrassment by making his money as a drug dealer, just iced my cake. I remembered the bartender and bouncer in the gas station that night in August when they told me Beau had asked a druggie to kill me. I also remembered all the negative things his mother, sister, and brother had told me on Easter three years ago. David was sent to isolate me and kill me here in the boonies where there would be no witnesses and the police wouldn't care.

The next day Mark, the BMW mechanic, called me and said David had come by bullying him again about fixing his car. Mark, his wife, and the other mechanics demanded him to get his car and take his bad attitude out of there as fast as possible or he would call the downtown cops and have him arrested for trespassing and his car would end up in the police impound yard. David went ballistic on Mark. Mark could see how dangerous this out of place New Yorker could be. Now David was the vulnerable one without his car or any allies, with only one very unpopular drunk woman as his friend.

The tow truck came quickly, lucky for David. But, Mark went up to him and said, "So help me God, if you go within one inch of Frank, you will find out how we handle trash like you down here in these parts. And believe me you won't like our style of southern back road justice one bit. Now get the hell outa here and never come near any of us again". Wow. I had to smile.

The first night was stressful alone. I still had a few more terrifying nights to come and hopefully go. It turned out there was only one nice, honest young cop on the island, and the Mayor liked him like a son. The Mayors wife demanded, out of guilt, that he check on me all night on his late shift and he would go around my place with a flashlight and check my lower yard every night until I left from midnight until seven a.m. It wasn't like he had anything else to do. It was the middle of the week and the island was dead. He apparently, saw all the corruption, since the real cops were taking over in April after the new Mayor was elected. He surely didn't want to lose his job. He had already applied to join the downtown force. The new Mayor would be firing "Chief Buttwipe" and he would be unemployed soon for not doing his job protecting innocent folks, like me for example. Both good old boys would be sent packing to the unemployment office with bad references. All I ever saw the chief doing was partying and he was never in his office when I called during the whole time I was being terrorized.

There were no police reports filed and missing evidence. In August, a young couple was robbed and their girl was raped, at knife-point. Nothing was done about that huge crime, just a few blocks from my house, in the daylight. The chief and the same fat lazy cop were on duty that day. The chief was being investigated for that as well. He now, because of me, had been being investigated since early December. Turned out I was the example the Feds used to make their case against him not doing his duty. He purposefully put my life in danger just because he could abuse his power as chief. I had an order for protection that he was obligated to uphold under the law in every state including this one.

I never knew this until the night before I left when my dog sitter came and took me to a late birthday dinner, when we happened to meet the new Mayor to be and his wife. He and his wife personally asked me to stop packing and stay. They assured me that the downtown cops would be taking over in just a week, my case would be investigated, and I would be truly protected and able to stay there and be happy. I told them thanks but it was already too late and I was forced to go. My Fed friend had kept her word but it was too late, and my safety was still compromised because Beau knew my street address. I had to relocate no matter what. I am sure that is another reason why the new Mayor was confident and kind to me. My case would give the island a bad reputation and that alone was bad for tourism. I felt like I could breath again. That last night was fun. I finally had a little fun before I left with my friend. The new Mayor to be and his wife celebrated my birthday with us. Just a few hours of no stress would do, after what I had endured physically and financially. I actually slept great that night.

The next morning I confronted Bill about being friends with the drunken woman across the street. He said he didn't know her. Funny, because she had the gumption to come over and ask him specifically, where

I was moving. I told the movers to say Mexico if anybody asked. I yelled, "None of your business". Then I just sang James Taylor's epic hit "Oh Mexico" all day really loudly. She and David were watching everything we did like hawks. I said, "Take a picture. It'll last longer". Since they were already photographing everything I did anyway, everyday, for four months.

The four movers went first to my storage unit and packed up what was left of my grand parents antiques. Then they came to my house afterward at noon, when I returned from the bank, to let them in. The men worked very hard the first day and had the truck half packed with all of the huge things and the many tubs I had packed. I think Bill under estimated the amount of things I had, when he gave me his first estimate to help me move, back in February. When the men were finished for the day, the house still seemed pretty full.

I was really nervous that night. Not just because of my things, but because the huge truck blocking the good cops view of my place. The house was already hidden in the woods, and with the truck backed in, it was impossible to see anything going on at my house unless you snuck around the truck. The countdown was on. Only 24 more hours left until I was far away and alive, if I was careful. I was up most of the night cleaning since I couldn't trust strangers in the house at this point. I was nervous enough after what Dan told me about Bill. I had a gut feeling I was in for something bad before I left the next afternoon. I lay down and prayed for a miracle.

Chapter 78

I awoke to the movers at my door. I had put my purse, personal documents, and extra car keys in a bag. I had also put my new lap-top, all my notes, and connectors in the computer bag. I had all my dog stuff in another. I had four slim, light bags all in a row placed on the foot of my fireplace so I could keep an eye on them all day while I cleaned and supervised. The puppies were out on the back screened porch. As the 85 degree sunny day crawled onward, I worked tirelessly to clean every inch of this place to perfection so I could get my full deposit back. The lady at the rental place was not very nice and I knew she'd use any excuse to screw me out of my deposit.

Finally at about three o'clock, my next door neighbor, Toppy, came by to help. He was a nice man who mowed my yard for me for just a bottle of cheap wine for a year. Bill informed me that my brand new washer and dryer wouldn't fit and I had to leave them along with ten other nice things I had and loved. Toppy said he'd trade me to clean the house for me for all the free stuff. I was quite upset, but exhausted at this point. My gut feeling the night before was becoming a reality.

Toppy was great. He helped the movers and took all the stuff off of my hands for his nice daughter who was my friend. She just got her first apartment and was broke and had nothing. At least my things were going to nice folks who hadn't grown up with all my luxury. Now I would have to rent a washer and dryer when I got to the mystery destination. I thought that was my bad news of the day besides being watched like a hawk by David across the street. Toppy saw him watching me, and he didn't like it one bit. Toppy grew up there and wasn't happy about strangers, like David, coming onto the island, and driving folks like me out. He liked me and my dogs living next door to him. His daughter loved my decorations. Good, because she got tons of my stuff. Oh well, it was only stuff that I had my whole life. God probably wanted me to lighten my load and change my style.

Toppy had the vacuum cleaner, broom, and mop zooming through the place. He had a pool cleaning business and could clean anything really thoroughly. I was happy for the help. I had a chance to take the doggies out back to the pond to run free their last time, for a half an hour, before the taxi was to take us away. When we got back, one of the movers was missing. I peeked out the front window and David was glued to my front yard with the drunken lady next to him holding a glass of wine. My move was their focus. I wanted to sneak over to the beach and run into the ocean and scream, but it wasn't safe. It was a perfect day and I was trapped on my safe turf. I even felt trapped the day I left. It was a sickening feeling. I was so glad I decided to leave. No one should have to live like this. I had felt like I was in jail since December and it stunk.

Toppy had everything out on the front porch when I came out of the bathroom after I had changed my clothes and freshened up to leave at five-thirty p.m. It was now five-fifteen. The truck was almost completely packed. A few of my chairs wouldn't fit in. I had to leave them. Toppy called some buddies and they took the washer and dryer to his place next door. He told me not to worry. That he would make sure the place was impeccable so I got my deposit back. I was at the mercy of strangers with all I had in the world. I was getting the dogs on their leashes for the taxi and I went to grab my bags for the over night stay in the airport hotel, when I noticed my computer bag was missing. I went nuts. I watched it all day like a hawk. It was hidden between my purse and other bag. The guy that left had stolen it. I couldn't believe it. Toppy couldn't believe it either. I paid these guys good money and tipped them and they stole my most important new thing I had with all my study notes and important in formation. I was furious.

Now Bill had to answer to everything since it was his hand picked crew who he said he trusted and had worked with for years. He swore no one had ever been robbed, ever. Ya right. I called the guy who gave him the great reference at the U-Haul place and screamed at him and told him what happened. He was apologetic, but offered no help. I was so pissed that I was finally blowing a fuse. I made the three of them call the guy that left. He didn't answer his phone. I made them search their cars and van. While they were doing it, the taxi driver appeared early, and the Mayor just happened to pull into his driveway across the street at the same time. I was like a tornado. A screaming angry tornado. It was fine time I blew up. I had had enough. David and Tipsy were my audience. Good. Not only was I pissed at the stalkers, mover, and Mayor, but I was worn out and pissed off, period. I had the chance to call out the useless Mayor and humiliate him in front of everyone for doing this to me, finally. I vented at how could he let, as I pointed at David and Tipsy, them destroy my peace and safety.

And here I had to move and it was all his fault. And that "putz" of a police idiot buddy "Chief Buttwipe" who refused to help me and cost me a fortune in hotel bills. I was screaming at him like he murdered my life. I ran him over like a freight train out of control, verbally. His wife, my friend, was standing behind him smiling at me with thanks glowing from her heart through her eyes. She had confided in me months before at how she wished she had never married him, that he was 16 years older, and a "red-neck". She is from near where I was from and had to learn the hard way as I did. It stunk being degraded by "red-necks". She knew my story and could relate to my situation. "Hello! The slaves have been freed!" -She and I both agreed that was the bottom line on how southern men treated women still to this day. She regretted everyday since her Mom pushed her into marrying the soon "to be ex-Mayor" and unemployed husband she would have to support.

The taxi driver was waiting behind my house at the old Mayor's place. He snuck over and offered to help in any way. I sort of knew him already from the hotel I had to stay at downtown for six weeks. That's why I asked for him, specifically, to drive me. I asked him to grab my dogs and their carriers and put them in the car first. Then he searched all of the movers stuff for my computer bag. He was nice to me. He was a huge Italian man with long black hair. He had an enormous nose. It was even bigger than Beau's huge beak. Was that possible? He was like a knight in shining armor.

No computer. Gone. I threatened Bill and so did Toppy and the taxi driver to make sure my stuff arrived at my destination with no more robberies or destruction. I don't like to say, "Everyone is the same everywhere". I so hoped this was the end and it wouldn't happen again. My dogs and I snuck through the ex-Mayors yard and vanished. No one but Bill knew my destination. If someone found out, I would be forced to call Quinn.

I had never been to this airport. It felt like it was hours from the city. It was rush hour and about 100 degrees inland. The roads were very old with potholes and the neighborhoods were severely rundown. New Orleans wasn't even as bad as this. You'd never know this depth of poverty existed when you lived at the beach. It was like downtown Cleveland in the sixties. It was a sad, rundown, never ending ghetto. I recall it vividly. There were only the ultra rich and the folks who worked for them. No middle class.

We got to the airport hotel safely and checked in. I was so angry about my computer being stolen. I hadn't eaten or slept in days or nights. I was in a state of shock and exhaustion. I called my neighbor to ask if the movers had left yet. He said they were closing up the truck and getting ready to leave. He was supervising for me. He said that David and the drunk lady came over and were trying to find out where I was going. He told them I was off to Mexico. At the time, a lot of the island folks were moving to Costa Rica so my move made sense. Plus Beau knew I used to live there. He wouldn't dare try to come there. He was scared to go anywhere he couldn't control. He knew I would have him in deeper shit if he came there.

My neighbor said he kept the things that were left over. I said it was fine. I had too much stuff anyway, always. He was grilling the movers to tell who stole my computer and told them it would be nice if it showed up in the truck at my new place as a miracle. I was up to my eyeballs in stalkers, thieves, and liars. I gave it up to God and went down to eat in the hotel restaurant. I needed a glass of wine and food. I sat quietly and ate slowly. I could barely lift my glass or fork at this point. I was beat in everyway. I dragged myself up to bed with my puppies and had the best sleep I have had in years. The hotel had that "Sleep Number" bed. Wow. What an amazing bed.

I woke up happy and ready to go start my new life again. I wondered how many other women had been through this or were going through it the same time as me. I took the dogs down and out for a walk then put them back in the room so I could have a good slow breakfast and relax more. I called the driver of the U-Haul for an update. He had left at four a.m. No news about my lap-top being found. Dan was right; they robbed me. I just prayed he didn't tell David and the drunk lady where I was really going. He promised he didn't tell. He didn't know that one of my best friends from college was coming to my house to help me move in with his son. I wouldn't be alone when he arrived in five days. And if he broke or stole anything he was going to have the crap beat out of him. I had muscle of my own in my old state where I was headed. My flight wasn't until one-thirty. Nobody knew what hotel I stayed at. I felt safe. For some wonderful reason everything was really easy. The dogs and flight were a breeze.

Our flight was actually 15 minutes early arriving. I grabbed the dogs and put them on the cart and wheeled out to wait for the realtor to pick us up. It was a beautiful evening. I lit up a cigarette and smiled. I took a deep breath and blew out massive stress. It was like a dark cloud that instantly turned blue and pink. I took the dogs out of their carriers and they were happy too. We all just sat a few minutes and were grateful to be in a new safe familiar world. It was 21 years since I lived in this state. It was so green and pretty. It was April Fool's Day.

A grey car pulled up and a blonde woman got out and so did a man. They said, "Hello. Welcome. We will take you to your new place and you will love it. It's like a paradise palace." I thanked them for coming to pick me up.

She drove like a maniac. She talked a thousand miles an hour. He husband couldn't get a word in edgewise. He was nice and mellow. I got a call as we were entering my new gated community, that the Fed Ex car carrier was already there with my cars waiting. The realtor took me to the house. It wasn't the house I saw and rented on the Internet photo. I started hearing the Talking Heads song, "Once in a lifetime" in my head. I had to pay a year's cash in advance to disappear and I get a nut job for a Realtor who can't even get the right house I asked for. I said, "This isn't the house in the photo". She said, "Shut up. This is what you're getting. I don't want to hear about it!" I responded, "I paid for a beautiful paradise. This looks like a dump". The next-door neighbors saw and heard her. They were horrified. She couldn't find the key. She went nuts running around the house in circles. She called the agent who lives at he end of the street and he wouldn't pick up his phone. She left him yelling angry messages. She made us get back into her car and we ran all over the town trying to find out where the key was. She was speeding and running stop signs. It was that crazy. She dropped her husband off to get his truck at their house. I had no idea where I was since I had never been to this town before today. I said," Just get me back to get my cars off. I'll put them in the driveway. Then I'll just take us to the closest hotel until you sort this problem out".

She had a screaming swearing fit. She was nuts. I also had shipped a huge box with my foam and bed stuff, dog stuff, teakettle, clothes, etc. I always do that when I travel or move. It makes life easier for me. It wasn't waiting on the doorstep like usual. She freaked out like I have never seen. She was cursing like a sailor. I told her to calm down. So did her husband. She ignored us. This was a major f%*k up for her. Apparently, she had never bothered to look at the house before she rented it to me. She had no idea about anything regarding this particular property and business arrangement other than the big chunk of money she got for her commission. She was mean and nasty to me because she didn't do her job. She finally got the listing agent on the phone and he told her the key was just above the meter. She called him out. She must have been on some crazy drug that made her psycho. She stole my joy as best as she could. She was acting like her con was fudged and she was busted. And she was guilty of legal fraud now.

It was just getting dark when the truck rolled up and she unlocked and opened the front door. She flicked the light switch on. My box was inside, behind the front door. She was shocked. I asked her if she had ever been in the house before. She tried to lie and say she had. Everyone could see she was full of bullshit. She was mean and bitchy and in a big hurry to leave. I couldn't wait for her to leave. I was so used to nut jobs like her by now. She got angrier. She didn't know I am an expert on dealing her kind. I act happy and excited like a kid in a candy store. I ignore mean idiots and stay calm. It drives them away. The guys with my vehicles opened the truck and she saw my cars. Her husband exclaimed, "WHOA!" She took a peek and knew she was going to be sued for every penny she had for this con.

The house was musty and moldy. It smelled like it had been flooded and the carpet not cleaned since. The painting wasn't even close to being finished. It was just started. Just the lines around the doorways and ceilings. The place was enormous. Two thousand, five hundred, and eighteen square feet. The fireplaces were capped off so you couldn't have a fire. It was cold like a meat locker. I asked where the thermostat was and she didn't know or care to help me in any way. There was no fridge or washer and dryer. It was filthy and nasty. She announced that she had to go and had some place to be. I asked whom to call to have the carpet cleaned, the painting finished, and grass put in for the dogs. There were only dead flowers and no landscaping at all. The whole street was picture perfect and lovely for a track home community. Mine looked like someone died there. The nasty realtor woman told me to call the agent he next day. She tried to say I arrived there too soon. I exclaimed reasonably, "It's the first of the month and I paid every penny for what was advertised on the Internet".

She refused to give me his number and knew it would all come back to her so she was very difficult. She was acting like a witch. She marched out the door, in a fury, and left me there in a the "Taj Ma-Hell". It took two and a half hours to get the vehicles off the truck. The same time it took to put them on. The men were great and very professional about their care for their cargo. I liked them and they thought I was nice and interesting. They were used to rich folks cars, not women in the Witness Protection Program. They had hearts. They knew I was in a very scary place and wanted to help make my life a little better if they had any power to. I appreciated that very much.

I needed all the help I could get at this point. I was scared for my life. They knew I had a Hit Man assigned to me. They smelled my fear. They were extra nice to me. They went out of their way to make my life more manageable as best they could. God Bless them. They came into the house to see I had been ripped-off. They were sad too. It reeked of black mold and the toilets wouldn't even flush. When they went to wash their hands we discovered there was no hot water. The future year in this dump, camouflaged as a palace, was going to stink worse than I thought.

Chapter 79

The realtor's husband came in his truck and wanted to try and help. His wife had screwed me over and he knew for sure now that the car guys were acting like big brothers and tried their best to make comments on the importance and urgency of the situation at hand to the situation to the husband in hopes that he would share this urgency of the situation with his wife later on that night or at breakfast the next morning.. The car guys commented about the plumbing not working properly right away. They gave the husband looks of dismay and shook their heads back and forth with disbelief. They actually were in complete disbelief that the house they had a photo and address of for delivery, was a façade and made loud comments in disgust. I loved them for that.

He went to the store and got me some wine and juices and put them in his old beat up cooler filled with ice from work. He felt really bad. He hung around and helped with the cars and helped me with my box and stuff. He said the house should've been ready and perfect. He didn't even understand how this happened to me. He seemed really sad. Not playing or kidding at all.

I was trying to deal with the dogs because the fence was too wide and they could get out into the street. Nothing in the house was what it advertised on the Internet photos. It was a scam. I was conned and robbed again huge. I was just happy to be safe. I thought for sure everything would be repaired and made right the next day. Finally, at ten thirty that night, every vehicle was safe in my new garage. Relief. I had not had a garage in a year and a half. It felt like peace to me. I put my foam on the floor with my bedding and went to sleep up in my new bedroom.

I woke up early because of the time difference and the extreme traffic noise. My bedroom was above the loud, busy road with a traffic light right on the other side of the wall. No wonder this was a rental property and not a real home. I wanted to get up to wash my face and brush my teeth, I tried to open my eyes, they wouldn't open. They were blood red, swollen shut and burning. I could barely squint. It was a nightmare. How could I drive to a doctor? I couldn't even open them to get down the stairs, to the neighbors or to my car. I heard my new neighbors talking below, so I cried for help. They were very nice to me and gave me drops in a jiffy.

John and Trina were their names. They were very nice to me right off the bat. They handed the dropper over our connecting wall. I put the drops in and my poor eyes teared and teared and burned like hell. I asked them how long the house I was in had been vacant. They said a year. I told them how I found the house and what the agent said. I also asked if they knew the agent. The said yes and that he lives just ten doors down the street. They gave me his phone number. They thought it was terrible that I was conned. They said the realtor was not good and was not popular in the community. The other folks before me left because the man had two heart attacks in the house. I could see why. I couldn't breathe in there. All the window cranks were broken too. It was a work out just to try to breathe the first day. I didn't want my stuff in dirty place like this. No way. Everything was going through my head. I was supposed to be relaxing finally, for a year or more safely. This place was not paradise in any way what so ever. It felt like a cold dingy expensive prison. I had paid for paradise and got tricked instead. I was miserable, stressed and almost broke.

I had to keep putting the drops in my eyes until noon. It took over three hours to get so I could see well enough to drive. The new neighbors told me there is a medical clinic right below my house and a market. I went to the Urgent Care place as soon as I could see. They gave me some medicine and drops and told me I had to see a specialist. They gave me his card to make an appointment. I then went to the store and got some food that didn't need to be refrigerated. It was Saturday afternoon. I had no idea where I was. I felt like I was dumped out of one nightmare into a new bigger one. I called the agent. He told me to call the owner and gave me the number. Everyone was passing the buck. My friend was due in the next day. I was having trouble breathing in the house so I opened all the windows. The air and heat didn't work at all. I was stuck in hell.

I called the owner and they said they would come and get the work done soon. I told them I already had to go to the emergency place and got a serious eye and sinus infection. They said they'd have the house cleaned and painted by the time my stuff came on Wednesday night. I told them I'd stay in a hotel until then and they'd have to pay for it. They told me please just wait until Monday. They said to just air it out. My friend and his son were coming with sleeping bags. We would all be on the floor, stuck. I still had to rent a fridge and washer and dryer. I was running out of money. I was supposed to pay the driver of the U-Haul 15 hundred dollars cash when he arrived with my stuff and unpacked it. Moving is very expensive and stressful. Accomplishing it in twenty-four hours is even more so, especially when you are running for your life from a hit man and a mad man.

I just wandered around my new street with my dogs and waited for my eyes to clear up and catch my breath. I met a few of my new neighbors. They were all very friendly and owned their homes on that street for twenty years. I felt safe, but sick and tired of being taken advantage of.

Chapter 80

My friend The Fox and his son T came the next day. He is a mover and a shaker. They arrived at one p.m. I hadn't seen The Fox since college graduation in 1985. He was a dear friend of mine who had been going through hell too. No one is exempt from attracting folks with mental and drug problems as it turns out. As I greeted him and his son, we were standing in the big empty, dingy, unpainted living room, suddenly there was a huge earthquake. The chandelier was swaying from side to side almost hitting the ceiling. We were grabbing for each other. We all started laughing and remembered it was just like the good old days back in college. Welcome back. The Fox said, as a joke, "You always have a huge impact everywhere you go, Ruthie". We were cracking up laughing.

We took the tour of the house and inventory of all the problems. The Fox is a filmmaker, so we did a virtual tour on film with my camera. It was very funny and pointed out all the problems. He and I agreed I would have to hire a lawyer on Monday to sort it all out. I surely had been conned. We took off in my car after, and went on a tour of the town and area. We found all the stores and beach and Mexican restaurants. We went by to surprise an old friend of ours from college. Turned out she is an agoraphobic and can't deal with people. She had no desire to open her door and come out with us. We were sad about her problem. She used to be my best friend and was the funniest person I had ever known in my life. My heart went out to her. We found a tiny surfer taco place with 80's music and went there to eat and wind down. This turned out to be a really cute little town. Friendly too.

We got up early on Monday with several missions to accomplish. The Fox and T threw up all night because of the dirty carpet. They said it was toxic too. Their sinuses were bothering them as well. They were coughing up stuff all night. We were all awake all night. Since it was empty the acoustics made it all the louder. I was not imagining the mold.

First was to get in touch with the owners to get the work done in the house before the truck came. We called and they wouldn't answer their phone. Next was to get to the hardware store to pick up something to keep the dogs safe in the yard. The Fox got chicken wire and zip-ties. He went on Craig's list to find me appliances. We went to see if there were any available. We drove out in to the middle of nowhere and found the address of a man who's add on Craig's list said he had fridges, washers, and dryers.

The Fox, T, and I pulled up in Fox's Diesel Ford monster truck and parked on the side of the house. The Fox got out and walked up to the garage to meet the man and see his wares. The man opened the garage and there was a junkyard of broken down crappy appliances. The Fox was the kind of man who could fix anything. He looked at the appliances and told the man they were unacceptable. The Fox got picky and the man got weird. The man didn't speak English, only Russian. And the Fox didn't speak Russian. The Fox pointed out the broken down problems. The Russian started yelling. The Fox yelled back at him. T was in the back of the double cab of the truck saw and yelled, "Start the truck, Indie!" I reached for the keys because I was in the front passenger seat, but The Fox had them on him. No luck.

All of the sudden The Fox came running like his pants were on fire, and jumped into the truck and stuck the keys in and fired it up and we bolted out of there as fast as a truck could go. We were laughing so hard my face hurt. I felt like I was in a foreign country again. Why? We went to another address and accidentally met a real estate agent who's daughter's 'Ad' on Craig's list got buggered up and said they had appliances for sale. We told the father the story. He knew who screwed me and gave me the name of a nice reasonable lawyer. We found the lawyer and called. He took my case right away so I retained him to represent me to get my money back in order to be able to move to a suitable clean house. We gave him the DVD we made and a printout of the house I was supposed to get and didn't. He loved this case. He called the woman agent, and told her off right there and then and reminded her of the laws. It was beautiful. He told me not to unpack my boxes when my things got there and just try to find another place to live a soon as possible. He told me just to make it livable enough to sleep and cook in for a while. In the meantime he would go after the agents and owners for fraud. He was affordable, but rents weren't.

This move had used up some of my savings already, so I was in for a tough time ahead. Plus I had to go buy a new Lap-top and that was expensive. I couldn't believe, nor could The Fox, that this kind of thing could happen to a person. This was all too much. We worked really hard and got tons of things accomplished in just two days. We also had a good time telling old stories of how and what our old friends are doing now. We found an appliance rental company and called got the appliances delivered and installed in the empty house the next morning at ten. The yard was dead and had no grass for the dogs at all, so we went to Costco and bought a fake grass rug for them and an umbrella plants and a lounge chair for the patio. We tried to make it bearable for now since I had to spend a lot of time outside in order to breathe.

The ten by twenty foot patio was polluted by the acoustics of loud traffic noise and had black moldy concrete and an old unpainted wall covered with black mold on it too. It was so dirty and ugly and acoustically overwhelming. We were all irritated by the fact that I was conned out of a boatload of cash. We cruised around, trying to discover and enjoy the new place and warm weather until my U-Haul arrived because after the truck arrived I would be in "box and sorting" prison for months ahead considering my circumstances from the last move. I had labeled everything before we left S.C. and packed very slowly and carefully. I had tried to memorize what was given away and what stayed. Since I had lost so much weight, I had given away almost all of my clothes to the Shelters. I hardly had anything new. All I ever wore when I was in S.C. was a bikini, pajamas, jeans, sweaters, and a windbreaker basically. It was an island I had escaped from, not Paris.

Chapter 81

The driver of my truck called and said he'd be arriving around six on Wednesday evening. His flight was booked to return him back to S.C. on Friday morning. Bill the driver would have just enough time to unload, relax, and return the truck; I thought. He said he used to live here and had a friend, who was sick with Cancer, that he wanted to see on his way out of town who was near to the airport an hour away. I thought to myself, 'I will be very grateful to have what was left of my things safely delivered all this way'. I wanted to be happy about just about anything good at this point after all the bad luck I was having since Beau got his hooks in me. It was coming up on two years of this bullshit he was putting me through. How in the world could someone trash another person's whole life and belongings and keep getting away with it? I couldn't get anything back that he had taken away. It was all sentimental to me. I remember the very few times I was in his home four years ago when he had nothing and I had taken months to help him carefully shop and decorate it nicely. I made his empty shell, after Gin moved out and took everything with her, a nice comfortable luxury home for him. He, in turn, had broken and tore my sentimental comfort zone to pieces.

Now a "Hit Man" was sent to kill me and I had to move in a jiffy again. All of this trouble at my expense. I thought of all my hard work going down the toilet and flowing through the sewers of the East Coast. I was really sad. In fact, I was so sad that I asked The Fox what to do. He told me he had been through the whole thing already and to just let go. Walk away, throw away, and tow away if necessary. Whatever. His advice helped me a lot that Wednesday morning during breakfast. I had such a huge knot in my stomach. We just hung out and waited for my truck to arrive. We just wandered around the house seeing the damage, wondering how this mistake with the property could happen to me, how we could unload my stuff, and where to put it. I had the whole thing planned in my head from the fake photos I saw, but now had to choose which room to use as storage for the things until I was able to move to a decent place. We chose the upstairs left guest room. It was so sad for me. The place they advertised looked so beautiful in the photos. Now the reality was nauseating and I was having a major panic attack.

We had made plans to go to the taco place with the U-Haul driver for dinner later on. We knew he would be starving by then. Six o'clock arrived and Bill and my truck pulled up outside and parked. Bill had driven straight through and not slept for two nights. He looked like death warmed over. He was short and skinny when I saw him last Friday, but now he looked emaciated with his bulging bloodshot eyes and nervous body language. When he pulled up and got out of the truck, he wouldn't make eye contact with me. No matter what I asked or The Fox asked, he eluded our answers. We all decided we would unpack the truck in the morning. This seemed reasonable since the guy had busted his boney butt driving all the way across the continent. He told me to pay him after he was done unpacking and ready to leave. I said, "O.K."

We all went out to the taco place and relaxed and ate dinner. It was difficult for me to relax because of a million reasons. The mover saw how bad the house was. My computer was stolen by one of his employees and I had a feeling there was a new surprise in store for me. I could just feel it in my tummy. It was not going to be a good surprise either. I asked him if David or the drunken lady had asked where I was going. He acted edgy and used being tired to elude the answer. The Fox and I knew something was up at dinner. The Fox tried to get it out of him by drinks and buddying up to him, but he was holding something in tightly.

They had about five beers and a few rum and cokes. I was designated driver, so I was sober and miserable. I actually needed to get drunk at this point. I was burdened down with responsibilities and wasn't allowed to relax at all. The Fox and T wanted to stay in a Motel because the house was making them sick. The motel was only 70 bucks down by the beach. It was a very stressful night for all of us because early in the morning we would open the back of the truck and have to haul my material life into this dump house. I was trying to reason with Bill, before we went to sleep, about who stole my Laptop. He was feeling trapped then.

He was in the new façade house in person, seeing

with his own eyes, how bad my life was about to become, and even worse in the morning. I had some wine and took myself up to bed. Bill went in to my guest room. I had made a bed for him on the floor with pillows and blankets. The vibe between us was dark and bad. I was asleep by eleven. I had bad dreams all night and tossed and turned. I couldn't breathe properly with the musty floor. At least it was the last night on the floor for me.

Chapter 82

I woke up around nine o'clock, tired and wheezy. I snuck downstairs quietly so Bill could sleep in a little. The puppies were quiet. I made some tea and waited for Bill to come downstairs. His door was shut still when I peeked down the hall. I was trying to organize my thoughts in my head for the busy day ahead of me. The Fox and T showed up at ten. They were ready to help unload my things. I went upstairs to wake Bill up. I knocked on his door politely. I waited and had no response. Then I said his name and knocked again. Nothing. I gently turned the handle and opened the door and the makeshift bed had not been slept in and the room was empty. I screamed and ran down the hall and stairs. The Fox and T ran towards me. I said, "He's gone". They exclaimed, "What!" I just shook my head and burst into tears and sobbed. The Fox hugged me and poor T didn't even know what to do at age 12. It would take another man or two to do this job. I was so upset that I couldn't even breathe. The Fox calmly told me, "Don't worry. We'll do it. We'll find a way. Relax". I was so upset I threw up. Here was my answer. Bill was in on something bad and was scared The Fox would beat the crap out of him or I'd have him arrested for theft of my computer. He ran scared and without pay.

The Fox and T went outside and opened the U-Haul. As they slid the huge door upward open, an avalanche of my belongings, broken into pieces, slid down violently and toppled on top of them! They had to jump back in order to escape injury.

I was standing in the driveway in shock. I cried even harder now and just fell on the dead grass. I couldn't hold it together through one more disaster, at this rate. The Fox and T were standing there, shaking their heads in disbelief and looking at the ruination of my life.

I heard my cell phone ring in the house, but let it ring and go to my voicemail. I just laid on my back and screamed at the sky, crying.

The Fox and T just picked up pieces of my broken belongings and assessed whether or not they should be trashed or repaired. T got the recycling and trash cans from next to the house and dragged them out to the truck. This was a major disaster.

It was as if my life and everything I owned had gone through a tornado and was whipped and broken and warped into a million pieces. As the two of them pulled at the next layer, more beautiful things busted into shattered pieces came sliding out onto the street. The crashing of my belongings was deafeningly loud.

The first thing I saw was my beautiful patio umbrella broken in half. The spokes were bent and its fabric was all ripped into pieces. It went straight into the recycling can. Next, antique chairs that were smashed with the legs broken off and the seat all ripped up. I opened a few tub lids to see if the stuff inside was safe like I packed it. My things were ransacked and tossed. Things were missing. It was complete and utter premeditated vandalism.

I had to hire a neighborhood gardener to help for two hours and assist me in returning the truck on time. It was way too much for my friends to do.

I got lucky. The men were so nice and very sympathetic for my losses. They hadn't seen anything like this intentional cruelty before. I was like a zombie. I had no feeling left in my head or body. I just pointed at the house or the cans all day. It was like directing traffic, only it was my entire life of family and art. It was a complete disaster. I had been done in. I felt like I was dead. Rock bottom.

The Fox, T, and I went inside for a coke and to rest for a few minutes. I was grey as a ghost. It was a visible sign that all of the life had been sucked out of me. I took an aspirin and sipped on a coke. We were quiet. This was beyond bad. It was downright ugly and nasty.

I went and grabbed my phone and saw there was a voice message left on it. I pressed play to listen. Everyone was silent while I listened closely through the phone's earpiece.

The message was from Bill.

The message said, "I left in the middle of the night. You don't have to pay me. He got to me and made me do this to you, but I wouldn't tell them where you are."

His goal wasn't to kill me anymore. It just was to kill who I was and who I am.